London
December 1970.

DUNKY FITLOW

DUNKY FITLOW

TALES BY

A. E. COPPARD

JONATHAN CAPE
THIRTY BEDFORD SQUARE
LONDON

FIRST PUBLISHED 1933

JONATHAN CAPE LTD.   30 BEDFORD SQUARE, LONDON
AND 91 WELLINGTON STREET WEST, TORONTO

PRINTED IN GREAT BRITAIN IN THE CITY OF OXFORD
AT THE ALDEN PRESS
PAPER MADE BY JOHN DICKINSON & CO., LTD.
BOUND BY A. W. BAIN & CO., LTD.

CONTENTS

for
PINK CRITTALL AND MAY CRITTALL

DUNKY FITLOW

THE SMITH OF PRETTY PETER

IN THE HAMLET OF KEZZAL PREDY PETER, WHERE he was born and had thrived, Alphabet Ayres was well regarded by himself — and indeed by his neighbours too; for though he did not care to hide his light under any bushel, it showed as a rule a green ray; a masterful man but kindly, with a few pounds in the bank, a spare suit of broad-cloth, and a walking stick made of a mysterious substance from the Canary Islands. As a bachelor of sense and care he was thought to have attained a settled disposition, but by the time he was forty he had mutton-chop whiskers and a gloomy face; then he went and suddenly married Amnesty Rockall, a smallish much younger woman with tightly folded dull hair (and not a lot of it either) who cackled, walked jerkily, and wore spectacles; but no matter for that, she had a cheerful face and brought with it a fortune of five hundred pounds.

As they emerged from the church and passed under the lych gate Amnesty paused and laughed aloud.

'I say, Alf, I don't want you to exhilarate me too much.'

'All right, Annie, never fear,' says he.

And he did not. They dwelled together for years and years in a gloomy cottage with a monkey-puzzle tree in the garden, and then Amnesty began to go so-and-so. That is to say, not actually mad, nothing so furious as lunacy, but she did occasionally drift, like a dry leaf from a thicket, into some by-corner of melancholia, and then she would go roving for a time up and down the neighbouring lanes, bearing under her arm a large wooden box with a bird's-nest in it. Nobody knew what the box was for (it had got 'Maconachie's Lobsters' printed on it), or why she harboured an old thrush's nest, but everybody knew her home was neglected, that she was a silly woman who tormented her husband with spiteful accusations.

'Ah, she's queer, right enough,' said Alphabet to his nephew Archy Bottrell, a tall pale faced builder with loose clothes who had prospered and bloomed on bricks and mortar. 'I never could understand her. And if I could, the Lord knows there's nothing to understand. My dog understands; he knows what's good for him, he minds my door and bites rats. But that woman knows nothing, does nothing, understands nothing; she abuses me. Why, she is a heavenly ruffian, and I shouldn't like you not to know it.'

Uncle and nephew hobnobbed of an evening in the taproom of *The Cow and Hare*, to drink beer and talk of the things that were uppermost in their minds, it might be gardening or politics or sport, or else local affairs and personal troubles. The nephew had an invalid wife who had been going to die for years but didn't quite die, and the uncle had a wife who had been going mad for years but had never quite gone. Archy Bottrell was a well-off man, he could afford a nurse and a servant, his house was adorned with grand furniture and large pictures of 'A Cornfield in Suffolk,' 'A Surrey Garden,' 'A pine tree in Japan' and so on, and his wife was no trouble to him at all — she was merely a responsibility. Alphabet Ayres on the other hand had a poor time of it; got his own meals, mended his own clothes, and lived a life apart; all on account of his unreasonable woman, who was an incubus.

'For forty years I was a man of my parts such as they be,' the smith declaimed. 'I cut and shut an axle with the best that breathed, and quicker than most. As for horses, it didn't matter what, there was none to touch me after George Fullamer went off on his preaching tour as the converted farrier. I was always great friends with George; he taught me much. Forty years, and then I fell into the claws of a wretch. It makes you wonder what is the use of behaving in a good decent way. You'd 'a thought Providence would have taken care of a man as showed respect for himself.'

'Uncle,' replied the builder, who was almost of an age with the smith, and generally addressed him as Alf unless he wanted to be impressive: 'Uncle, there is neither care nor favour to be looked for where that sex is uppermost. Mind you, I don't say it's not deserved, but I do say it can't be looked for since that long-whiskered female sort of a serpent got into the Garden of Eden. When that serpent crawled out of Adam's ribs — that was no decent way to be born, either! — Adam made a great mistake not keeping her under his thumb.'

And Archy was crushing his thumb on the tap-room table as if he had got a maggot there.

'That's true, and it's true,' said the forlorn smith. 'No man with the fear of God before his face should have allowed her.'

'Where Adam made his great mistake, uncle, was playing second fiddle to that caper. He was the father of mankind, but weak! It was his weakness, I tell you. There's been a cross on the world ever since. Don't you go on making his mistake, Alf.'

'I've done my best,' the smith assured him. 'There's nothing I'm ashamed of, or that I wouldn't do again. I took care of her lovingly as long as I could, as long as she'd let me, and what's more I've taken care of the money she had. Five hundred pounds it was. I've done well with it,' he whispered. 'I've done well. And that she can't stomach at all! She can't abear the thought of all that money under my control. But she's a foolish woman, she's not responsible.'

'Quite right, Alf; you can't give them faith or credence.'

His uncle had taken up his pot, but put it down untasted.

'She is a foolish woman. Easy come easy go, I tell her. Where would it have been now had I not taken care of it for her?'

'You can't trust a woman with money, uncle, course you can't; nor a fool with a weapon.'

Ayres took up his pot again, and said: 'I don't suppose you can.'

'Suppose! Hearty Saints of God, don't I know!'

After repeating 'Where would it have been now!' the smith managed to take a good draught of his ale. Then he set the pot back on the table very carefully. 'And ever since she've been with me, of course she's gone mad. Not really mad, you know, but still, not quite responsible. It's the moon.' He tapped his forehead with morose significance. 'No accounting for a thing like that. It's pitiful and all how dislike of a man brings a woman down. With another one, some rascal perhaps, she'd a been as right as rain. I dunno.'

The builder leaned forward and peered solemnly at his uncle.

'Listen. You're not a young man, Alf. I'm not myself. But an old well-fed tree bears the sweetest codlins. Something ought to be done about her. You give her half the money and tell her to pack herself off.'

The smith turned his eyes away, pursed up his lips and shook his head, put out his hand to the pot but thought better of it.

'No, Arch, no; that cock won't fight. And would she go! No fear, not much! She'll never leave me. I can't explain that to you, but I know it for certain. If I gave her that five hundred pounds, she would only be five hundred times madder than before; she would have her fling, the money would be spent, and here we'd be again five hundred times worse off. Besides, the money's invested and it's doing well, O no, Arch, no.' And the smith kept on shaking his head and saying, 'no' until he had repeated it seven or eight times. Then he burst out: 'You may say it and say it, Archy boy, but there's nothing I could do. I'm done for.'

The nephew just flicked his fingers: 'Get rid of her, get rid of her,' he said.

'But how, my good chap! It's all very well to talk like that, and she *is* a bad wife; but that's only a hardship, it's not a crime.'

Archy gave a temporizing cough and said:

'We don't want to talk about crime, but a hardship like her I would not put up with.'

'Well, then, now you tell me! It is easy enough to say "Get rid of her" and "Pack her off" and suchlike, but that is not to be thought of, it's impossible. What I mean to say is: how is it to be done? There now, Arch, come on!'

And Arch sat up and growled: 'Brrr! Give her a bucket of salts, Alf; that's the dose for a sick elephant! I beg your pardon, uncle, but I tell you I'd have the hair off her inside and out before I'd let her tantalize my mind; inside *and* out.'

'Hush man; don't,' said Ayres. 'Don't pander to the unseemly.'

They parted outside the inn in brightest moonlight, the builder going up the road towards the chalk pits and past the palings of the park, where he could see cypresses like parasols, poplars like bodkins, and a beech holt resting on its eminence like a sponge; while the smith went down the road towards the watercress beds and a silent brook. He could smell the dewy dust of the road, and hear frogs crying from the dyke like shrill young rooks. The air was cold for May. There had been a foggy March month. 'Fogs in March, frosts in May' muttered Ayres. 'It will freeze to-night, I shouldn't wonder.' And he sighed, remembering that Amnesty was always at her worst when the moon was full; it seemed to interpose a crust of ice between her and her mortal fancy.

Sure enough, his wife was standing on her box in the midst of the road before their monkey tree. Her old hat dangled in her hand, the moon shone on her bedraggled hair, gleamed on her spectacles, and made a wretched wreck of God's handiwork. As Alphabet approached she lifted one arm exhortingly and cried out:

'Ho, ho, my nice man! Mind your eyes, neighbours. Oo . . . oo . . .oo! Fair as a lily, and look at me now! Mingy man, never a ha'penny!'

'Get down off there and go indoors,' he said gruffly, pointing with his stick to their house. Amnesty got down and picked up her box.

'Put your hat on!' he commanded. 'Catching your death a cold like that!'

Amnesty stared at him belligerently and said: 'When I be dead I don't care what becomes of my hat. The good spirit knows it would be no use to me. I don't put my trust in any hat.'

He drove her in before him through the garden gate. As she opened the cottage door the moon-light shot into the room across a brick floor to an open hearth that had no fire on it. If there was any comfort in the room it was comfort that seemed to have lost its pride: a lamp unlit on a bare table, a dresser in disarray, old out-of-date almanacs on a wall, a long clock in a corner not ticking, the smell of a dog, and a gun over a mantel-shelf. Amnesty at once huddled down on her box with folded arms, while her husband lit the lamp and closed the door.

'I wish we was dead,' said she.

Ayres cut himself a crust from a loaf on the dresser, and put it on a plate with some cheese, and sat down at the table.

'You was always wishing for something you hadn't got.'

His wife sat up, her knees together, a hand on each knee.

'Well, what else could I wish for?'

'Why can't you be satisfied?' he asked.

'What with?'

'With the same as other people, and give up these capers. You was a good woman once.' And he began to eat carefully, pushing hunches of bread into his mouth with the fingers that held the knife.

'And what did I get by it?' she said excitedly. 'Look at you! You lost most of your teeth.'

'Is that my fault?'

'You let 'em fall out, didn't you! And there you are, you was bald before you was fifty!'

'Could I help that?' he asked imperturbably.

'O, don't talk to me!' she cried. 'You bought the wrong sort of hat — I always told you so.'

'Well,' mumbled Alphabet, 'you can't escape the ravanges of time. Look at yourself!'

Amnesty sprang up, her eyes blazing:

'I was fair as a lily, sweet as a rose. My parents slaved and saved that money for I. They starved themselves of comfort and pleasure and me of my youthful joys, and now look! First one died, and then the other, and so I married you and brought you my fortune. Yes, when you married me you came into a property — and look now! There was tears and blood on it ever since, and nothing else for me. I was fair as a lily, sweet as a rose — yes, I was. And look at me now!'

It is not well to look at a woman sobbing. Alphabet went on carefully parting bread and pushing it into his mouth.

'Go to bed,' he growled, after a tough swallow, and she went upstairs alone.

11

With the passing years Amnesty's malady neither grew nor declined, it just remained, and its persistence mattered less and less to most people; like the sour sloe or the bitter crab it was neglected; soon it mattered to none. In the village her strange manner had once been an excitement; then she became a laughing-stock, next a nuisance, last of all she was ignored. Except by Alphabet Ayres, who could not ignore her. It was not in him to treat her with active unkindness. It was something he had to bear with; he was a patient man, he could afford to wait. The worst that could be said of him was that he avoided her. At seven o'clock each morn he rose up and went over to the forge with his dog. After an hour or so of work he turned home to prepare his breakfast. Whether his wife was abed upstairs, or already tramping the roads with her box and bird-nest, he did not know, he had ceased to care. If he met her in the road he passed her without a glance, without a word, as indifferent as a cart-wheel. And whether she really went mad at the making of the moon, or whether it was all mere cunning and revenge, Alphabet never could decide. You would have thought she had once been a regular goddess for fine looks and had brought him riches as well, that he had wrested the money from her and ill used her beauty! Often she would plant the old box in the middle of the turnpike road and sink on it in reverie with her head in her hands until she was nearly driven over by some waggon or other.

One springtime Hannah Bottrell died. For a week or two Archy was bewildered by the strange state in which he found himself, and often surprised by the tears that dropped from his eyes at any odd moment, but he pulled round well. On fine summer eves that year you might have seen him at her graveside, stolid as a pole for minutes at a time, or bending down with his hands still in his pockets to stare at her blades of grass. His uncle would be sitting on a bench in the next field watching the cricketers, and beside him there would be old Culpepper the miller, a man with grizzled ginger hair and sharp eyes, who throughout the district was miscalled Coolpepper. Archy would join them on the bench, and beset by voracious gnats all three would watch the cricket and discourse of moody things till the gloaming came.

'Hannah was a good honest wife, Uncle Alphabet, and served me well. An invalid of course she was, but the pluck of that woman was . . . well, it was gigantic, and that's a fact. You remember, Mr. Culpepper, when the oculist operated on her? She had one of her eyes froze and watched the operation with the other. Gigantic, gigantic! I don't suppose I'll be able to get another like her.'

There was the tone of acute astonishment in the smith's enquiry: 'You're not thinking of wedding again, Arch?'

'Well, there's nature to be considered, Uncle

23

Alf; you can't eat the bread of life alone. Solitude is ruination. A man's a man, he must be, he's got to be.'

Uncle Alphabet, rolling his stick between the palms of his hands, looked thoughtfully away and said:

'Every man to his choice, Arch, but once my knot's untied you won't catch me in it again for a thousand pound.'

'Ah, Mr. Ayres, well,' the miller broke in gravely. 'You've had your full *share* of the misfortunes of matrimony. Every man has his share, we are all bound to have, but you have got your *full* share.'

'That's as may be,' the smith answered. 'I'm hard on sixty, and I've a hollow time of life afore me as would make most men weep in their handkerchiefs. But I've a bit of respect for myself yet. When I was a boy I'd submit to be pole-axed before I'd say black was white — if it wasn't. But times have changed since I was a boy, and they've changed smartish since I came to my prime.'

'I should think they *have* changed, Mr. Ayres; times have truly changed, sir,' said the miller. 'Take flour, now: there is flour *and* flour; 'taint all grist as comes from the hopper.'

'You are quite right, Mr. Culpepper, there is flour and flour,' Archy said. 'That chap Gobbett bowels above his strength, Alf; always did.'

'There is,' the miller said, 'and there must be, you may depend upon it; I have seen it and said it all my life, and I will to my dying day: there is grain *and* grain, and you can't odds it.'

'Bravo! That's bowelled his wickets. True, Mr. Culpepper, there *is* grain and grain.'

'And you can't odds it, I tell you,' declared the miller in some excitement. 'I will tell you another thing: there is beer *and* beer, Mr. Bottrell, as you very well know.'

'O, my! You're saying something now!' agreed Archy.

'There is beer *and* beer,' Culpepper repeated it with triumphant conviction. And even the smith admitted as much: 'There is indeed,' he said.

'Beer nowadays,' continued the miller, 'has *no* heart in it. . . .'

'None at all,' interjected Archy.

'. . . and *no* body.'

'No heart and no body nowadays, it's just bare skin and bone as you might say,' rejoined Archy. 'Why, I can mind the time, Alf, and so can you, Mr. Culpepper. . . .'

'Ah, I *can* mind that time,' the miller eagerly said, '. . . . when you could not get more than one single sole solitary pint of rare old stingo served across a public counter. They dassent serve you!'

'O, 'twas perilous,' the miller agitatedly agreed, 'perilous it *was*!'

'Gunpowder!' growled Mr. Bottrell. 'And now?'

'No heart in it.'

'And no body,' added the other. 'You might just

25

as well be a duck, swallowing dew. Change you say! Why, dear heart of God, this world goes spinning round at such a pitch I wonder the old King of Trumps Himself don't get dizzy of it!'

Alphabet scratched at the ground uneasily, with his stick, then folded his hands over the handle and leaned earnestly towards his nephew:

'Never abuse the Almighty, Arch. You cannot be too careful. We know He is dumb, but we don't know about His ears.'

'And it's all made for our welfare, Uncle, all this revolution in the space; a mile a minute is nothing to it, nothing at all! We can thank our lucky stars there's plenty of room, but you may be sure it can't go on for ever.'

Mr. Culpepper intervened with a puzzled air: 'What *be* you chaps talking of?'

'I was talking of the globe,' Archy answered promptly.

'And I of God Almighty,' the smith said.

'O,' Culpepper breathed, 'blow this preaching! I was talking of beer.'

'Well, if it's beer you're after,' said Archy, 'it's time we cut along and milked the old "Cow."'

So off they went together to *The Cow and Hare*, and as they passed along by the churchyard Archy gave a glance or two over the low wall and mumbled: 'Poor Hannah!' The smith said 'Hum,' and the miller sighed.

'My wife,' he said, 'has been dead and gone four

years come this next thirteenth of November. Poor
suffering soul! Twenty-three weeks she lay, but
full of life, *so* happy. Kidneys. No one knows, *do*
they? No one knows.'

'That Thatcher is a middling tidy batsman,
Alf.'

'He never seems to get many runs, Arch.'

'O, but he blocks the ball well.'

'I say no one knows, Mr. Bottrell,' said the
mournful miller. 'Do they now? No one knows.'

'It's a fact, Mr. Culpepper,' said the new widower
with great heartiness. 'They do *not* know.'

III

That same year Archy Bottrell began to build
his uncle a little double fronted cottage in a garden
to itself and under one roof, but having two doors,
each leading to a room down and a room up, so that
Alphabet could inhabit one half entirely to himself
and Amnesty the other entirely to herself, or as
near as might be. The builder had tried to persuade
his uncle to slope, to emigrate secretly or separate
publicly, to pack Amnesty off somehow, to put her
into an asylum, or even murder her; but to all these
proposals his uncle had right and rooted objections
and the double cottage alone satisfied his sense of
what could with propriety be done to improve his
situation.

When all was ready Alphabet and Amnesty

moved into the new cottage and dwelled side by side, severed only by plaster and wall-paper, and no sooner were they established there than the smith made up his mind to effect another remarkable change. Having pondered long over some small books, and calculated with a pencil on some large pieces of paper, he concluded that it was a ripe and favourable time for him to retire, so he sold his horseshoe business to an asthmatic cockney who was something to do with bicycles, and resolved to labour no more.

He inducted himself gradually into his new leisure by making odd household contrivances, mostly of iron, and tilling the new garden. Amnesty, rather baffled by his constant presence before her, seemed inclined to forgo some of her ancient follies, and she would sit in the garden watching Alphabet, who did not mind her so much now — found himself indeed growing affable to her! At times they even shared a meal together, for she often ran short of some commodity or other that he kept a store of. Ayres still bought and paid for everything, he had always done so; sometimes he gave Amnesty a shilling or a sixpence, but she only spent most of it on toffee.

One morning she went out into the garden and took a mouse to him. It was caught in a trap cage, and what with fright or some other mishap the captive had given birth to five pink piglike morsels no bigger than bees, all dead.

'God help us!' said Alphabet. 'I can't harm that poor thing. Give it a feed of cheese rind and let it go.'

They pushed cheese through the bars but the mouse did not heed it any more than she heeded her five dead babes. The smith poked their bodies about with a hairpin; they were stiff and pallid; the trap with its dead and living prisoners filled him with acute distaste.

I don't mind a mouse,' he explained to his wife, 'but it's not my kind of partner in this blissful world. I didn't make the world, and I don't want much of it. I didn't make the mouse, and I don't want it at all. A four-footed beast goes its own way about things, got it's living to make same as the rest of us, but it's not my kind of partner in the blissful world. Long as it keeps itself to itself, and no larceny — all serene; but soon as it gets its nose into my cheese pot we got to have some everlasting understanding. That's my hunting temper, I suppose; but it's the same for us all, turn and turn about. If I was a mouse I know what I'd be in for — and that is good justice.'

'What, you!' cackled Amnesty, 'You never had any hunting temper!'

A little huffed, he said: 'You, what do you know? You know nothing at all about it.'

'I know you, and I know that much,' said she.

Alphabet corrected her in a surly manner:

'Every man has a hunting temper of some sort. Some hunt women, some politics, some money, and I don't know what all. I don't hunt money, though I shouldn't rush home out of a shower of it if a storm came on! That I wouldn't. And I never hunted women, I was never a hound to that sort of hare.'

'No,' said Amnesty, 'you never caught much, did you?'

'Was never anything to catch,' he answered.

She had apparently been surprised and subdued by his unwonted chatter, but here she recovered herself:

'Ho, ho, wasn't there, Alphabet Ayres! I was fair as a lily, once; sweet as a rose, I was. And I was manhandled many times and never told you of it, see!'

The smith sniffed disgustedly: 'Get away with you!'

'But I was! And more than once or twice. And it wasn't with any old soldier, either.'

Ayres stared his entire unbelief: 'No, I never knew that. You never told me.'

Amnesty was scoffing: 'Not likely. I'd something better to think of!'

'Who was it?' he asked. 'When was it?'

'Tra la la la,' sang she.

'You was always a cunning thing,' the smith said slowly. 'I don't believe a word of it.'

Swiftly she replied: 'I was never cunning enough

in this world, not by half, but we'll see how I gets on in the next, please God.'

'I don't believe a word you say.'

'You needn't,' said she.

All day long he was bothered, and he plied her with question after question, now direct, now subtle, about this new strange aspect of his wife, an old aspect though new to him, but Amnesty would reveal nothing more and she enjoyed a sort of triumph over him at last.

The next morning his wife sat in a chair outside her door watching him at labour with a hoe. After a silence while Alphabet paused in front of her and leaned on his hoe:

'I had a rare dream last night — dreamt I was just married to a nice young gal! A lovely creature she was, as pretty a piece of fabric as a man could wish to handle.'

'Dirty creature!' exclaimed Amnesty.

'All right. All right,' he answered pacifically, and resumed his work.

'Look, neighbours!' she cried, to nobody in particular for there was none but themselves in view: 'Look at that heathen man, petting his potatoes again!'

Her husband straightened his back and said laconically:

'She was lovely; never had to do any courting.'

Amnesty said no more.

The dream may have been a true dream, or it may just have been fabricated by him to oppose to his wife's disagreeable hints, yet from that time Alphabet did really begin to dream astonishing things by night and do peculiar things by day. Something seemed to be working to an explosion within him. It was not the mere affliction of leisure, though what a scope it gave for brooding! — nor remorse for his sins, whatever they were; it was as if Amnesty had been urging a rock over a crumbling cliff, and at last it had fallen. It was *he* who went mad, and, unlike Amnesty, there was no half and half about it either. He had got the devil one morning on an anvil in his sitting room — so he thought — he was cutting him out of the axle of the world, and with a heavy hammer he clouted and smote table and chairs and fireplace and dresser and windows, crying out: 'Jehovah!' and 'Sweet sinners!' until all was crashed to splinters and he had destroyed the place. Neighbours and strangers rushed along but they feared him, and he scattered them all for hours until a doctor came with men and beguiled him off to a madhouse.

He was never let out again. Amnesty was left by herself, but although she thus became sole mistress of the cottage she never used but her own half as before, keeping herself alone there, waiting and moping and visibly growing older. The box and bird-nest were done away with and no more seen, and she did not walk the roads. At all hours of the day she would go, ah, and creep all hours of the night, to his door and knock upon it, though there was never an answer to be got nor the hope of one. The door was not locked, yet she never touched the hasp to enter, but knocked and stood and called and asked for him.

POSTE RESTANTE

*(This tale was written upon a theme set by John Fother-
gill for his 'Omnibus', and is here reprinted by his kind
permission.)*

As a rule Arthur Hart was a lucky man, but
there were times when fortune, without really
failing him, did not seem to be helping him very
much, and then he was baffled. But he was never
baffled for long at any one time, being a lucky man.
Physically, mentally and socially Hart was a good
average sort of person with pink cheeks, coal black
curly moustache, a romantic disposition, and a habit
of clothing himself in suits so very dull that they
verged on the vulgarly unimpressive. Yet he must
not be unkindly blamed for this, having been or-
phaned early in life. At thirty he was still a bachelor,
with a prosperous factory for making lavatory basins
and such-like ware on the outskirts of North London,
left him by his father; in other words he was in a
position to be envied by orphans of many degrees and
a fair number of other bachelors.

Arthur and his prosperity were also in a position
of some exposure to women, eligible and ineligible
alike, but a shy man who blenches before his own
desires helplessly assumes an armour he detests
and longs to discard. Romantic though he was,
he had never been able to conquer his graceless
inhibition and meet the desiring challenge of any

pretty creature. It was therefore in a state of extreme excitement that one day he read a rather intimate letter addressed to him from an unknown lady, a Mrs. Wright. The circumstances which brought this unusual letter into his hands were themselves by no means unusual; one of those controversies was raging in the column of *The Daily Signet* upon the topic (or topics) of Love and Marriage, in which it seemed to Arthur Hart that both pros and cons were understating their experiences, and conceiving this to be due to popular regard for the delicate nature of the theme he composed a letter embodying views of more than ordinary candour, derived mainly from his browsing in the published case-books of various psycho-analysts. He signed his letter *Pro Bono Publico*, with the honourable addition: 'I enclose my card,' and the letter duly appeared. The controversy continued its raging career, but Arthur did not write again because he had received this letter from Mrs. Wright and straightway embarked upon a private correspondence with her.

Her letter to *Pro Bono Publico* was transmitted to Hart by *The Daily Signet*, and it stated that Mrs. Winter was in profound sympathy with the views expressed in his letter and would like to correspond directly with him upon the matter. The letter was typewritten on a quarto sheet, faintly pink and perfumed. It bore no date, address, or name, but pinned to it was a stamped envelope addressed to

Mrs. Wright, Poste Restante, at some office in the district of Ealing.

Arthur Hart turned the letter over and over in his mind. Never in his life before had he received a personal private letter from a woman, and it excited him as much as her presence would have embarrassed him: an unknown creature, pink and perfumed like her letter he was certain. For an hour or two his imagination played with all the romantic possibilities offered by the piece of pink paper, until some tiny shoots of doubt began to burgeon in his mind. Why had she not given her real address? Why was she hiding under cover of a suburban post office?

Well, for one thing she was married. And then of course she had no idea who or what sort of person *he* was; it was only natural that she should want to assure herself of his bona fides at the outset, to know who he was before giving the clue to herself. Besides, there was her husband, who presumably was not to know about the matter. But why had she not at least *signed* the letter? There was not a scrap of handwriting, not a Yours truly, not even a name upon it, all was typewritten, even the envelope, and that was stamped as if she very much desired an instant reply.

It was truly romantic, mysterious, and inviting — thought Arthur Hart — but soon he had a further misgiving: it might be a joke. By God, yes, it was a practical joke. Some ass was trying to play the fool with him, some man perhaps, who would get him to commit himself and then hawk the letter round his club: 'Ho, ho! D'ye see this! My dear Mrs. Wright. Love and marriage. Won't you, will you; will you, won't you? Ha, ha! Look, Look. That fellow Hart! What a dog!'

Yet there was something veridical in that pink and perfumed invitation, the sort of truth that Arthur was eager to put to the test. Already to his fancy Mrs. Wright (if this letter *was* genuine) would be dark and beautiful; the letter itself was a witness to her romantic intelligence; it might be a crass blunder to ignore her because of his fear of being victimized by a joker. Nothing venture, nothing win. So he replied that very day declaring his willingness to continue the discussion with her, in the hope of arriving at some sincere conclusion about these questions through their mutual sympathy. But in order to safeguard himself against that possible joker he adopted the same means as Mrs. Wright and typed his letter and did not sign it. Moreover, he attached a stamped envelope addressed: *Alaric Delmaine*, *Poste Restante* at some post office in North London.

By such crude courses do people like Hart embark upon their clumsy adventures. He took a false name and a post office as defence against a practical joker; on the other hand, it would intimate to Mrs. Wright that what is proper for goose must be good for gander.

Mrs. Wright answered his letter in the same form

again, with pink perfumed paper and stamped envelope addressed to her *Poste Restante*. She intimated in a graceful way that while she preferred them both to remain impersonal she wished the correspondence to be as personal as the subject demanded and circumstances allowed.

Hart still feared the joker's heavy hand, but having begun he would not withdraw, and trusted to his own wariness to escape ridicule; so they continued to write to each other anonymously until all his suspicions were allayed and he too became as frank in his attitude as the lady had been from the beginning. He wanted to know her Christian name; Mrs. Wright, he pleaded, was a mere abstraction that gave him no image of her. Also he wanted to meet her; could they not do this now, and realize all the joy of their letters?

She told him her name was Charmian, but that she was a wedded wife and never could they meet, that his letters were the great solace of her life so tinged with darkness, that it was impossible for her to step beyond the barrier of their letters. Within these limits she would do anything for him, it was a delicious intimacy, a marriage of minds. Never would she forget how thrilled she had been by his own beautiful name in the first letter; he was always Alaric to her.

From now onwards the letters were cumulatively love letters. Hers were almost always written in exalted tones, and if her language was somewhat

39

extravagant it must be remembered that this is the common issue of vivid emotion. Mrs. Wright was undeniably a woman of goodwill and generous tendencies. Her knowledge of human nature was perhaps not very profound; she seemed to think that the machinery of life could be run by mere kindness and that every complication could be resolved by simple treatment. It was a sort of spiritual arithmetic, her two and two always making four. When that sum refused, as it often did, to compose itself so readily, she attributed it to the evil disposition of the factors and not to her faulty arithmetic. There were things in the human heart, she admitted, that *could* not be accounted for. At such times Hart felt ashamed of having assumed a false name, but he could not bring himself to confess it to her, and anyway if they were never to meet it was a harmless subterfuge, and did not matter. At other times Charmian's letters were the outpourings of an amorous woman revealing her tempting self to a man from a safe distance; she was thus free because he could not observe her, in his presence she would have been restrained.

For over a year they exchanged their inflaming notes and Hart did not again press her to meet him. Save for an occasional tantalizing desire to meet this beloved woman in the flesh he was content with the anonymous relationship. Confronted by her he too would certainly have been confused, possibly ashamed; he could not have faced with equanimity this ruthless partner in illicit intercourse. There was, too, the obstacle of her husband, for although Mrs. Wright never referred to him again he remained an insurmountable and dangerous problem. By this scheme of theirs they had made their position safe; their fantasy of love had bloomed like a flowering tree, it was most beautiful, but a touch of reality would blight it. Charmian was a woman of rare free spirit, but not, O most certainly not, one to be flattered, fluttered and flirted with.

They might have gone on thus until in another year or so, maybe, their devotion had wilted and dried in its own sterile husk, but the Great War crashed upon them and Arthur Hart went for a soldier. Both agreed it would be impossible to correspond when he went off to the War.

'Let us say good-bye,' wrote Charmian, 'and keep only the memory of what we have been to each other. We are strangers in the flesh and I could not bear to hear of the dangers you will meet. But always remember you are in my heart, and when war is over we may come together again. A hundred unexpected things may happen before then and so if you *do* care, put a line in the personal column of *The Daily Signet* (it brought us to each other). I shall surely see it and reply.'

Hart the more readily agreed to this because it absolved him from the embarrassment of confessing his real name. He tried to persuade her to meet him just once before he left for the front but she answered that it was impossible, that even if it had not been impossible she could not think of breaking the frail romantic thread they had woven around themselves.

Hart thought vaguely that this was a little callous, but he soon found out that human slaughter, filth, horror, starvation, and wounds, were more tremendous things than pink notes from unknown women, and at length he ceased to think of Mrs. Wright.

Three times he was wounded, and on the last occasion he stayed pleasantly through the end of summer and autumn in a Brighton hospital, where they had amputated two fingers of his left hand and repaired the remnants of an ear that had been torn away. In consequence he did not return to the front and the Armistice found him sufficiently in love with a V.A.D. nurse to propose marriage. Edith Stone had shown a tender interest in his case, had treated him with singular kindness and behaved devotedly, but in the end she married him.

At breakfast on the first honeymoon morning they sat facing each other in the hotel over the question of what to eat, and Arthur was enchanted to learn that his wife shared his predilections for coffee and haddock.

'Now I know one thing!' he cried, picking up his knife and pretending to sharpen it on his fork.

'What?' asked Edith.

'I think we shall get on well together.'

42

'Do you,' said Edith, whose finery made her look almost pretty; 'do you really?'

'Of course we shall,' answered her husband.

It is perhaps beyond human power to maintain any relationship at an ideal level, least of all marriage. Arthur and Edith were married a month after the cessation of war, and they went to live in a sweet little house at Kew, with a cook-general named Mackerel, whose jobbing-gardener of a cousin came and forced rhubarb for them and produced anaemic lettuces three times a week. The Harts had not known a great deal about each other except that they wanted to get married. Edith was an orphan, without any relations; her father had been an artist; she had undoubtedly made the best of her situation by marrying Arthur, but she was fond of him and they were happy for quite a while. But as time went on and the minor disillusionments ensued he could not help sometimes comparing the rather dutiful response of Edith with the ardour of Charmian's love. One was fire and the other, if not ice, was cool. And her coolness made him cool. just as Charmian's fire had inflamed him. He did not tell his wife of that episode, and the letters he still cherished were kept under lock and key. He did not complain to Edith, he was not a complaining man, but whenever he re-read the letters, and he began to do so rather often, he could not help but see Edith in her rather meagre properties. And it seemed to him she was less like a woman than a corset-bust in a woman's shop window. There was the curve of a bosom — made of wax — the fall of hips that served no sensible office. In her eyes there was more drought than dew, in her speech more vanity than understanding, in her love more function than emotion. Edith was not at all handsome, nor endowed with any special graces. Once she had been tender and devoted, now she was dutiful and efficient, though occasionally he was aware of strange moods in her which were hostile to him and warned him to keep at arm's length for days on end. At such times her brown hair seemed coarse and harsh, her grey eyes smouldered in the pale face with gleams of unuttered ill-will, her face grew more emphatic in its plainness, and her touch chilled him. There were headaches then, and little ills which she imagined to be the preludes to some fatal sickness, apprehensions of a decay which she sought to arrest by resorting to patent medicines. Edith never criticized *him*, or quarrelled with him, not even about his common respect for omens, a failing which undoubtedly annoyed her. She had no superstitions, absolutely none, and reduced every omen to its farcical ineptitude. But still, when a strange cat crossed her path she was pleased if it was a black cat and disturbed when it was not. That was merely because although she did not like cats at all she preferred cats to be black. It would never do to walk under a ladder, anything might drop on you; and if salt were spilt at table she cleared it up at once because she disliked untidiness.

Frankness and pride she declared were the noblest qualities in life, and begged Arthur never to stoop to artifice or descend to pity; he was to speak freely to her about everything that concerned themselves, with truth, the whole truth, and nothing but truth. Yet once, when moved by the lack of warmth in their relationship he ventured to speak about this she declared she had never been so insulted in her life, that he had a vulgar mind and a disagreeable temper, that he imagined . . . O depths!

'Ah, you don't understand,' muttered Arthur huskily.

'But I *do* understand. Quite well I do. What *is* there to understand?'

'I was merely saying . . .'

'What? O Arthur, why are you so weak, so silly!'

Baffled, he interrupted her denying tirade by handing her a pair of nail scissors and saying:

'I wish you'd just clip my sideboards for me.'

So it was inevitable that his comparison of bleak Edith with the passionate Charmian nourished a sense of loss, but after a year of wedded fortune he recognized resignedly that women are as variable, unstable, and incalculable as the waves of the sea. Fashioned of wind and water, all alike hurrying to the shore, these resemble each other though changing from moment to moment. But the shore they break upon does not know in what mood or shape they come, and before it can know this they are gone. And yet, there are others, waves that have yet to break, pink and perfumed waves!

One morning at breakfast, on opening his *Daily Signet* he was astonished and agitated to see a notice in the personal column:

'CHARMIAN TO ALARIC. Where are you?'

For minutes his blood seemed to do nothing but swarm into his breast and then discharge in frightful showers to every limb. He shot a stealthy glance at Edith, who was rather blithe this morning and did not notice his perturbation. Putting aside the newspaper he made an effort to consume his food, but all appetite was gone.

'Aren't you feeling well?' Edith asked.

'O yes,' he brightly replied.

'But you've not eaten anything.'

'Just don't fancy it this morning.'

'Is it your liver? Have one of my tabloids?'

'No, no. I'm all right. It's nothing.'

'I wish you would.'

'I'd take one if I wanted it,' said Arthur. 'I'd absolutely love to, *but* I don't want it. I do not, really.'

'Are you going? Already?' she asked, as he got up from the table.

'Yes, I want to get off to the office early. Got to leave the car somewhere for the brakes to be overhauled, they're slipping a bit. Bye, bye.'

As he bent and kissed her her hand casually picked up the newspaper and she asked:

'Do you want this?'

'I might as well take it,' he said, but before handing it to him Edith glanced up and down the columns and it seemed to his guilty fancy that her gaze hesitated upon that invitation from Charmian! Just that very one thing! He was horrified.

'Here you are,' she said, folding it up for him. 'Don't be late this evening.'

'No,' he answered, 'no, I won't.' And off he drove to his office and factory, chanting absurdly to himself. There is nothing more remarkable than a lavatory basin manufacturer in the transports of a mystical passion. The cool glazed commonplace exterior seethes and becomes magniloquent, rhetorical, melodramatic and fatuous, and our friend kept murmuring:

'Alaric, where are you?'

'Beloved, I am here!'

'Beloved, where are you?'

'Alaric. I am here!'

and so on, until he came to the office of *The Daily Signet*, and there he left an advertisement for its personal column on the following day.

The succeeding twenty-four hours were spent in a discordant distracted state and the throes he experienced were those of a scoundrel, a victor, a coward, a god; he was all these rolled into one, loyalty to Edith contending with the re-awakened passion for

Charmian. The issue was never in doubt, and it may be suspected that his sense of loyalty was little more than fear of the consequences of discovery.

When *The Daily Signet* came at breakfast time he saw his own advertisement in the personal column:

'ALARIC TO CHARMIAN: Write to old address. Enchanted.' Immediately above it her own announcement was repeated, with an addition:

'CHARMIAN TO ALARIC: Where are you. Write to old address?'

Away his thoughts whirled in wild-cat imaginings, until he heard his wife petulantly call:

'Do put that paper down, Arthur. Your breakfast.'

'Good!' he cried. 'By Jove, it's getting late, I must hurry.'

'You're not to,' she admonished. 'Are you feeling better this morning?'

'I could eat a horse,' he declared.

'Are you sure?'

'Not about the horse, but I'm all right.'

That evening he posted a long letter to Mrs. Wright, *Poste Restante*, at the old office in the Ealing district. It began by announcing — he wanted to be perfectly straightforward — that he was now married, and then it continued, in the traditional way of such letters, that his marriage was an unhappy one, his wife was cold and unresponsive and did not understand him. She was an Edith Stone, it had been a momentary attraction

48

due to his weak state in hospital where she was nursing him. He had lost two fingers of his left hand in the war and a part of his ear was shot away, otherwise no damage but a few scars.

'She told me her father was an artist, but do you know I found out since that he only designed umbrella handles. But enough of such troubles, we have found each other once more. Your last letter said to me: *Always remember you are in my heart*. I want to hear from your lips if that is true now. You must meet me, you must, I insist. It is stupid to waste our love on mere letters.'

That and more like it was the kind of thing he wrote. He was grown up now. Having been to the war and lost some of his fears, he recklessly plunged.

Next morning on his way to business he popped into the North London post office he had designated.

'Any letters for Hart?' he inquired of a pretty girl behind the counter. After searching in the rack she told him 'No.'

Disappointed he turned away and then it flashed upon him that he had made a stupid mistake. The name he should have asked for was Alaric Delmaine, not Arthur Hart! It was impossible to ask the girl again for a different letter; she would think him an impostor. Blast it, he would have to wait. Twice again during the day he peeped in at the post office and each time the same girl was in attendance, he dared not go in, and it was not until he was driving homewards that evening that he found a different official there and secured the letter for Alaric Delmaine. He slipped it into his inner breast pocket, he could not bear to open it there, it would keep until he had a few calm moments alone.

At home he was soon able to obtain them, for Edith had a headache, wanted no dinner, and so after bustling about tenderly for her, her indisposition having made him feel something of a villain again, he left her lying on the couch in the drawing-room with a tube of aspirins and a cup of tea. Then he went in to his dinner, and alone in the dining-room he opened Charmian's letter.

O, it was a strange upheaving revelation, written by hand, not typed, and the paper was neither pink nor perfumed. Yet it was full of the old passion.

'I am a widow now. Perhaps if you still care for me, it will be possible for us to meet somewhere. My husband is dead, but you know how unhappy I have always been with him, so I cannot pretend any sorrow.'

But then came a passage that turned his heart blood and brains into buttermilk and cheese.

'He did not understand me, no one has ever done that except you; he had none of the fine feelings and the glow of my Alaric. But what could you expect of a man who made lavatory basins and things like that. He was a well-meaning man, a good man, and did his duty in the war, he was wounded several times and lost two fingers and the part of an ear.'

And the handwriting was Edith's! Yes, it was

that guilty thing lying in the other room, that piece
of dry pumice, who had fooled him with monstrous
balderdash. She was Charmian! And she had got
his letter, too, by now. Sure. Jesus, Joseph and
Mary, they were properly bowled out! O the hell,
the hell! Edith was Charmian, Charmian Edith! O
marvellous! Olympus had been in labour and produced this . . . this . . . pincushion! It was stuffed
full of poisonous pins.

Half an hour later he went into the drawing-
room; it was impossible to postpone the discussion
any longer, they were in it, up to their necks, together. Edith sat on a hassock, staring into the fire,
her face huddled in her hands. Hart went and stood
looking down at the top of her head.

'Well,' he said casually. 'I got your letter. Did
you get mine?'

Silently she nodded her head.

'So I'm dead, am I?' he cried angrily. 'And
you're a widow, eh?'

'You've done just the same as I have,' she
answered dully, 'and perhaps for the same reason.'

'What do you mean?'

'You take assumed names and make love to girls
you think are married. Have I done worse?'

'That's what I want to know.'

'I have not.'

'You wished me dead. Dammit you *make* me
dead.'

'I'm sorry, Alaric, I did not know you.'

'Who the devil was Wright. You never told me you had been married before. Did you kill *him?*'

'No,' she said sullenly. 'I was never married before. There is no Mr. Wright, there never was any Mr. Wright, he's a fiction — like Alaric Delmaine.'

'And like Charmian!'

'No,' the answer was sharp, 'she's not a fiction.'

'O, I'm all wrong, and you're all right, I suppose. Well, for God's sake explain it all to me.'

But Edith remained as quiet as the wall in that teeming silence, until he blared out:

'Well, what have you to say?'

Wearily she rose and confronted him:

'What *can* I say?'

'That's what I want to know.'

'I'll try to tell you,' she said, 'if you'll sit down and be patient.'

There was such a deprecating humbleness about her appeal that he dropped into an armchair, while she sat down on the hassock again and faced him.

'Think of me as Charmian, will you? You know *her* well enough. There are all our letters, yours and mine, you know me only too well. Perhaps I am a romantic fool who *thinks* passionately but never *feels* passion, but I can't believe it, even yet. I was never attractive to men but I yearned to be loved, and a good many years ago I got into correspondence with a man I did not know, and we wrote letters without seeing each other. They were not very nice letters, his to me, but he persuaded me to meet him, and when we met I was repelled. I never saw him again, nor wrote him, but I missed the letters terribly. That was what I wanted, to pour out my intimate thoughts and feelings to a sympathetic man in a way I dared not do face to face with him. I suppose I was a very virginal type of creature, who feared the realities of love and was satisfied with the romance. I did not want a real love-affair, I wanted a fantasy. This kind of thing happened half a dozen times, I think. I wrote to men, and they responded, and though they never gave me in their letters the fine thing I dreamed of I was fairly content until they wanted to meet me. That always proved fatal, the glow and charm faded immediately on seeing them, I could not write to them any more. So at last I determined I would never meet a man in such circumstances again, never, never, it spoiled it all. It sounds so simple to me, all this, but I suppose you find it hard to believe.'

Arthur Hart shrugged his shoulders vaguely.

'But it is true,' she continued. 'It *is* true. Then I wrote to you, and your letters gave me all I had ever craved. All, all. And I was so afraid of spoiling it that I would not meet you, and I did not.'

'Not as Mrs. Wright,' he said, half laughing.

'I called myself that, and pretended that I was married to give it as an excuse for our never meeting. I am glad somehow that you respected that and did not insist on seeing me, and yet you were the only one I ever longed to meet. That is all.'

53

Her husband sat staring into the fire; then he said, turning to her and fidgeting in his chair:

'Well, it has cleared up things a bit, but it leaves matters pretty hopeless.'

'I suppose it does,' she admitted.

They were silent for a long time, and then she said:

'I shall write no more letters.'

'Why not?'

'To no one now,' she said sadly.

'Not even to me?'

She leaned forward and scratched at his knee reflectively with her finger nail. 'Would you like that? Would you care? Would you care as much as before?'

'Would you?' queried Hart. It was a fascinating enigma still. She replied:

'Would letters be necessary now?'

Strange excitements were stirring him, incredible blisses.

'Ah, but you've killed me off,' he said brusquely.

'That was only symbolic. I wanted to put out of my heart anything that interfered with my feeling for Alaric. That has been so perfect I felt your letters were more than words, just as mine were really me.'

'Six men,' he grumbled.

'You were the last. I never wrote to another. You were perfect to me, something I'd been trying all my life to find.'

'As Alaric?'

'Yes.'

'But not as myself?'

'I did not know your real self. It was hidden. I only knew an Arthur Hart and he never loved me as Alaric.'

'Nor you me as Charmian. I only knew you as Edith.'

'Don't you think,' said Edith slowly, 'that we have found each other now?'

'I wish,' he said, 'you had not sneered at my lavatory basins.'

'You sneered at my father's umbrella handles.'

'Did you really wish me dead?'

'No, no, Alaric, no,' she eagerly clasped his knees with both her hands. 'Don't you see that I've found all I've been striving to get, and I'm no longer afraid? I was frightened this morning when I got the letter and realized all, but O, my dear — do you really think I am cold and unresponsive?'

'Depends on whether you are Edith or Mrs. Wright,' deliberated he.

'Then doubt no more,' she whispered, rocking his knees fondly. 'Alaric, where *are* you?'

Bending down, he caressed her flushed cheeks between his hands, murmuring:

'Charmian, I am here!'

ARCHIE MALIN, A YOUNG SAILOR JUST OFF THE SEA, rambled into a tavern one summer evening with a bundle under his arm. There was hearty company, and sawdust on the floor, but he was looking for a night's lodging and they could not do with him there, so they sent him along to the widow Silvertough who keeps a button-and-bullseye shop down by the shore. (You would know her again; she's a mulatto, with a restive eye.) And could she give him a night's lodging? He would be off by the first train in the morning — would a gone to-night only the last train had beat it — just a bed? She could; so he threw down his bundle, bought a packet of butter scotch, and went off back to the tavern, *The Cherry Tree*. Outside it was a swing-sign showing about forty painted cherries as fat as tomatoes on a few twigs with no more than a leaf apiece. Inside there was singing, and hearty company, and sawdust on the floor.

'Happy days!' said the sailor, drinking and doing as others do.

Well, this fair young stranger, you must know, was not just a common seaman; he wore a dressy uniform with badges on his arm, and looked a dandy. He could swop tales with any of them there, and he sang a song in a pleasant country voice, but at times his face was sad and his eyes mournful. Been to Sitka, so he said, but said in such a way that nobody liked to ask him where that was, or where he was bound for now. They thought, indeed, that maybe some of his family had grief or misfortune come upon them, and no one wanted to go blundering into the sort of private matters that put a man down; but when someone spoke about the numbers of people dying in the neighbourhood just then, the sailor became rather contentious.

'Baw! Plenty of people die every hour, but you don't know any of them. There's thousands die every day, but devil a one of them all is known to you or to me. I don't know them, and you do not know them, and if you don't know them it's all the same, death or life. Of course, when a big one falls — like President Roosevelt, it might be, or old Charley the linen draper over at Crofters — you hear about that; but else you don't know them, so what does it matter to you — if you ain't acquainted with them? I tell you what, it is very curious how few of the people you *do* know ever seem to die; but it's true — they don't. I knew my own father, of course, as died; and a friend or two that died was well known to me; but I don't know any of these other corpses, nor what becomes of them I do not care. And that's as true as the dust on the road.'

'Young feller,' an oldish man, drinking rum, said, 'you are young yet. When you get to my age you will find your friends a tumbling off like tiles from a roof.'

And what becomes of them?'

58

'They'll get their true sleep.'

'That all there is to it then?'

'O, there's goodly mercy everywhere. Accarden to your goings-on before, so it is. Whatsoever you does here must be paid for there.'

'Aye,' said the sailor, with a general wink, 'even up yonder money talks, I suppose?'

'God help you! To be thinking of that!' the old man cried. 'Money talks, 'tis true; but there's only two ways it gives you any satisfaction; one is earning it, the other spending it.'

'There's many though,' the sailor said, 'as spends a lot they don't earn.'

'Ah, that's their own look-out,' said the other, with his glass of rum in his hand. 'And you can take your mighty oath it's the sacramental truth. You can't thread a camel through a needle's eye. Dust to dust, you know; ashes to ashes.'

'Here!' growled the landlord. 'Tip us a lively song, someone. I feels like I was going to be haunted.'

So they persuaded the young sailor to sing his song.

What's become of all the lassies used to smile up on
    a hearty?
  Luck my lay, luck my laddie, heave and ho!
What's the news of Jane and Katey with their
    mi-ra-fah-so-lah-ty?
  I dunno, Archy Malin, I dunno.

Where's the lass as swore she'd wed me when I
    shipped again this way?
    Luck my lay, luck my laddie, heave and ho!
Was it booze, or was it blarney? Was it just my bit
    of pay?
    I dunno, Archy Malin, I dunno.

O, young men are fond of pleasure, but the girls are
    full of vice,
    Luck my lay, luck my laddie, heave and ho!
Is there ne'er a pretty creature who's as simple as
    she's nice?
    I dunno, Archy Malin, I dunno.

They gave him a hearty clap for singing it,
though it wasn't very lively.

'I never heard that ballad before,' the old rum
man said.

'You wouldn't,' replied the sailor.

'And I thought I knew most every song as ever
was, most of 'em!'

'You wouldn't know that one,' the sailor said,
'because I made it myself.'

'Ah!' the other gleefully cried, 'I knew; I knew
there was some craft about it.'

'And it's true,' added the singer, 'true as the dust
in the road.'

With that he got up, pushed his drink back on
the table, and away he went.

With a bit of a lurch now and then he strode

DUNKY FITLOW

This new collection of Coppard's tales consists of fourteen stories written during the last two years. They show considerable diversity, and are likely to appeal to a large circle of readers. It is popularly held that collections of stories are seldom successful because readers of books prefer a continued narrative, while short stories are read only in magazines and other periodicals. However true this may be, and it is partly true, in the case of Mr. Coppard it is different. He is a short story writer and has never attempted the novel. All his collections have a premium value as first editions, and interest in his writing has caused each volume to be reprinted a number of times. *Dunky Fitlow* can be recommended to all Coppard admirers whether they be collectors of first editions or not.

Readers who have only a limited acquaintance with his stories are recommended to seize hold of *Dunky Fitlow;* it is likely that they will find their experience enriched and their pleasure increased. Knowledge of human nature coupled with close observation of people who, for the most part, live close to the soil, are qualities which are manifested in all Mr. Coppard's writing. A sense of humour and insight into character are apparent in everything he writes.

moodily along the sea wall of the little harbour. Most of the shops were closed, and a calm midsummer dusk was nestling on street and sea. At the end of a rocky mole protruding seawards he was quite alone and leaned on a parapet. The moon rose drowsily over the bay, whose silent waters only moved when near the shore; the waves frilled pettishly on grey rocks veined with silica. A ship passed over the sad evening sea, its lamps faintly glowing, and a few houses on shore beamed with lights as well. The mountains around were black already, though the sky behind them was pearly. Somewhere a bell was ringing.

He wished himself gone out of the dull little town, but he was bound to stay until morning, and so after sighing away a half hour or more he turned at ten o'clock to ramble back to his lodging, but on the border of the town he took a turn up on to a little rampart of the hills, a place newly laid out on its banks in municipal fashion with shrubs and young birch trees and seats on winding paths. Up there he lounged down on one of the seats under the slim birches, between whose branches he saw the now risen moon over a darker bay, the harbour with its red and green lights, one or two funnels, a few masts and spars. And he could hear, though he could not see, a motor passing below and the clatter of a trolley. Half full of beer and melancholy he began to drowse, until someone passed quietly by him like a shadow. The night was come, and despite the moon's rays he only took in the impression of a lady, richly dressed and walking with a grand air. There was a waft of curious perfume.

Now the handsome sailor had a romantic nature, he was inclined to gallantry, but the lady was gone before he could collect his hazy senses. He had not seen her face, but she seemed to be wearing a dark cloak that might have been of velvet. He stared until he could no longer see her. 'Smells like an actress,' he mused, and yawned. Leaning back on the seat again he soon fell into a light slumber, until roused once more by a feeling that someone had just gone past. The path was empty, up and down, but though he could see no one, or hear anything, that strange perfume hung in the air. Then he caught sight of a little thing on the seat beside him. In the chequered moonlight it looked white, but it was not white. The stranger knew it was unlucky to pick up a strange handkerchief, but he did pick it up. He found it was charged with that elegant smell he had imputed to actresses.

The moon glittered on his buttons, the patterns of slim boughs and leaves lay across him. *I dunno Archy Malin, I dunno!* he hummed, and stuffing the scented handkerchief into his breast-pocket he sat blinking in the direction he had seen the mysterious lady take. It was late, she had gone *up* the hill; she ought to be coming *down* again, soon.

'That's a nice smell, so help me,' he observed; and he pulled the handkerchief from his pocket again. 'I bet it's hers.' While twiddling it musingly in his fingers he maintained an expectant gaze along the upward path. 'Couldn't have been any handkerchief there when I sat down, or I'd have seen it.' As he replaced it in his pocket he concluded: 'I bet a crown she dropped it here on purpose. Well, you done it, Jane; *you* done it.' Leaning with his arm along the back of the seat he sat so that he would be facing her when she came down the hill again. And he waited for her.

It was in his mind that he ought to have followed her — she might be waiting for him somewhere up there? But she would be coming back — they always did! — and he felt a little unwilling to move now. Time passed very slowly. In the gloss of the moon his brass buttons shone like tiny stars; the patterns of leaves and branches were draped solemnly across his body and seemed to cling to his knees. He held his breath and strained his ears to catch a sound of her returning footsteps. As still as death it was. And then the shock came; the sudden feeling that there, round about him, just behind, some malignant thing was watching, was about to pounce and rend him, and he shrank at once like a touched nerve, waiting for some certainty of horror — or relief. And it gave him a breathless tremble when his eyes swivelled round and he *did* see something there, sitting on the seat behind him. But it was all right — it was her!

Calmly he said: 'Hallo! How did you get here?'

(God Almighty, his brain had been on the point of bursting!)

She did not reply. She sat gracefully, but still and silent, in the black velvet cloak, one knee linked over the other. Whether she had a hat or not he could not tell, there was a dark veil covering her head and face. But none the less he could tell she was a handsome woman all right. Her arms were folded under the cloak, where her fingers must have been clinging to hold it tight around her.

'I saw you go by,' began the young sailor, 'but I didn't hear you come back.'

Well, she did not answer him then, she did not utter a word, but she certainly did pay a lot of attention to what he said to her, and her eyes gleamed quite friendly under her veil. So Archy kept on chaffing her, because he was sure she had not dumped herself down there beside him in that lonely spot, at that time of night, for nothing; and of course he felt quite gay. She nodded a lot at the things he said to her, but it was quite some time before she opened her mouth to him, and then he was rather surprised. Because she was a fine well-built girl, with a lovely bosom and all that, but her voice really did surprise him.

'I have never been here before,' was what she said, but her voice was thin and reedy, as if she had asthma or something. 'I happened to see you — so I came along.'

'O, that's dandy,' said Archy, and he hauled up to

64

her and was for putting his arm around her straight
away.

'No. . . .! You must not do that!'

And although she did not move or shrink away
she spoke so sadly that somehow that jaunty sailor
was baffled; she was a perfect lady! He sat up and
behaved himself.

The girl stared through the trees at the lights
down in the harbour, and you could not hear a
whisper down there, or anywhere else in the world.

She said: 'I was lonely.'

'I bet you was!' was his uncouth reply, and he kept
his own arms folded. This was the queerest piece he
had met for a long time.

'Please don't be angry,' she said, turning to him.

'No. Sure,' he answered heartily. 'I'd like to
know your name, though. Mine's Archy Malin.
I'm a sailor.'

'My name?' She gave a sigh. 'It was Freda
Listowell.'

'Well, ain't it now?' he quizzed her.

She shook her head.

'Married?' pursued the sailor.

'No.' The question seemed faintly to amuse her.

'You lost it then?'

'Yes,' was the grave reply.

The young man was beginning to enjoy these
exchanges. That sort of chit-chat was part of the
fun of making up to girls like Jane and Katey. This
one was a lady — you could not doubt that — and so

it surprised him a bit. But all the same, he liked it.

'Freda Listowell! That's a nice name, too good to lose.'

She shivered, the moonlight had grown cold.

'Shall have to help you find it again,' he continued.

'You could not do that.'

'Could I not! Are you staying in this burgh for long?'

'I am not stopping anywhere at all. I must go back soon.'

'You can't get far to-night — it's late. Where are you stopping, then?'

'You would not believe me if I told you.'

'Me! Not! I'd believe you if you said you was an angel from heaven. Unless you've got a car?'

She slowly shook her head.

He began to feel he was not getting on very well with her, after all. Somehow they were making a poor show together. But he could tell she was an actress; it was not the things she said so much as the way she spoke them. Taking a cigarette from a packet, he lit it.

'I've never seen anything like him in my wanderings!' He held the packet towards her indicating the picture of a fat-headed seaman with whiskers and the word 'HERO' on his hat. 'Have one?' he asked her, but she declined. So he leaned his elbows on his knees and puffed smoke at the ground between his boots. And she had very elegant shoes on, and silk stockings on her fine legs — he couldn't take his eyes

off them. But what was she trying to put across?
Where did she live then? Without turning, he
spoke towards the ground at his feet:

'Are you all right?'

'No,' she replied, and there was despair in her
voice that woke an instant sympathy in him. He sat
up and faced her: 'What's wrong, Miss Freda?
Can I butt in at all?'

For the first time she seemed to relax her grave
airs, and echoed: 'Can — you — butt — in?' It almost amused her. 'O, no. Thank you, thank you,
thank you; but no.'

The refusal was so definite that he could not hope
to prevail against it; he could only murmur half
apologetically:

'Well, if you wanted my help, I'd do my best.
You know — say the word.'

'Ah, I was sure of that!' was the almost caressing
rejoinder. 'My dear, dear friend — but you — ' In
agitation she sat up, her hands clasped together slipping out from her cloak. He saw them for the first
time, they were gloved. Then she parted her hands,
and almost hissed: 'What do you think I am?'

It startled him; there was certainly something the
matter with her.

'You'd better let me see you home. Serious, Miss
Freda.'

'But I have nowhere to go,' she cried.

'What are you going to do then?'

'Nothing.'

67

'But you *must* do something.'

Raising her veiled face she gestured with one hand towards the moon, and said:

'I am going to vanish.'

'O, ho!' In the flash of a second the sailor perceived that he was not dealing with an actress at all, she was dotty! She was going to commit suicide! That was what had baffled him — she was a lunatic, lunatic! A pretty fine lot to drop in for!

'You see, I am what you call a ghost!' she solemnly said.

Well, that clinched it; the poor things generally got worse at the time of the moon. He was keeping a wary eye on her; he liked women, got very fond of them, especially nice young women on moonlight nights, but he did not like them mad.

'You don't believe that?' she asked.

He tried to humour her. 'It's a funny thing that I was having an argument about ghosts with a fellow, once before to-night. And now, here you are, the second one that's trying to persuade me. As a matter of fact, take it or leave it, just as you like, I wouldn't believe in ghosts not even if I *saw* one!'

Very calmly she said: 'What do you think I am doing here?'

Archy fidgetted for a moment or two before replying:

'Quite honest then, I never thought you were a ghost. First I thought you were — you know — a nice girl out for a bit of a lark. . . .'

He paused for her comment on this. It was a very cold one.

'Go on,' she said.

'Ah, well. Then I thought you were an actress.'

'I'm not.' There was a flash of petulance.

'But then I saw you must be in a bit of trouble of some sort.'

With hesitation she agreed: 'Yes, I am.'

'You know — lost your memory, or. . . .'

'No,' she sharply interposed. 'I've lost my life.'

'Well, something like that,' he said pacifyingly. 'Do you come from . . . er . . . from down there?' He nodded towards the town.

Quietly she answered: 'I come from heaven.'

The poor fellow was almost suffering with bewilderment; a sailor lacks subtlety, and he was adrift, so he almost leaped at his little bit of a joke.

'Ah! That's it! You're an angel — I guessed that.'

'There are no angels in heaven,' cried the girl.

'Ain't!' he said.

'No, I have never seen one there.'

Archy mumbled that that would be a great disappointment to him later on.

'What do you think heaven is?' the lady asked. He was obliged to admit that he had not up to that moment been able to give very much thought to the matter.

'I can tell you,' she said gravely.

'Do.' She was so patient that somehow he was

giving up that notion of her being just mad — and anyway, he did not know how to deal with a lunatic.

'When I died, about three years ago . . .' she began.

'You know,' the sailor turned laughing towards her, 'you *would* make a blooming good actress!'

Wearily she stirred: 'Listen!'

'What was you before you died?' he jeered; he was not going to let her mesmerize him like that.

'I was young and rich and foolish then, I had only one thought or passion in my life: I doted on clothes, fine clothes. I suppose I must have been mad. Nothing else ever really interested me, though I pretended it did. I lived simply to dress myself in quantities of beautiful garments. I think I was beautiful, too — perhaps you would have thought so. . . .'

'Let me see!' Archy made a snatch at her veil.

'No . . .!' There was such a tone in her denial that his marauding arms shrank back on him, and it seemed as if the echo of her cry fluttered for a moment up among the faint stars.

'Take care . . .!' Her gravity quelled him. 'That was my life, that and nothing else: day by day, even hour by hour, to array myself in the richest gowns I could procure. What vanity! And I believed that I was thus honouring my body and delighting my soul. What madness! In everything I did my only thought was of the clothes I might wear, what scope the occasion would give me thus to shine. That was all my joy. Life seemed to have no other care, meaning, or end; no other desire, no other bliss. I poured out fortunes on silk, satin, and brocades, and imagined that by doing so I was a benefactor to all.'

'O, but damn it!' interjected Archy. She stopped him with a gesture and then sank back in the corner of the seat, wholly wrapped in her velvet cloak. The sailor leaned with his arm on the back of the seat and surveyed her very wearily, thinking that if she did not go very soon he would have to clear himself off and leave her to her trouble. He felt like yawning but somehow he did not dare. As far as he could make out she was the picture of misery, and he was veering once more to the belief that she was crazy. Harmless enough, but what could *he* do with a daft woman?

'Then I died suddenly,' she went on. 'Imagine my disgust when I realized, as I soon did, that I was buried in a stupid ugly gown of cheap cotton, much too big for me! Ugh!' The lady shuddered. 'For a long time I seemed to be hanging in a void, like a cloud of matter motionless in some chemical solution, alone and utterly unapproachable. My sight was keen, but I could *see* nothing. All was dim and featureless as though I was staring at a sky dingy with a half dead moon.

'Then my thoughts began to swirl around and come back to me, my worldly thoughts; and though I knew I was dead, a waif in infinity, my thoughts were only of what I had prized in life itself — my wonderful clothes. And while I thought of them, they too began to drift around me, the comforting ghosts of them all — gowns, petticoats, stockings, shoes.'

The sailor sighed, and lit another cigarette. The lady waited until he composed himself again.

'But there they were as real as I was, real to me. Ah, what joy that was! I tore off my hideous cotton shroud and dressed myself in one of those darling frocks. But I soon tired of it. When I took it off it disappeared, and never came back again. I remembered other things, I had enjoyed in life, but none of those ever came to me — only the clothes. They had been my ideal, they became my only heaven; in them I resumed the old illusions.'

'Christ!' muttered the sailor. 'I shall! I shall have to clout her in a minute.'

'Pardon?' cried the lady.

'I said: time's getting on, late you know,' he replied.

In the ensuing silence he could almost *feel* her hurt surprise. so he turned to her quite jocularly:

'Well, you *are* giving me a sermon, Miss Freda. What I'd like to know is how you dropped on *me* like this!'

'They all disappeared after I had worn them once; one by one, they left me again. I did not realize that for a long while; and in my joy at getting them back I wore them and changed and wore others, just

72

as I had done in life; but at last all had departed except these you see me in now. When these are gone, I think something strange is going to happen to me . . .'

'Huh!' said Archy.

'. . . but I cannot tell.'

When she stopped speaking the sailor wriggled his cigarette with his lips; the smoke troubled his nose, and he sniffed.

'There ought to be *something* else, don't you think?' she sorrowfully asked.

There was moonlight in the buckles of her shoes, the leaf patterns lay across her neat legs and graceful body.

'Sure!' he answered consolingly. 'It will be all right in the morning. Have a good night's sleep, and you'll be as gay as Conky's kitten to-morrow.'

The lady did not speak or move for some minutes, and when the silence became too tiresome the sailor had to ask:

'Well, what are you going to do now?'

'I wish,' she sighed, 'I could be buried very deep, under the floor of the sea.'

'Baw! You'll get over that!' he heartily assured her.

Then she seemed to be summing him up, as if he only irritated her now. 'But I am dead, I told you. I am nothing but a wraith in the ghosts of my old clothes.'

Her persistance annoyed him; he could not

believe she was a lunatic, and this other business was the sort of lark he did not take kindly to.

'O, cheese it, Freda! Where do you live? Come on. You've been trying to put the dreary on me all this time, but I'm not that type of jacko. I'm a sailor, I am. So suppose you give us a kiss and say Night-night, and toddle off home like a good girl.'

And yet — he waited for that gesture from her. It did not come.

'You do not believe me?' she asked.

'No. I've been doing my best, and you're a bloom-ing fine actress — aren't you? — but I can't bite it. Can't!'

Up he stood, almost indignant. The girl sat where she was and the sailor lingered. For, to tell the truth, he still did not want to leave her; after all, she *might* be queer, he was still adrift; perhaps if he walked off she would follow him. He had taken but one step away when he heard her voice mur-muring. With a frown he listened:

'I could prove it very easily.'

'How?' He swung round.

'By taking off my clothes,' she said.

My! Wasn't that a good one!

'Your clothes off! Here!'

A silent nod was the answer, and it revived at once all his extravagant fancies.

'Aw, now you're talking Freda!'

He flung himself back on the bench beside her again. 'Will you? Come on!' He knew she was going to do it, he awaited her restlessly. 'What about it?' he urged, glancing up and down the paths. 'It's all right. Come on. There's no one about.'

At last she got up, and as he moved too she hissed: 'Sit down, you fool!'

For a moment or two she stood there in the path, guarded by the bushes and little trees, fumbling with her clothes, under the cloak. And she was very cunning, because before he knew how it happened all the clothes dropped and lay in a heap there.

And that was all.

There was no slender naked girl awaiting his embrace. Freda Listowell was gone, dissolved, vanished; he had seen nothing of her, not even her hands. Only her ghostly garments lay in the path with the moon shining on them; the cloak and the shoes, the veil, the stockings, flounces, frills, green garters, and a vanity bag with a white comb slipping out of it. So cleanly swift and yet so casual was her proof that he was frightened almost before he knew.

'She was there. She did not move!' he whispered. 'I could pawn my soul on that!'

For a space the doubting sailor dared not rise from the seat; his hands clung to it as a castaway's to a spar, as he turned his fearing eyes to right, to left, and behind him.

'I don't believe it!' he muttered stoutly, and tearing himself away from the bench he cringed in the path.

'Ahoy there!' he whispered. 'Where are you?'

Sternly he straightened himself, and walked erect among the near bushes. She was not there. Nowhere. When he spun round again her clothes had gone too. 'Hoi! Stop it!' he shouted, but he knew she was not hiding — there was nothing of her to hide. With his heart threshing like a flail he breathed appalling air. 'What was it?' He wanted to fly for his life, but he could not. His nails were grinding into his palms as he braced himself to grapple with his shocked brain.

'Foo!' he gasped, twining himself round and round, not daring to stand still. 'Foo!' Sweat was blinding him, and thrusting one hand to his pocket he pulled out a handkerchief. It was the perfumed wisp he had found on the seat an hour before. As he caught its scent again, he remembered. He held it out in the moonlight, and stared at it, muttering: 'I don't fancy that. I don't. . . .'

Something invisible in the air plucked it from his fingers.

CROTTY SHINKWIN

THIS WAS A LITTLE MAN I'M TELLING YOU, CROTTY Shinkwin, a butcher once, with livery eyes and a neck like a hen that was not often shaved. He knocked out a sort of a living by the coast of the cliff and the sandy shore of Ballinarailin, a town full of Looneys, Mooneys and Clooneys, the Mahoneys, Maloneys, the Dorans, Horans and Morans, but if you were to ask what was their scheme of life it could only be said they were seen gathering weeds from the sea and stones from the shore, which is poor stuff anyway to be passing the time of day on.

In his young youth Crotty bought cattle alive and sold it dead. You would see him going into the kitchens with the large hack of meat in one hand, a saw in the other, and a great coulter of a knife in his mouth, and when he came out again you would observe there was the less meat on him to be carrying. But he was married ten years to Eva Clohesy, a hard woman, and so he was forced to give up that kind of life — it was too much altogether for a man that did not know the wishes of herself from one moment to another.

'Why,' says he to Peter Sisk, 'if you ask me what she likes, or what she wants, you have me beat. *She* could not tell you. It would take the help of God Almighty to keep up with her. Napoleon couldn't do it; he could not.'

So Mr. Shinkwin took to fishing, or to looking after

the holy well, and little handicrafts like that, for there was nothing else to turn a hand to in that drifty place.

'Holy and sacred medallion!' says she to him then, 'and what are you about at all?'

She was glaring at him with her two cat's eyes, but a fine woman, one of the Clohesys she was, as brisk as a Connemara cow, and two hairy arms.

'I am not well,' says he.

'What's on you?'

'And I never *could* be well again,' he says, 'not in this mortal world, and what's more — I *will* not.'

'Och! For a man that's about to be dying there's a deal of talk and porter in it yet!'

Crotty looked at her: 'The devil knows, you strap, and everyone knows, I've a drowsiness in my bones and a creepiness in my stomach. I'm sick and I'm bad. It's wrecked I am.'

'O, you goat!' says she. 'You shanandering goat!'

'But . . . but I endure it,' Crotty said, 'as a man I endure it; I do not give in to it. By my soul, you can't daunt me, and I do not sink to my bed.'

She gave a great spit, like a man with a quid:

'The kingdom of heaven be yours, little or much.'

'And if I should come,' he continued, 'to my expiration, do not go for to put your hands on me and rouse me again.'

'The devil a hand,' says she. 'Let you walk out to the rocks now and catch me a couple of crabs, or by the harp of the Jews it's your corpse itself I'll be lathering with holy water this night.'

So Crotty would go perch himself on a stone to watch the half mile of surf roving in from the bay, and the nuns from the convent bathing in it. Giddy and gay they would be, bobbing up to their ribs and groaning, but they were dressed in blue sacks of nightgowns and long baggy trousers and offered no nice allurements to Mr. Shinkwin's eye. If they took an orphan down to bathe with them, it should undress and dress on the stones outside the bit of a box they dried in, for though it blew hearty and crisp the child could not be let come into their holy boudoir.

'It would be queer and all,' thought Crotty, 'if the child was the nuns just now, and the nuns was the child!'

And here was Tarpy Ryan and his ass-cart loading weed, and far out in the bay was Inniskalogue, a big hump of an island with nothing on it but grass, and smooth as a button. No one lived there, neither priest, peasant nor gentleman; nobody visited it — it had the bad name; no one owned it and nobody wanted it. If you asked a fellow about Inniskalogue he would twist his eyes, or he would shake his head and scratch it (or his haunches) until you wished you had not inquired of him. But it lay on the blue bosom of the sea, the sunbeams glistening, a fine sparkling pasturage with the gap of a cliff here and there.

One nice day Crotty and young P. J., a handsome lad, sailed over the bay in a yawl, and in about an hour they got so close to one corner of Inniskalogue

79

that they could see the stones, but not a bird on it or any other living sign. And P. J. cast anchor there for to do a little fishing. Down went the hook, the cables leaping and growling after it and after it until there was no more cable, and still they had not got a hold.

'By my soul, there's a power of deep water under us!' said P. J.

Just then, down comes a draught of air from a cloud and it puffed the yawl out round past the corner of the island. They went roving round to the far side with the anchor trailing, till they felt a jerk and the little boat shook.

'She's got a hold,' cried P. J.

And by the souls of the sainted martyrs, she had! The wind gave a great twist, the yawl reeled, and there was that island, hooked underneath by the anchor, tearing after them and following them.

'What is it and all!' Crotty shrieked, for his seven senses had gone black on him, and P. J. was too dazzled to loosen the sheet. They could not see the mainland for the island hid it from them, hundreds of acres it was, and it moving like a cork on the hills and hollows of the sea. They fell on their knees in the boat and prayed to God.

'Sir,' gabbled Crotty. 'We are perishing! For the love of heaven, mercy! Throw back that walking world and sweep the head off me, for my soul has no thirst for the waves of water. Jesus, Joseph, and Mary! Sir, if you please! Amen.'

Then, in the very nick of destruction, the island stopped, and the boat stayed and began to move backwards until it was rushing backwards towards the island. As they looked at it the island itself heaved up and twirled over like a great plate on a hinge until it was upside down. It turned as easy as a porpoise, casting no splash, with only showers dripping off it, but the great black half moon of it when it was up-ended, was as much as a side of the whole world falling, and threw a cold shadow across the yawl. It stayed upside down, and there the boat stayed too, anchored fast and the sail throbbing, and the sea rocking gently as a cradle now.

'We're stuck!' cried P. J., heaving on the rope. 'Crotty, we're stuck!'

'O, God alive!' Crotty said, pointing. 'Will you throw an eye on that?'

And he did so. The island was topsy-turvy now, its green hump was below and the roots of the island had come up from the ocean; they could see a neat little town sitting amid the drainings of a flood. The water was sweeping from it like sand from a barrel, but it dried on the moment. The weeds began to become grass and pretty fuschias and long creepers to hang over the walls. Some big fishes that had got caught gasping in the hedges flipped into the fields and changed into sheep and went crying for their lambs. There was a little church with a steeple chiming — the bell had a pitiful note like the chink of two stones — and a score of cabins but no people seen.

'Will you tell me, Crotty, what is that there now?'
P. J. was pointing towards the church steeple.

'What?' said Crotty.

'On the cross of the church? Do you see it?'

'I do see it.'

'It's my anchor!'

'God's fortune!' said Crotty. 'And how did it climb there at all?'

'And the rope of it stretching from us across the fields.'

It was true enough. The anchor had hooked in the cross of the church itself when it was upside down, and they had pulled it right over.

'I can't lose my anchor,' said P. J., 'it's Andy Mullen's anchor.'

'It is,' Crotty said.

They hauled on the anchor cable until the slack was dripping above the sea, and they pulled themselves right ashore against the path that ran up to the church.

'Go and get the anchor, Crotty.'

'O,' grumbled he, 'I was never that sort of climbing man, I haven't a wing to my elbows.'

P. J. went on coiling up the cables and readying the boat, and spitting in the sea, and staring at the island.

'Go and get the anchor, Crotty.'

Crotty, sitting on a thwart, gaped at the church steeple with repugnance. It was a small steeple, but still it was high and the anchor was on it like a crow's nest in a tree.

'I'm thinking,' said he, 'there's a bank of bog betune this and that; a man would murder himself going there. And what's a bit of a hook? I'll take a pull on it anyway.'

He pulled and pulled on the anchor rope until he was sore and tired.

'Go and get the anchor, Crotty,' said P. J. again.

Crotty sighed and sat down. 'A deceitful island,' he mused. 'No one knows the half of it, sleeping or waking. Am I alive, or is it dead we are? Is my head my head, or is it my rump?'

'Go and get the anchor, Crotty.'

'Ah, to hell with the anchor,' replied he.

P. J. stood up. 'I wonder,' said he, 'if there's a police barracks in this place.'

'Maybe,' Crotty said. 'Maybe there's a booking-office and a train to Dublin!'

P. J. took off his hat and flung it ashore.

'There goes my hat,' said he, 'and where it goes I must follow.'

So saying he stepped on the gunwale and leaped to a rock.

'God save all here!' he cried.

No one answered, but Crotty scrambled over and stood beside him. P. J. walked towards the little road, but Crotty kept still and called out: 'P. J.! Let you take a sniff round first!'

P. J. paused: 'Come on with you! Here's a notice on a board. Come and read it.'

Crotty went and read it out to him.

NOTICE

RATEPAYERS WHO HAVE FAILED
TO PAY THEIR RATES NOW DUE
FOR SOMETIME ARE HEREBY IN-
FORMED THAT STEPS ARE ABOUT
TO BE TAKEN IMMEDIATELY TO
ENFORCE PAYMENT

(Signed) *Crotty Shinkwin*

'By the powers above, P. J. or the powers below,
'tis a disgrace to my native land. I've seen the like
of that notice before, barring the name. I never
thought my name was so common, I did not. The
buttons on your coat are the one buttons with mine,
but your name is not Shinkwin, and my name is not
your name. Who is this nigger-driver of a tax-man?
Or am I doomed to a watery grave, is it? Will I be
collecting the rent from a few shrimps, d'ye think?'

'Come on with you!' said P. J.

They went on, but they did not use the road going
to the church; they took a step aside on the turf that
led them up a hill, good honest turf, a little damp
maybe, but thrifty and sound. Up, up they went,
and what with the steepness of it and the sun's
warmth Crotty was soon wishing that he had never
come that way or met such a contrary island, or gone
in a boat with such an ecclesiastical turn of hook.

'I've a drought on me would blind a salamander.'

Looking here and looking there he saw no sign of life or laughter till they came to the top, and there it was a high cliff they were on, it dropping to the sea sixty or seventy or eighty fathoms down. Behind them and below were the church, the cabins, the sheep, the flowers; patches of field, and a wood of thorns; they could see all over this turned-up island. And all round it was the tranquil sea, but there was not a sight of the mainland or Ballinarailin anywhere in the quarters of the hemisphere, nothing but the sea only and the place they were on. They were stricken with the surprise of that, and the fear of that, and the silence of it; the power of the wind would not have loosened the flax from a ripe thistle.

'Where in the world is the world?' moaned Crotty.

From the edge of the cliff they watched the blue seas move, white gannets diving, and three porpoises rolling slowly along. Halfway down the cliff a dead pig lay tumbled on a rock, a white pig with a long red burst in its belly.

Crotty was timid as a sheep, but P. J. was staring like a man well on the road to heaven.

'Peace to my soul,' he murmured softly. 'This would be the grand place to live in with the woman you wanted and she loving you at all times. It is planted with sweet herbs, and the air is gentle with the kiss of their blossoms.'

'What is it? What is on you, P. J.?'

'Here, on this cliff for my holy tower and the wide sea shining, to go in strength and virtue like the fleet and careless birds. Or to walk with the burden of love till I might find her sleeping on the shore.'

'Ach!' growled Crotty, 'and she glaring at you with her two cat's eyes.'

Just then they saw the little man; he was sitting on the cliff with his legs dangling over. They walked up to him.

'The blessing of heaven on you, good man,' said P. J., 'but that's the queer place to be fishing!'

The man did not answer. He had the face of a weasel, and fingers like the claws of a crab.

'Is it deaf you are?'

The surly man took no heed of them at all, but was pulling up a long stout cord from the sea below. Over and over he coiled the white cord, a mighty stretch of it, until it dripped with sea, and there at the end of it was hooked a fish. The man gave its head a clout and cast it into a creel by his side. As soon as he had stuck a mussel on the hook he threw down the cord again and sat still as stone. Presently he looked round, but he said nothing. It was as if he did not see them, although they were standing so close they could notice a flea was feeding on his ear.

'Is it blind you are?'

And Crotty bent down to tap him on the shoulder, but when he did that his two fingers sunk into nothing, as if the man was but a vapour.

'Jesus, Joseph and Mary!' yelled Crotty. 'Let me

out of this!' And he ran off so fast you could not see his two feet moving at all. When he came to the boat again P. J. was beside him, laughing:

'Wait, Crotty. D'ye hear that, you stag!'

Crotty heard the church bell clinking faintly.

'There's the little anchor to fetch,' said P. J.

Back he turned up the road that led from the sea to the church, and Crotty could do no more but follow him. They hurried along the road past the wood of thorns to the village itself that had a shop and some houses, but not the sign of another soul did they see, and they got to the church where Crotty took a good dab at the Holy Water. Then they stood under the rope, taking a strong squint at that anchor hung on the cross of the steeple.

'I get that,' said P. J. 'I'll get it.'

So they went and opened the door of the steeple and saw a chimney, with a ladder of wood rearing up to the bell-chamber, all covered with barnacles and hairy weeds.

'Go out and hold the rope, Crotty, till I throw the anchor down.'

And he did that.

Crotty stood holding the rope amongst the grave-stones and they leaning this way and that in the churchyard. There were pools of water round the gravestones and the leaning ones looked as though they were peering down to read their own inscriptions in it. One stone near him gave Crotty a twist of the heart when he had spelled out its words.

Eva
the faithful wife of
Crotty Shinkwin,
sometime of
Ballinarailin.
'Sweet heart of Jesus,
be thou my love.'

He let out a great cry but his comrade did not hear it, for he was crammed in the steeple.

'God rest her soul,' said Crotty, bending over the stone. 'Did a man ever see the like of that! God rest her soul — and soften it, too,' he added. 'Bad it is, for the grass grows on her tomb, and there's muddy water between her and heaven. But good it may be, for the world is made of a roguish nature, and wouldn't it be hard if there was no profit on misfortune at all! I was wearing out my life with both hands, waiting on her tooth and nail, and when I'd a mind to rest she would glare at me with her two cat's eyes!'

He looked round fearfully, as if he might see her tracking him even there! A voice cried: 'Mind yourself, Crotty, she's coming now!' But it was only P. J. pushing his head and arm through a hole in the steeple to take a grab at the anchor. The bell stopped clinking, and down came the anchor at Crotty's feet. Without waiting a moment he heaved it on his shoulder and ran off alone to the boat and cast the anchor aboard. Then he coiled the cable and readyed the boat and set the sail. By and bye he saw

P. J. come stepping along with a bundle under his arm.

'Hurry on,' he shouted, 'hurry now!'

'Be easy, Crotty,' replied his comrade. 'I've the treasure of the world in my arms.'

'What is that, P. J.?'

And P. J. showed him the bundle was a pig's bladder, blown up like a balloon and tied at the throat with a blue ribbon.

' 'Twas hanging high up in that steeple. 'Tis a bag of air from the garden of Eden itself. A saint brought it away.

'A saint! What saint?'

'Some holy man, Crotty, but he's gone dead with the hundreds of years.'

'And what's the virtue of it?' Crotty asked.

'Sure,' said P.J., 'and we'd never sink with this aboard. Mind yourself. I'm jumping.'

He took a good leap and landed in the boat. At once there was a terrible scrambling noise in it.

'What! What!' they both cried, stiff with the fear. For the anchor had taken a great jump on to the shore, like a thing alive, it was tearing up the road back to the church, and the rope rushing after as a long snake would.

'It's the anchor!' screamed P. J., and he made a grab at the runaway rope, but as he did so the skin of air from Eden's bower caught in a hooky nail and burst with a noise. Like a big gun, it was. Zip! And P.J. was blown up into the sky until he was no bigger than

a pin and then Crotty saw him no more, for the air
let out from that bag was like the blast of fifty storms
congealed in the crash of one gale. It tore the buttons off his coat and left the roots of thread dangling.

Away rushed the yawl on the crown of the sea,
with Crotty alone and the island following him, for
the hook was in the steeple again. The wind soon
slightened, but Crotty's wits were all scattered and
they went journeying upon the waters of the world
for two days or three before the gossoon had the
sense to cut the rope. And then he cut it. And when
he cut it the island stopped, it heaved up in the sea
again and turned right over to its own old shape and
pattern; the church, the steeple, the pleasant fields,
and the wood of thorns, sank in the heart of the
ocean and you could see no more than the bare hump
of pasture it had always been. The yawl sailed on,
and Crotty heard a bird piping. He scanned the sea,
and by the safety of God, there was the mainland
again, and Ballinarailin again, and Inniskalogue was
where it always had been! He set a course and —
signs on it! — it was not long before he was there
where the nuns were bathing, and Tarpy's ass-cart
was loading weed.

He fastened up the boat, and he hurried home with
the look of decent grief upon him, but by the suit
of Satan it was not grief at all when he met Eva Shinkwin at the door, as sleek as an eel, and she glaring
at him with her two cat's eyes! It was like the cold
nose of a calf pushed in the small of his naked back.

He wished he had been able to buy her the makings
of a costume, or something.

Where in the name of the king of thunder had
he been? Devil and all, what traipsing females had
he been after ruining now?

Well, if she *wanted* to know, he could tell her. O,
yes. Give him a civil word or two, and he would tell
her. And it would be the truth. And the whole truth.
And nothing but the truth. It would form the forma-
tion of all he had to say.

But, holy and sacred medallion, she could never
believe a thing like that!

THE WATCHMAN

L ESTER COOLING, THE PETTY CASHIER AT PONTING'S
Pill Factory, was short in his balance again.
Not much, about twenty-five shillings all told, but
it was not the first time, or even the second, this had
occurred. On the last occasion the boss, a tall, thin
man with piercing dark eyes and very white cuffs,
had stormed at him dreadfully.

'If you can't look after a small sum like ten pounds
without losing half of it from day to day you're not
fit for your job. How old are you?'

'Twenty-eight, sir.'

'Twenty-eight, and you're married? Well, I can't
help that. I *will* not have any more of this shortage
in your cash. It has got to stop, see?'

'But, sir,' explained Cooling, 'I'm certain somebody is stealing it.'

'Who the devil *could* steal it? And who *would*
steal it? Who do you suspect?'

Cooling didn't know.

'Of course not. Don't go making these vague
accusations until you've got some proof. It's nonsense and utter carelessness, that's what's the
matter, Cooling. You hand out the money to
someone or other and you don't make a note of it,
you forget all about it.'

'No, sir,' said Cooling firmly.

'You lock it up in the safe at night?'

'Well, no, sir, I can't sir. Mr. Burns the head

clerk keeps the key of the safe, and he always leaves before me. I have to wait for all sorts of things, the men want 'subs.', or the carters come in for cash, and sometimes the travellers, and things like that. I have to keep the cash-box in my desk, but of course I always lock *that* up.'

'You don't go betting, or anything of the sort, do you, Cooling?'

'O, no, sir.'

'Well, don't. But understand this now, I warn you, it is not to happen again. I'm sick of it.'

So that night Cooling thought he would walk along some time after ten o'clock and have a talk with Fox, the night watchman, about it. And he told Fox, and asked him if he had ever noticed anybody hanging around the offices after hours. Could he suggest anything? Fox was a tall, raw-boned laconic man who did not care very much for clerks anyway, especially when they were rather good-looking, as Lester Cooling was. The only people he was civil to were the foremen and the girls who rolled up the pills; wherever he met *them* he was quite affable. But still, he gave Lester his attention while he explained the situation to him, and at the close he summed up:

'Of course I keep my eye on the offices, it's what I'm here for. If I had noticed anything wrong I'd have reported it. It's what I'm paid to do. I expect you've made a mistake, added it up wrong or something, and if it ain't that you can take your oath it's

94

not at night anything's done. If it was done at night they wouldn't take a few shillings, they would take the lot, wouldn't they?'

Cooling was much impressed by the strong common sense of this deduction. He knew his own honesty, and it confirmed his opinion that the thieving took place during the daytime, in spite of Mr. Ponting's incredulity, so he resolved to set a trap for the miscreant. Which he did. But no matter how he contrived it, the peculations continued, and at last the boss discovered that the cash was short again. Unluckily Mr. Ponting was in a very bad temper that day (he often was!) and he sacked Cooling on the spot, as if he had been a mere fat-headed labourer; paid him two weeks' salary and packed him off at a minute's notice. Cooling went home in a sort of tearful rage, but he fumed at his wife, Agnes, who wept because she was perfectly certain he had 'been up to something' and would not be able to get another job and they were ruined. Well, that wasn't helpful, though it was partly true. It is astonishing how unpleasant truth generally is! The only recommendation he was likely to get from Ponting's Pills was the character of a cashier who had been sacked at a moment's notice because his cash was always short. Nice treatment, that, for a man who had served them loyally for over seven years! Victimization! and Agnes howling her eyes out and blaming *him!*

Lester Cooling was, to say the least, as honest as

95

the day — and yet, he was not *quite* innocent. Lying in bed sleepless that night he suddenly remembered. At the office, in a cupboard used for storing old derelict documents and the odd truck and lumber of a business house, he had carefully hidden a bundle of his own private letters that it would not do for anyone else to see. Good God, in the excitement of his sudden dismissal he had forgotten them! He kept them there for secrecy and safety, and he had left them there, left them behind in the cupboard! Sweat began to ooze out of him, but he remembered that it was a very good hiding place indeed, and no one would be likely to come across them; at any rate, not for a long time. That thought calmed him a little, but he knew he dared not leave those letters to such chances; he would have to get them, and quickly too. They were love-letters from a girl, and she wasn't his wife either, in fact she was the wife of one of the foremen at the works, a beast of a fellow named Backhouse. What *would* Cherry say? What a mess-up! They were grand letters, Cherry was a wonder, but he had been a fool to keep them. If Agnes got to hear of them she would raise hell, and if Cherry's husband got hold of them there'd be, well, there'd be murder! O, he would *have* to get them. He'd run along to the office to-morrow and say he had forgotten some of his personal belongings. That's how he would get them.

Next day he met George Malpas, one of his fellow clerks, the most decent of the lot, and to his astonishment and indignation George passed him by without stopping, without a word, as though Lester had been a thief. Absolutely! There was no doubt about it and it unnerved Lester completely. So that was what they thought about him, already! Mean, miserable skunks! Well, but still, he'd have to go and face them, he had got to retrieve those letters somehow, but he put off the ordeal, and from day to day he continued to put it off. He had not heard from Cherry yet, he guessed she knew the why and wherefore of his dismissal, but he could not bear to face her until he had dealt with that shocking danger hanging over both their heads. Lord, but she'd laugh when he told her, afterwards! And soon a bright alternative struck him, one by which he could avoid the sneering eyes of the other clerks; they might even refuse to let him enter the place! Instead of that, he could just simply go along after ten at night and get Fox the watchman to let him in when the place was empty. He was a surly devil, but he wasn't a bad sort really, and he couldn't refuse a simple request like that.

So, late at night, Cooling slipped off to the factory. It lay in a rather out-of-the-way corner near a canal, and at the best of times was not a cheerful-looking place. But that night it seemed as gloomy as a prison with its lofty dark façade and its iron gates under a black archway. Quite close was the office, with a dim gleam through the fanlight over the door. He rapped on the door and waited, but there was no reply, so he tried the handle. The door yielded, and he peeped into the well-known hall with its staircase and clock. On the left was a door leading into the Inquiry Office, and that was where Fox made his quarters for the night. Cooling entered the Inquiry Office, but Fox was not there. The electric light was on, and a fire burned comfortably, for the night was chill. Cooling waited nervously for some time, feeling guilty, but no one came. Where on earth was Fox? He must have gone into the works for some reason. Cooling was nervous and uneasy. A pretty fine watchman indeed! Door open, and you could walk *in* as you liked and walk *out* with what you liked, and no one to stop you. It was then the silly idea jumped into Cooling's mind. An electric flash lamp lay on the mantelpiece; Cooling picked it up, and muttering, 'I can't stop here all night!' he hurried out of the room and crept quickly up the stairs to his old office. It was a long, roomy place, with half a dozen tables and desks, some cabinets and cupboards, and everything was in darkness, but with the aid of the electric torch it only took Cooling two or three minutes to secure the incriminating letters. He shoved them into his pocket and was closing the cupboard when he heard the front door below shut with a loud slam, and the clatter of a bolt. Cooling was suddenly almost petrified with fright, but when he heard the steps of the watchman lumbering up the stairs he instantly crouched into hiding beside the cupboard and put out his lamp.

With a fluttering heart he heard the watchman draw near, switching on electric lights as he passed them, and then stop at the door of Cooling's office. The light suddenly gushed on, but Cooling was well hidden. The watchman entered the room and shut the door. He was humming. The sweat grew on Cooling's forehead; he neither breathed nor stirred. He heard the watchman walk half a dozen steps — and then stop. There was the clicking of a key in a lock, the sound of a drawer pulled open, the rattle of a tin box, and the chink of coins.

'My God!' thought Cooling, a great light breaking on him, 'he's at my table!'

With infinite caution he peeped, and there was Fox standing by Cooling's old desk, with the cash-box open on the table. He was pocketing some coins.

'Got you!' yelled Cooling, springing out. 'Caught you red-handed, you swine!'

The watchman shot round and saw him; with a sly movement he slid the cash-box behind him out of sight.

'What are you doing here?' he asked sternly.

'I've seen what *you're* doing here,' said Cooling. 'Bah! I always had my suspicions of you.'

'What are you doing here?' repeated the watchman, quite unperturbed.

'What have you just put in your pocket?' sneered Cooling, moving slowly forward. 'I saw you!'

'In my pocket?' said the watchman softly, and he

felt in his pocket. 'Just stop where you are, Mr. Cooling. Put your hands up, Mr. Cooling.'

'What d'ye mean?'

'Put your hands up,' repeated the watchman.

To Cooling's horror, Fox was pointing — of all unexpected things in the world — a revolver straight at him! It was just like one of those absurd situations Cooling had often seen on the films.

'What's that?' he said, backing away. 'I say! Don't Fox!'

'Put your hands up!' shouted the watchman. 'And quick.'

And so, just like those silly asses on the pictures, Cooling held his hands up over his head. He had to.

'This is a revolver,' Fox said, resting at ease on the table. 'How did you get here?'

'I came in the front door, just now.'

'Anybody with you?'

'No, Fox. I only came to get some things belonging to me.'

'Did you get permission to do so?'

'It was my own personal property,' explained Cooling. 'I'd forgotten to take it away.'

'Have you got a permit?'

'No.'

'O!' said the watchman, mildly. 'So you sneak in at this time of night, all in the dark, without anybody's permission?'

'Well, I waited, I did, Fox; but you weren't there.'

'I was about,' Fox replied. 'Did you get what you were after?'

'Yes.'

'What was it?'

The clerk tried a little bravado: 'That's none of your business,' he said.

'No? Do *you* carry a gun, Mr. Cooling?'

'Search me!' said Cooling, with a reckless attempt at irony.

'I will,' said Fox. And he did. All he found was a fat bundle of letters.

'Leave them alone,' said Cooling. 'That's what I came for.'

Fox silently transferred them to his own pocket, and then, at the revolver's point, he ushered Mr. Cooling downstairs and locked him alone in the Inquiry Office. The window had iron bars, but Cooling did not trouble, he was too delighted at having caught the thief red-handed. With a pistol too! But as time passed it dawned upon him that Fox had locked him in there while he made good his escape. Damnation! And there was a telephone in the next office if he could only get at it; but the door was locked, the window was hopeless. Funny how it cooked your goose when a door was locked on you!

It was the matter of an hour before Fox came back, and when he came he brought a couple of policemen and gave Cooling in charge for breaking in and attempting to steal. He had explained it all to the police; how he had caught Cooling red-handed at the cash-box and how he had been only just in time to frustrate him. The police inspected the unlocked desk, the cash-box and the cash — yes, that was intact, not a halfpenny short — and their examination left no doubt of a verdict. It was a clear case.

At the trial Fox gave his evidence with a modest air, very quietly and simply, and was complimented by the judge on making so smart a capture. As for the prisoner's plea about some private letters, the judge brushed all that aside. It was obvious nonsense, a flimsy futile pretext. The stupefied Cooling got twelve months, and it was not long before Mr. Fox entered into communication with Mrs. Backhouse.

THE BEAUTY SPOT

AT SEVEN O'CLOCK ON AN AUGUST MORNING A sour-looking man stepped out into the back garden of his little house at Clapham Common. The sun was bright, long shadows were contracting almost perceptibly, and there was a promise of pleasure in the air, in the garden, indeed in all save the sour-looking man himself. At that hour Bantry Fossett looked everything a man — in age about thirty-five with a nose as blunt as a bee's — should *not* be, everything he in fact *was:* uncombed hair, face unwashed, beard unshaven, shoes unlaced, braces unfastened. Carrying a teapot he slunk from the kitchen door and approached a lilac bush at the end of the garden. He took the lid off the teapot and stooped to place it carefully on the ground; then he jerked the leaves from the pot and they fell under the lilac bush. For some moments he stayed gazing into the empty pot as though it might have been a tunnel in which some accident had just occurred, and he said:

'I'm *not* the kind of person such a thing ought to *happen* to. *I've* done no wrong and I can't understand it; there's no sense any way you look at it.'

He stooped for the teapot lid and as he replaced it he murmured:

'You can't think how *tho*roughly, *vi*gorously, and enthusi*a*stically sick of her I was!'

Speaking stoutly to himself he crept back to the

house. 'I was, I was, indeed I was.' And he prepared himself porridge and tea on the gas stove in a kitchen that was painted in some long-lasting wholesome colours and smelt of sour spice. He was alone, very much alone. While the breakfast boiled he washed his face and hands at the scullery sink and dried them on a dirty towel.

'I was, I was, indeed I was,' he repeated. But you need not believe him.

'A pretty fine thing, I must say, for a wife to do!'

With a grunt he slapped down the towel and went and combed his hair at a mirror on the wall behind the door; then he dropped his arms hopelessly, shrugged his shoulders, and opened his hands.

'All right, Eliza, all right. Very well. If that's your temper you can sit on it, my good woman. And your character, too. You can't think how sick of *you* I was. Huh! That would make her wild if I told her. And I would if I could. Yes, I would, and serve her right; she was too imperious. And what was *she*, after all?'

With a disagreeable air he put on a collar and tie and then sat down to his meal. But there was nothing to console him in that, the oatmeal was gritty, the tea sour, sugar bowl empty — damn it all! Damn everything!

Fossett conducted a concise conversation between himself and somebody not present, and this was punctuated with angry exclamations and protests, such as: 'But what you fail to realize, my good woman!' or 'I absolutely fail to comprehend you,' or 'Yes, and above all, my lady, above all, understand this!' These fragments might have been prologues or perorations, they were not completed, and Fossett sat brooding, with one hand on the table, tapping with his fingers.

'I gave you everything your heart and soul could wish for, my dear; I did, really.'

Well, this Eliza, this wife of his, was missing; and when your wife is missing nothing is any use — you are bound to feel depressed. That is the curious thing about even the worst of wives, and nobody could say Eliza had been one of those; she might be a bad woman, but that remained to be seen. Eliza was missing, had been missing for some weeks, and she was likely to remain missing for a long time. Frankly, she had decamped; she had bolted, it was understood, because she was sick of Clapham Common and Bantry's tiresome ways. That, of course, was not good enough. Good enough for what? — you quite properly ask, and the answer is, Not good enough for Bantry Fossett. She was altogether too imperious.

Eliza was five years younger than Fossett and had married him only two years before, because, as a charming woman of ability she had grown tired of exercising that ability in a sub-post office, and Mr. Fossett, born of an epileptic butcher and now a man of no profession except house property, had at last just simply provoked her into sharing his private means. So he had taken the little house, engaged a little servant, and he and Eliza embarked upon a little life which Eliza shared as amiably as she could with him because there was little else to be done about it. She was a tall pale woman with bronze hair, who always dressed in brown with cream-coloured trimmings and polished her nails frequently and superciliously, but she had an active mind whereas he had slovenly airs. Bantry Fossett was not a gentleman either in the strict or the loose sense of the word; he was indeed the sort of man — Eliza soon perceived it — who would have gone out to dances with his laundress, and Eliza's rippling high-flowing spirit began to languish in its hymeneal suburb. At first they bickered playfully, then they quarrelled actually and actively, and after that they brooded. They wrangled over the most trifling things. Going out together somewhere, do you know, he stopped at the gate—

'Dash!'

'What is it this time?' Eliza asked with a sigh of scorn.

'My umbrella. I've forgotten it.'

Eliza sniffed derisively.

'I know what you are thinking!' he said hotly.

'I'm not. But you don't want an umbrella on a day like this, and if you *do* bring it you are bound to leave it somewhere and lose it.'

Fossett stared at his wife, injured and amazed.

'That is not true. I don't believe I have ever lost a single umbrella in all my born days.'

'O, go on and get it, stupid. You've the brains of a lamb. Look sharp!'

But he turned and drawled: 'A lamb, eh! Well, up to the time I met *you*, my dear, I thought I was a bit intellectual. Only a bit, mind you. But I soon found out that you can't be intellectual and practical at one and the same time.'

'No?' Eliza was guilty of a sneer. 'But you might try to be one *or* the other, darling, whichever it is.'

And then, of course, he *did* go and lose that umbrella, the first umbrella he had lost in the whole of his life, and it rather incensed him against Eliza. She had a nasty habit of generally proving right, and that was fatal to any composition between them; it enabled her to despise him quite cheerfully, but it made him despise her with something like hatred.

Now she had cleared off altogether, and right away from him, far far away, she was indulging in the exciting pastime of losing her reputation; he did not know exactly where, and it did not matter a bean to him. The little servant had gone, and there was already a board up on the front of the little house apprising Clapham Common — which is not at all the common part of Clapham — that a desirable residence was To Let. Fossett had packed off the little servant because he would not bear to have so close a witness of his humiliating plight, and he had a notion that she suspected him of murdering her mistress. All this was enough to divert even an angel into the swamps of misogyny, and so it was quite easy for Mr. Bantry Fossett to wander in that delusive tract, where the change for any common coin is generally counterfeit and the heart appears to revel in self-inflicted wounds.

The year waned towards winter, and still he was alone, the house unlet, his predicament unresolved. Eliza, it was certain, was not coming back to him, and he could not go to her even if he had — O good lord! — wanted to. She was alive and well, but he could not find her; she had walked away and did not wish to be followed — not by him.

'It has been a mistake,' she had written, 'Least said, soonest mended.'

Fossett could not help admiring her pride, for she had taken nothing from him, and wanted nothing; and yet that too displeased him, for it seemed to frame her with an independent glow that was *not* for him and had never *been* his.

II

Friends seldom came to visit him. Fossett was not by nature unfriendly, or unwilling by design, but he was slow in responding to the genial eye and so his friends were few. However, there was Ashley Barnes, a short man clothed in grey, chemist or something of that sort in a distillery and fond of botanizing amongst wild flowers. At his forty years of age you might, with no offence to his appearance, have thought him fifty. Often his crimson face, white moustache and interrogating spectacles, on one side of Fossett's hearth would confront the sour man's blunt nose across the fireplace and comfort it with mysticism.

'What am I do to, Barnes? I'm not the sort of man such a thing ought to happen to. It was just an evil chance, I suppose.'

'No, no, no! I assure you, Fossett. Some purpose is served, must be served. There is purpose, there is design, even in calamity. Not a sparrow falls to the ground but it is noted, and so on. There is no such thing as an accident in the workings of nature, no such thing, I assure you most positively. What is done is good, and equally what can't be undone must be the will of the universe, the contrivance, in short, of God. Must be, mustn't it? Ultimately all is good; it may not be so at the moment, that may lie far ahead of us; but ultimately, ultimately — it is the law of moral gravitation.'

'That,' said Fossett despondently, 'is all very well if you live as long as Methuselah — but you don't.'

'Tut, Fossett, tut! Why do you want to be a Methuselah?

> "A thousand ages in Thy sight
> Are like an evening gone."

You remember that, don't you?'

The earnest eyes behind the chilling spectacles

beamed benignantly. 'Come, come; in the battle of life you may sit down and rest awhile but you may not bivouac in it. I shall take you out, come on, and we'll have a run round somewhere to liven you up.'

And Ashley Barnes took his friend Fossett up to a cabaret where they were expensively starved amid a troupe of lovely half-nude dancing girls, little urchin boys sweating at limelights, an orchestra that boomed and puffed and zimmed, insufferable waiters, and hilarious onlookers who seemed mysteriously certain that they were roving in a very paradise of enjoyment. But Fossett knew that there would not be any chairs — no, really, there couldn't be! — in paradise, nor any of this other, except perhaps the lovely half-nude girls. Blissfully shocking it was; Fossett felt dismally out of date and Barnes, too, was not unperturbed.

'Look at all these oblivious people,' he sighed. 'What do they know or care about ageless beauty? I don't suppose they have ever even heard of Savonarola!'

And when Barnes told Fossett who Savonarola was it occurred to Fossett that Savonarola had certainly never heard of *them!* These people were living — he protested — they looked gay and might be happy, and he did not care for history, anyway. It was just dead people and dead events. He agreed with Barnes that the past *might* have been beautiful, but it was not history that made it so. If it came to that, wasn't it the present alone that *made* history?

And the present was life itself and not mere recollection.

'I don't follow you at all, I really don't, my dear Fossett. You seem to have a mind like only one end of a telephone and I can't get your meaning until I hear the other end as well.'

'I can't tell you any more than that,' said Fossett; but all the same he went on talking and talking one-endedly so long to poor Barnes after they left the cabaret that Barnes at last dashed off crying something about his last bus and Fossett was left to walk home the last two or three miles to Clapham Common. So very late it was to be walking those empty dark long-necked streets, at the end of which, forever receding, was the drip of stars to a mysterious horizon. But under the solid black roofs there were ten thousand beds in which people were sleeping, or preparing to sleep, in peace and love; the kneelers, the dim prayers in the light of candles or paraffin lamps; the virgins, the adulterers, the men, the children, the whole body of the world. Yes, in peace or love — he had to believe that, although . . . ?

Well, one night, one night they set out together again.

'I feel terribly like another binge to-night, Fossett; let's go and have a livener.'

'Another what?'

'Come on, man,' said Barnes urgently, 'there's a lot of heart in a loaf beneath the crust.'

So off they went, and dined on the heart of something or other that looked like spaghetti and liver, and then they dived into a bohemian tavern called *The Clay Pigeon* where everyone stared at them quite morosely for a while. They sat down at a round table and Fossett first flicked some specks off the table with his finger and then bent and blew off some crumbs. The only agreeable people there seemed to be the potman and the servers behind the bar; the others were there to make (God cherish them!) merry, which they did with the penny piano and its ancient airs sombrely, with their drinks lugubriously, and with discussions tempestuoso. The men were the sort who made quite an affair of taking off their overcoats, and affected to like crayfish, *pâté de fois gras*, and other edible offal. The women were the sort that Fossett never could endure. He didn't *mind*; he did not on principle dislike people or things or ideas which were commonly thought wrong or which he could not understand, but whatever he could not endure he always thought must be wrong in itself somewhere. That, of course, was the sole reason of his dislike.

The people who came into this bar seemed inclined to stay there the whole evening, as if they had nowhere else to go and nothing else to do; it was, you might say, a rendezvous of loose ends. If you listened to them awhile, as Fossett did, you would fancy that these shabby persons had read all the new books, seen all the new plays and films, contemplated all the new art, and were now crapulously stirred by the mere mention of the besotted hierarchies which fostered such impudent disintegrations.

The two friends were drinking bottled beer, and Fossett after taking a deep gulp sighed:

'I'd been living by some sort of light, you know.'

'Yes, I know, my boy; and the light has gone out.'

'No,' corrected Fossett, 'the light hasn't gone out, it has simply been taken away.'

'I see.'

'It's gone, Barnes, it is somewhere else.'

'And you want it back?'

'I don't know.'

'You want to go after it, then?'

'No, I don't.'

'Then what *do* you want, my dear boy?'

'I only wish it had not gone.'

Friend Barnes brooded for some moments; then he said: 'Drink up.' But before emptying his own upheld glass Barnes began to burble:

'If you *must* follow a gleam, be sure it comes from a pillar of fire, not from a candle in a sieve. Set yourself by a man-made scale and your judgments will be awry. Before you can act upon them, before you can say "Swish," time has passed into the Nothing.'

Fossett was decidedly baffled by this declaration, but he managed to conceal the fact from Barnes by saying: 'Well, if that is so, God help us!'

Having no other reflection to voice he seemed to leave the matter to God. Anyway, there was the drink: 'Here's precious!' he said.

'Aye, aye,' responded Barnes airily.

Fossett put down his empty glass and suddenly enquired: 'What are you making faces at?' To his astonishment he discovered that Barnes was ogling a plump lass sitting alone in a distant corner. And she was smiling back at him!

'Succulent, isn't she?' Barnes commented.

The flexuous creature was dressed in black, as though in mourning for someone, and she had the face of a tinted fairy. Fossett passed a single ignoring glance at the girl, and then returned to his own private musing.

'You know, I never thought I should ever feel like I do about this.'

'Grief,' said Barnes, 'makes many a man acquainted with himself.'

'I thought I hated her, Barnes, but instead of Eliza it's myself I hate. Myself!'

'O no,' the other assured him. 'You've just a grudge against nature, that's all; against nature itself. And there's nothing more futile, Fossett, nothing. A man must live according to his lights. Take me. I'm partly English, part Irish, part French, and what is the result? When the English is uppermost I am reserved and thoughtful; when I'm Irish I'm rather vivacious; and when I'm French I can't keep my eyes off a pretty girl!'

'What's the matter with you, Barnes?'

'By jabez, Foss, she *is* rather succulent.' And he nodded towards the pretty girl in the corner.

'O, that!' Fossett moodily sighed.

'Not at all, old man. And yet — why not? O dear! By the bye, why don't you file a petition against Eliza for — er — restitution of these — er — conjugal rights?'

Fossett made a very wry face. 'What's the good? What *is* the good of that? If Eliza wanted to be restored she would restore herself, wouldn't she?'

'But don't you see, man,' Barnes said hastily, tapping the table with his forefinger. 'If she didn't come back to you then, you could divorce her, see!'

'And silly things like that!' Fossett sneered. 'Thanks, I don't want them.'

Barnes slumped back in his chair: 'O well, if you want *her!*'

Fossett shut and opened his eyes sharply several times. 'I want *her* to want *me*; that's what *I* want.'

'But if she doesn't want you, eh; how about that?'

'Can't help it. I still want *that* — I shall always want it.'

Barnes drummed on his knee with impatient fingers, stretched his face by opening his mouth hugely and pushing out his tongue; then he became animated indeed!

'Pah, Fossett, you are an infatuated booby! Women! Pooh, they all have high flown notions but very low morals. Plenty of them, there are thousands. A few are worse than hopeless and the rest are none too good. Shall I tell you a story?'

'No,' said Fossett.

'About the nun who . . .

'I've heard it,' interjected the other.

' . . . went up in a balloon with a nigger.'

'Please, please!' Fossett protested.

Barnes subsided with a giggle. 'It's a very neat yarn.'

'Old as Adam,' was Fossett's laconic comment.

'So is the Christian religion,' insisted Barnes, 'but what's the use of grumbling at it?'

'I'm not grumbling,' Fossett declared, 'I don't grumble, I never grumble at all, leastways not very often, or unless I've a cause to. What makes you say I grumble?'

'I don't say it.'

'Well, why do you think it, then?'

'I don't think it either, my dear fellow. My remark was merely a remark, just casual.'

'Eliza,' continued Fossett, 'said so too. She was always accusing me of grumbling, and I never could make out why. I've something better to do, I should just about think I have. But she was always at me about something or other. For instance: some time ago I had a dream, thought I was walking along a dark street at night and came across one of these automatic slot machines in a doorway. I thought I wanted a cigar so I stopped at it. It had two slots, one marked *Eternal Life* and one marked *Damnation*. I put my hand in my pocket and found it full of half-crowns and as I felt like having a cigar I poked one of the half-crowns into this *Damnation* hole without really thinking. I dunno why I chose that one, but anyway I *did*, I put the two-and-six-pence in and it went down with a chinkle, and nothing came out, but a little red light just sparkled for a second. So I popped in another two-and-six and kept on and on and on until the whole pocketful of half-crowns was gone, hundreds of them, and not one cigar did I get. So then I shouted at the blessed machine: "The same to you!" and of course I woke up. Well now, that's all it was, but when I told Eliza about it next day, she said: "Just *like* you. Half-crowns for cigars, too!" So I reminded her it was only a dream, after all. "Pooh", — she said — "what does that matter, it was just exactly that kind of thing you *would* do. Why didn't you try the other slot?" I told her it didn't seem as if I could help myself in the dream — you know what dreams are — but she said, quite nasty, "No, you wouldn't!" And she went on at me with a lot of nonsense about analysing your dreams and finding out your secret thoughts, until I said "But dash it all. Eliza, it was only a dream!" And she said, that only made it worse! I can't bear such ungovernable superiority, Barnes, I can't. And the funny thing is, Barnes, I never patronise slot machines, I've never done such a thing in all my life. I made it a rule not to.'

Barnes grunted and laughed: 'Now why on earth did you make a rule like that?'

'O,' replied Fossett, with an air of wisdom, 'you can't live at all unless you live by rules of some sort, so what I say is: you might as well make the rules yourself, eh?'

Barnes ordered two more bottles of beer.

'If you had heard her,' Fossett continued, 'you would never have realised we were only talking about some dream, you'd have thought I'd wasted a hundred pounds trying to get one cigar. I tell you I simply could not bear her ungovernable superiority. You can't think how sick of her it made me.'

'I don't know, Foss; I always admired Eliza. I thought *you* were a very lucky man.'

'Me?'

'Yes, you seemed very fond of each other, too.'

'O, in a way, of course. But it was like this: she would be for loving, or she would be for quarrelling, and dammit, I had to be one with her somehow, didn't I? But still, there you are. Do you know, Barnes, I never even kissed another woman in all my life, never. Silly, isn't it? But there you are.'

'Well, you're a free man *now*,' said his friend consolingly.

'I don't *want* to be free, Barnes! But I suppose you can't understand that.'

Barnes' big spectacles gleamed sternly. 'Nonsense!' he said softly. 'Freedom is the — um — the great gift to the world, Foss.'

'I don't want it,' Fossett hastily decided. 'There's nothing *in* freedom except loneliness.'

Barnes' spectacles hovered speculatively over such treason.

'Getting your own meals,' continued Fossett, 'and sleeping alone.'

'Ah!' cried Barnes. 'What you want is a change, my boy. When you let your house . . .'

'I *have* let it.'

'What! You have! O well, well, there you are then. What are you going to do now?'

The forsaken one sighed, looking the Figure of Gloom. 'That's the mischief; I really do not know. Now that I've got to clear out I don't want to stir. What am I fit for now?'

Barnes ruminated for some moments. 'For myself I should like nothing better than to retire from society and live in the Kyles of Bute, but what I would do if I were you,' he announced at last, 'is this: I would pack myself off, and go and live in the country and raise things.'

'Raise things?'

'Yes, pigs, you know. And bees, chickens, gardening. There's money in it; not that that matters to you, lucky dog; but it is real life for a man to be breeding and breeding.'

'Pigs?' Fossett thoughtfully inquired.

'And bees,' aded Barnes.

'Chickens?' Fossett mumbled.

'And gardening,' Barnes said. 'I'm very fond of flowers.'

'Yes,' Fossett replied. 'Beans and greens.' And he began to meditate stolidly until his friend broke in upon his reverie: 'Excuse — a moment'.

Up rose Barnes, marched across to the young fairy in black, and sat down beside her. Left alone to his vegetable musings Fossett chewed the cud of the fancies just imbibed from his friend, and it neither sickened nor choked him; it was good, wholesome cud. When he noticed his bottle was empty he turned round and saw Barnes still bubbling and burbling beside the pretty young woman. Her round face looked painted, her hair looked gilded, she listened to Barnes without a smile; but she seemed warm and cosy and her figure was trim and expressive.

'Two-pennyworth of fluff,' was Fossett's contemptuous thought, and he ordered a single bottle of ale.

The idea of going away and becoming a husbandman in place of husband brought a ray of relief into his beleaguered mind. As he lived now, he was but a lost dumb fool. The twirl of mysterious fancy had swung him into Eliza's arms; warm and cosy *they* were at first, so warm and cosy, but soon to become cool and discomforting, then cruel and repelling; so she had moved on. But instead of relief he felt only the old prisoner's longing for his chains, and he could not have them — ever again. It had been a misfit, a sad misfit, but even a misfit was better than sheer nakedness. Or wasn't it?

The babble of the bar-room, the piano, the alter-
cations, the coming and going of people, faded from
his unconsciousness as he confronted his dilemma.
Eliza had gone, she had taken away his chains, but
this had not quenched his fondness — except just at
first, when he had felt glad for awhile that she had
left him. He *had* been glad. But still, she had sloped
off, and a man cannot stand such treatment, it is too
contemptuous. No; and even now, if merely moving
his little finger would bring her contritely back to
him he was not sure that he *would* crook it, even now!
There was no tuppenny fluff about Eliza; she was
tallish, with a sort of bronze hair and a pale fine face.
A very assured woman; she knew or seemed to know
something about everything. And that was another
thing: she despised him sometimes because he did
not know a great lot of things that did not matter to
him! But he knew enough to keep himself alive,
and what did all the rest matter? Ignorance! Well,
Clapham Common was not the Garden of Eden but
he had got to shift out of it (all through her!) and
go and grow some beans in the provinces. The
prospect of waiting on pigs, hens, and such fauna,
was *not* so tasteful to Fossett, but gardening was
agreeable. A garden did not want feeding or petting
or killing; it stayed where it was, it did not die or
run away or go stinging the neighbours or get some
putrid fever; it stayed where it was and did what
you wanted.

'Say, old man!'

121

It was Barnes, and the chit of a girl, confronting him.

'This is Miss Brown,' said Barnes, 'and this is my friend — er — Mr. Jones.' And he winked slyly at Fossett, who half rose, lifted his hat with one hand and with the other smoothed the thin lank hairs across the alcoves of approaching baldness on his brow. Then he hastily replaced his hat and stood erect, for the girl held out a greeting hand with a yellow glove on it and a black bracelet on her wrist.

'My name is Fossett, not Jones,' he corrected stubbornly.

The girl sprightfully said she was pleased to meet him, and that her name wasn't Brown neither. Certainly she was painted up and powdered, but her hair was all right, and she had a most expressive figure.

'Say, old man,' said Barnes. 'I'm — you know — I've just got to see Miss Brown off somewhere, and then — shall I see you later, or — or what?'

'I reckon you won't,' Fossett said.

'Well, *au revoir*,' chirped Barnes with relief, and the girl nodded austerely. Fossett did not watch them departing.

'I wonder how they go on,' he mused, 'people of that sort. I've never done it.' And it seemed as if he had surprised himself in some inexplicable omission.

An opportunity of reparation soon presented

itself. As Fossett stood outside waiting for his bus a short plump woman sidled up to him, and omitting all preamble urgently invited him to go home with her. Husky was her voice, shabby were her fashionable clothes, she had an odour of decay. Fossett was terribly embarrassed; he was like some untutored schoolgirl suddenly confronted with the apparition of a romantic duck. That the poor wretch was hungry he guessed at once.

'I'll give you a good time,' she said. 'I will and all, and it won't cost you much.'

He shook his head sternly.

'Come on,' she urged. 'It's not far.'

He shook his head decisively.

'Come on,' she pleaded, 'you shall see me naked.'

Silly thing — thought Fossett — just as if. . . . 'No!' he snapped, moving quickly away.

'Aw!' she growled after him, 'go and. . . .' But he did not wait to hear, he went rushing along the dark street until he caught a bus for home.

III

By March he was settled in a cottage in the Chiltern country. Born in London and reared in London he had seldom departed from that immense and ancient shrine; it had furnished him with some reasonable convictions, some reasonable ignorance, and the absurd notion that cokernuts came from St.

Mary Axe. Fossett had lived in streets that somehow did not permit you to fraternize with your
neighbours — there did not seem to *be* any neighbours, only people — and yet every house was plainly
though inscrutably numbered, the odds all on one
side, the evens on the other. There were millions
of these people and an abundance of other things;
more churches than there were streets in many a
holier city, more streets than there were churches in
the rest of Christendom and, being the Heart of the
Empire, it was (in all the best places) full of policemen, post offices, and palatial lavatories. But somehow our Mr. Fossett had never quite loved it.

Aforetime Fossett's father, the epileptic butcher,
had — almost unwittingly, you might think — pro-
tected his only child from the consequences of such
contacts by dying and leaving him the substantial
rewards of some speculations in house property,
whereupon Fossett the son, who was neither epileptic nor bloody-minded, had vaguely conceived a
desire to build himself a house, vaguely somewhere,
comfortable and tidy, warm and cosy, a lovely abode
with balcony, greenhouse for tomatoes, in fact a
real pretty piece in which he could pass his days in
amity and sloth. But although he often dwelt upon
this project he was not moved to compass the ambition; on the one hand because he did not want to
confine himself to any one spot for the duration of
his days, and on the other hand (you see!) he had
never yet noticed the spot in which even this might

be bearable. Later, when Eliza appeared and married him, he concluded it would be wiser to continue to dwell at Clapham. Yet now that opportunity had bloomed again and there were no more obstacles, he speedily descended from contemplation of things that *ought* to be done (but were rather difficult) to those things that *could* be undertaken whenever he felt so disposed. Moreover he justified himself by the plea that it was rather late now to put up a new house for the remnants of his broken life. Not anything like forty yet — but ambition is so pusillanimous!

So he bought a cottage on a slope of the Chiltern hills, a dwelling with an obtuse harassed-looking gable dominated by a docile chimney. It had a garden with trees for apples and bushes for gooseberries, space for beans and greens, a barrel for a dog he never kept, and a stall for two ponies he never owned. Later on he was to learn by sour experience that the quality of apples is oft-times strained, and that gooseberries of the kind seldom agreed with him.

Here he dwelt in a tiny world enclosed by the flanks of coloured hills sprawling from the west of the county to hover over this triangle of meadows and brooks. Great woods heaved themselves across the hills, and beyond the hills there seemed to be nothing but the sky of heaven, a cloud or two, and an odd bird at times. Even the landmarks and boundaries had delimiting names; Wood End, Lane End, Moor End, Tyler End, Peel End, even

Gravesend; and hard by that was World's End. Fossett's view from his hillside embraced no more than the hills, the woods, the sky, and this triangle of meadows and brooks with a village at each corner, and an inn. There was *The Axe* at Treddle just below him; a mile to the east, at Kilpack, was *The Bowling Alley*; then to turn south with Lovingdon Vale along the second side of the triangle brought him to *The Packhorse* at Clinton; all snoozy musty places, full of friendly neighbours with but one post office and one policeman for all three. There was a church with a vicar at Treddle, and another at Kilpack with a lovely Norman tower and no parson; but Clinton, where the post office traded and the policeman lived, had no church, merely a couple of chapels that looked ashamed of their secret selves, but were well loved.

Within a short time Fossett became acquainted with many of his neighbours, farming men, shepherds, woodrangers and keepers. He dug and planted his garden. Esther Kidling the carpenter's wife tidied his house each day, cooked for him and washed his linen. She knew of a hunch-backed lady who would do sewing for him, Miss Dew, who wrote little stories for children about the infant Jesus. So he sent some hose to Miss Dew, and in a day or two it came back in a parcel tied with odds and ends of string. There was a card inside, addressed to Mr. Fossett:

'Dear Sir —

'Allow me to present a small bill of 4d. I understand gentlemen in rooms pay one penny per pair
for sock darning.

'Yours truly,
'Emilia Dew.

'P.S. — I am engaged at the Vicarage on Thurs-
day.'

That was very nice of her, Fossett thought; he
was getting along excellently. And so now, how
about it? What had Miss Eliza got to say?

Eliza in truth must have had a bushel-basketful
of information to deliver, but he did not hear from
her. She had gone, quietly, soothingly, completely,
and now they did not communicate with each other;
he knew less of her than the devil did of the deep
sea. Yet Fossett was still at some remove from
tranquillity. He could not deny himself the thought
— was it hope? was it belief? — that she would one
day re-appear. She would come to the door one
evening as it might be, and he would welcome her;
they would sit down by the fire.

Early in April he set out one morning to go to
Clinton by a new path. There was no direct road
from Treddle to that village; you had to go crooking
round by Kilpack to avoid a stream. So he jolted
down the hillside to Treddle, where two old men
were felling a sycamore tree in the vicarage garden;
a red cow and a black horse lay at full length in the

croft next to it, breathing dreamily. Fossett crossed the highway and entered a track that trailed across Treddle Rise in the direction of Clinton. Teams were ploughing on the hill slopes under the black woods; there were violets and windflowers on the hedgebanks; three parts of the sky was in cloud, but there was warmth in the brisk air and the odour of things newly green.

Soon he came to the hill above Clinton and ascended a woodland track. The wood was dim although the trees were bare; not a bud had broken and old leaves lay matted and silent everywhere; but at the top of the hill the trees opened and the wood ended in a thicket of briar, crackwillow, hazel and cornel. Straight through the thicket for a hundred yards or so ran a wide green path, so seldom used that it was soft and elegant to the tread. He cut himself a handstick of cornel, a straight tough plant, and at the end of the green path he came to a stile, with a hill sloping abruptly down. Below him lay Clinton, with Lovingdon Vale slipping through a gap in the hills. The day was more bright now, the air sweet and kind, and the sight of the vast range of hills and black woods filled him with tonic excitement. Behind him lay the thicket and its quiet green path to the wood; the sallow blooms had puffed and were golden, bees hovered there. Exquisite privacy! Clinton, long streeted and sunny, basked among bleached furrows and green pastures. The stream which legend and history and gossip all declared dried up in winter and flowed in summer, belied them all by doing the reverse like any reasonable stream. It was blue, and very blue, its channel through the green meadows as aimless as the track of a snail. It lay across the civility of the village and did not seem to move; the road from Kilpack lay across the stream — and likewise did not move. Fossett could hear the cheerful anvil at the smithy and the hoom of a thresher at Shrubb's Farm. Fallow lands were covered with the dark dots of dunghills. A lark was singing above some adjacent acres newly harrowed, where a man by the name of Threadgold was sowing barley. He waved his hand as he strode; a little white cloud sprang out of it and disappeared. At the edge of the field he turned, took six paces back and began again, waving his hand as he strode, a little white cloud springing out of it.

What was it that moved Fossett so profoundly in the prospect? Was it the heave of those hills, that derided the little pricking fingers of man? Was it the arched vastness of sky, extolling the untrammelled hugeness of nature and making all one with eternity? To right and left and far ahead were hills, woods, roads, hamlets, farms and fields, and the blue brook veered across the foreground with a devil-may-care totter. A thousand features emerged, only to immerse themselves again in the general harmony. It was exalting, it enlarged him, he too had risen to a height.

He sat down on the footboard of the stile, the sun was insidiously genial and Fossett mused in a half-intoxicated state.

'Bright home of God!' he murmured; and although the sky was peerlessly beautiful he did not mean the sky alone; there was this gentle earth. Compared with that ranging beauty London was just a hutch — no more, no less. For awhile he bathed, as you might say, his poor soul in that scene of glory; it was a soul become momentarily as an archangel, but soon, as if he could no longer brook such amplitude, he began to feel uneasy.

'What a waste of land!' Fossett said it to no one in particular save himself. 'Something could be *done* with all this, sure, it could. All wasted on cattle and dunghills and fodder for their blessed horses! It's cruel; something could be done with it!'

There was nothing calling him hence, he might have stayed all day, but the desire to move on was insistent and he descended the bare slope that dropped down almost into the drawyard of *The Packhorse* at Clinton, a brick and flint inn thatched with straw and shaded by a walnut tree. Inside, a mason Fossett knew was sitting on the settle beside a log fire that carried a cauldron of potatoes boiling. Although it was but noon the mason was cheerfully unsober.

'Well, sir!' said the mason.

'Well, George!' was the reply.

Fossett seated himself and called for ale which

they drank together. George the mason had an old scar on his face where he had been clawed by a cat, a hole in his skull derived from some battle, and a lilt in one leg where a horse had misbehaved. He was a genial hard-drinking joker of forty, and was brought to bed of a quinsy once every year.

'Who does that land belong to, up there?' inquired Fossett, pointing back to the wood on the hill.

'That?' replied George. 'That Wood? All belonged to God Almighty once, but it don't now, however.'

He was rolling up a cigarette with some shag from a tin box.

'It's a pretty spot,' Fossett went on.

'Pretty!' cried the mason with a sort of comic ferocity, 'where?'

Fossett faltered: 'Why, up at the stile, where the green path is.'

'Waw!' spluttered the mason. 'Magpies and pigeons and a couple a dozen rabbits.'

'There's a lovely view, I've never seen anything like it.'

'Ah, go and stuff your sleeve! Major Markwick took it for a season, and he could shoot the eye out of a wren, but he got nothing up there, had nothing, and was none the better.'

A young carter with a large but thin red nose came in.

'Hey, George!' he cried.

The mason nodded to his pot of ale on the table. 'Take the top off a that,' he said.

The young carter smiled. 'I will, thankee, George, but I can't drink very hearty this morning.'

'Good!' growled George, at last licking the edge of his cigarette paper. 'I don't want you to drink so very hearty when you got your shirt collar undone like that.'

'Ah, well, here's good health and presence of mind, George,' said the young carter. 'May you live long and die happy.' With that, he completely emptied the pot.

'Good!' said the unperturbed mason. 'And I hope you won't be so bloody miserable when *you* has to pass away.'

'Hope not, George,' grinned the other.

'Because,' continued the mason, 'I likes your mother very well. But I hopes it won't be long, however, case I meets you in a pub again with your shirt collar undone.'

Mr. Fossett called for drinks for all three.

'Jim,' said George, 'who does that wood up yon belong to?'

The young carter meditated, but he could not exactly remember.

'Well,' growed the mason, 'you'd better bloody soon find out, cause I wants to know.'

'It's a gentleman as lives over in Glostershire. Begins with a T, I knows that.'

A woman's voice called from outside and there

came a tapping on the window pane. It was George's wife, beckoning to her man.

'Hullo, lovey!' he cried, 'what do you want? Come on in here.'

A middle-aged woman, very neat and tidy, with lively eyes, came in, and George rose unsteadily.

'Drunk again!' she said, in accents of disgust.

'Good!' he cried. 'Have a drink, lovey?'

'No, not with you,' she answered.

'Just a little drop of something short?' he pleaded.

'Come on out of this,' was her reply.

George lifted his heavy voice in a sort of plain chant: 'Behold, thou art fair, my love!' And his wife, leaning against the jamb of the door, could not help smiling at his hilarious voice. The brute looked so beautifully healthy and don't-care. Nothing seemed to worry him, not even his wife. Nothing ever had worried him, nothing would. He stopped his recitative and asked as he swayed:

'What d'ye think a that?'

'I think you're a dirty drunkard,' was her prompt reply. 'The Lord must have given you to me for my sins — I'm sure of it!'

'Good!' he shouted heartily. Swaying and grinning he put up his hand to adjust his cap, but his fingers fell upon his nose and so he caressed that member thoughtfully instead.

'Tell you what I did,' he muttered.

'Tell me nothing,' she retorted. 'Go to the devil.'

'Good!' But he went on, softly, persuasively.

'No, I tell you straight, 'twas on account a Freddy Musgrove. His missus has just got another little 'un and I bet him half a gallon as it would be a gal. Well, his old woman fell to bits last night.'

'God Almighty!' cried the mason's wife. 'And haven't I got a little one, and two of 'em, and three of 'em, and four of 'em! Pah! I could hit you as free as look at you, drunken thing!'

'Good!' he shouted with fervour. 'An' you'll only listen to me. . . .'

'I *won't* listen to you, you devil — you and your pretty johnnies, singing all them bawdy songs!'

And she departed, raging.

'Well, sir,' — George prepared to follow her, 'I'll see you to-night, sir, or some other time.' Then he whispered mysteriously: 'I'll find you who that land belongs to, and let you know. So long!'

He went away and Jim went away and shortly Mr. Fossett too went away. As he plodded round by Kilpack he was ruminating on marital affairs. Here, at any rate, it seemed that wives were faithful loving creatures, who ran after their husbands even when they were drunk. It was perhaps something in the air, the healthy contact, the unfettered play of nature, the little and large together, that made them so. Had Eliza lived with him there instead of in London she would have been a different woman, she would have made him a happy man.

IV

The friendly mason often met Fossett, one way
or another, but he did not remember to tell him who
was the owner of that lovely spot by the wood, nor
did Fossett inquire of him again. To Fossett, who
visited it as one might visit a shrine, the place
became a haunt of almost religious devotion. The
year won through its phases, spring, summer,
autumn, winter; whether fair frail foul or fiddle-de-
dee made no difference to Fossett, who lived on the
side of his hill contented and at peace. From his
window he could survey the Vale, cock an eye at
Treddle, behold Kilpack, and take a squint at half-
hidden Clinton. Come storm or shine it never
wearied him, it was always new, interminable, well-
loved. But it was the beauty spot (as he called it),
that nook at the corner of the wood on Clinton Hill
where the green path ended at the stile, which drew
him with its air of special sanctification, and its
grand view of Lovingdon Vale; that broad majestic
outflow of freedom and beauty symbolized in some
way (he could not tell how or why) an ideal of love,
for ever diverse, for ever constant. Gone now his
wonder at its 'waste,' forgotten now his thought of
'doing something' about it; it must be left alone,
unimpeached, unsullied. Though at times the
elements were uncouth and gales fought in the
screaming trees, those contours were always noble
and unperturbed, they neither ran away nor grew

gloomy. The long slow process of the yielding soil was the emblem of their pride; obscuring clouds might harry it, but they could not betray; the harvests illumined it, the fall of the leaf illumined it, and the snow glorified it, even as budded twigs and spring flowers in their season.

Twice or thrice a week Fossett would stroll there to renew his mysterious exaltation. Otherwhiles he became enamoured of carpentry, made odd articles of furniture, dog kennels and pigeon-cotes, which he gave away to people who did not want them but did not like to say so, and he built unaided an ornate wooden hut for the cricketers' field. He read books, plenty of books, standard works like *The Pilgrim's Progress* and the writings of Sir Walter Scott. He thought Christian's desertion of his wife and family a most ungodly deed, but of course he had a strong prejudice against people who ran away from home — it was not at all the nice thing to do.

So thus he lived, friendly with shepherds, woodmen, farming men, gamekeepers and drivers of carts, for more than two years before his friend Barnes — who had often promised to visit him — at length came to stay for a day and a half, in June.

Well, then, upon my soul, Barnes was no longer the nice clever person Fossett had once deemed him! His ideas were no longer striking, his appearance even was queer, and although he was just as full of words and sympathies, the sympathies were obtuse and the words like some part of a uni-

form he had acquired for social wear. It was extraordinary — but Fossett felt that he had actually
outgrown Barnes! And Barnes was one of those
people who never outgrow even their shoes — those
brown ones with thick soles and an unnatural gleam
on the leather! Fossett remembered them well;
across the blade of the foot were the neat unobtrusive
stitches of repeated repairs. After lunching on pig's
fry, specially recommended by the carpenter's wife,
Barnes sank back into an armchair in the old
familiar attitude.

'Well, Foss, my boy, this is really snug. Splendid
to see you again and looking so well. Are you well?
How goes life with you? You look well, but you are
very quiet, you know. You don't say much; is anything the matter?'

'No, not at all,' Fossett answered. 'It's not that I
haven't anything to say, at least not quite. I've
plenty to think about, but I can't always manage to
think about it at just the right moment.'

'Ah!' giggled Barnes, 'you're a sly card.'

From his prying innuendoes it divulged that he
suspected Fossett of some low intrigue with women,
and despite Fossett's denials the jolly little Barnes
was unconvinced. His friend was annoyed: 'Let us
go out for a walk,' Fossett said.

They tramped down the slope together. The mid-
June sun was aglare and the vale was at its brightest.
Passing Treddle school they heard the children
singing:

'Hearts of oak are our ships,
Gallant tars are our men,
We always are ready,
Steady, boys, steady.'

Crossing Treddle Rise Barnes stooped about picking flowers. Then he pulled them to pieces. They met a little gipsy girl, who asked:

'Mister, d'ye know where they sell onions along here?'

No, Fossett did not know. Barnes gave the child a penny, and asked her if she went to school.

'Yes, sir,' said she.

'Regularly?'

'Yes.'

'Sunday School, too?'

'I do, sir,' she answered. 'Sundays and Mondays and any other day.'

They saw seven hares playing together in a field, and a duck and a tiny pig eating a swede. The little pig ground his teeth into the root, while the duck stood respectfully by and picked up the crumbs.

'Do you ever hear from Eliza?'

Fossett met his friend's inquiry with a surprised glance. 'No, why should I?'

'Ah, well! Thank goodness that's all over.'

There was a long pause before Fossett said: 'I don't know about that.'

'What!' cried Barnes. 'I thought it was all finished and done with.'

'I don't know,' said Fossett again.

'But you surely don't mean — after all this time —
you don't want her back — and the way she treated
you?'

Fossett repeated lamely that he did not quite
know. Such vagueness was more than Barnes could
pass.

'Come, man, you *must* know; there's no sense
nonsense or philosophy in saying you don't know.'

'What is it then?' Fossett gruffly inquired.

'Ignorance!' was the sharp reply.

Fossett considered this, and then muttered:
'There's something more in it than that.'

'What, for instance?'

'The truth.'

'Pooh!' Barnes triumphantly snorted, 'just truth-
ful ignorance!'

'Well,' Fossett answered him, 'isn't there some
bit of a virtue in that?'

'None! No more than in falling over a log you
hadn't noticed.'

'I suppose,' Fossett went on solemnly, 'that's just
about what I've done.'

'My God, Fossett! Some people seem born into
this world simply in order to fall over things. Pick
yourself up, man, and kick the thing out of the
way.'

'The log isn't there,' sighed the other.

'And a good job, too, you ass! Why, you positively invoke some cosmic calamity.'

'O, well,' Fossett said apologetically. 'I live here very quietly, I have been here a long time now. Everything is very good here; I am happy, I am sure no one could be happier, and yet, somehow, life seems to be — you know — flowing *away*. It no longer flows *towards* me, something has gone. I suppose it will not come again, although I live here as if I were waiting for it.'

'For what?'

'I couldn't tell you, Barnes; I don't know.' And Fossett waved an almost exasperated hand. 'Silly, isn't it?'

'Silly!' howled Barnes. 'Why, you positively invoke some cosmic calamity, you do, really! You've evidently no purpose, no principle, in life, and *that* you *must* have.'

'O, Lord!' sighed Fossett, 'all this purpose and principle! What *does* it amount to?'

'My principle in life,' retorted Barnes, 'is logic. Life *is* logic, logic. And what more do you want? Logic!'

Fossett remained silent. They climbed up through the wood to the beauty spot by the stile. There they sat down and Fossett waited, waited for his friend to rejoice with him. There was not a ploughed space to be seen, the earth was all coated with greenery; meadows were clean as a cloth and quiet as a cloud. A wagon piled with hay had a dense black shadow under it. Some sheep on a down were sharply white, having been newly shorn. The bright heat leaned upon the soil as lightly as a feather, for a soft breeze fluttered from the north. Barnes said it made the foliage of the ash trees behave like a pianist's fingers, just before he begins to play.

It seemed that Barnes was not so mightily taken with Fossett's view; it was rather the velvety green path between the trees and the stile that took *his* fancy.

'Be jabez, Foss, what a place for a tryst!'

'Tryst?'

'Yes, wouldn't it be gorgeous! Look at it!'

Well, yes, that was delightful, too. 'But do you know,' said Fossett, 'when I first found this spot and saw that valley and the sky and the piercing sun, I found myself murmuring: "Bright home of God!" Just that. And it's curious, Barnes, and I don't understand it, because I'm not much for religion at any time — don't stop to think, you know — but there was I with this Bright Home of God! And it is always the same, whenever I come here, just that bright Home of God. It's holy, Barnes, it moves me.'

'That's true, that's true; but what a place for a tryst! Just here! What a place!'

'I'll keep it to myself,' mumbled Fossett.

'Covetous man! It's as fine as the Garden of Eden. Damn it, Foss, you've no principles, no logic. Ha, ha, ha!'

Barnes' mirth jarred distastefully on his friend; his coloured face, uncoloured hair, grey clothes, interrogating spectacles and glistening boots, were alien images there, and Fossett felt he could never again share that sacred spot with *him* — perhaps not with any one. As they strolled homewards Fossett doubted if he could share *anything* with Barnes now; they did not vibrate in the same way, or if they did it was on very different strings; and so when his friend returned to London the next day — with a reiterated injunction, and a confident promise, to come again soon — Fossett experienced a relieving conviction that he would not see him for a long long time. Barnes was a wise man, knew a heap of things about everything, but knowledge was not all; you might be a philosopher or a professor of something or other, and yet fail at cleaning your own boots or keeping your collar-box in order. His presence had given Fossett the same impression as a tree whose leaves autumn had touched with its scraping fingers, he was not new, he was no longer fresh or wise, he was not quite pure.

And that is how matters turned out; he never saw Barnes again.

v

And it was long, too, before he revisited the beauty spot. Some poor dejected mortal — Lester Killjoy was his name — owing to a disappointment in love or luxury one day made away with himself in Clinton wood, hanged himself on a tree there, and the place lost its savour. The quietude had grown sinister, it was haunted by startling conformations seen from the tail of a timid eye; the beeches hugely loomed, portentously stolid, their branches menacing claws; the rotten stumps of felled trees took on the appearance of crouching beasts and the sighs of dying men breathed from many a bough. To gain the stile it was needful for Fossett to traverse this wood, but it filled him with such sombre fancies that for awhile he could not go. As winter drew on, however, his qualms died down, and he set out once more to visit his sylvan sanctuary. This time the woodland path was barred by other obstacles — a fence and a board of warning to trespassers. Fossett suffered a mild shock, but he turned back with a law-abiding sigh. By the time he reached home he had grown indignant; those wretched rights of property were an unjust infliction, there were such things as public rights of way. The path was of no particular use to anyone, it was a dead path, it only led to a view, yet some rich gaffer had shut him out and warned him off and no one would bother. Curse him!

At night he strolled down to *The Axe* at Treddle to ask George the mason about it; something ought to be done. The dingy taproom was lit as much by its blazing log fire as by its one tin lamp. Four men sat at a long table playing dominoes, and at two other tables men sat drinking and smoking. George was not there, so Fossett sat down between old Henry Hackthorn and William Busby, a powerful but almost toothless man whose pipe sprouted from his face like a leafless sapling from a rock. They were conversing about Lester Killjoy, who had hanged himself.

'Of course,' said William Busby, 'the man was a fool, Henry. There's hard and gentle fortune for all alike, but he was a very foolish fool, and he couldn't pay his way and so he had to be made bankrobbed. Well, what could you expect? I sold him some hens myself once, soon arter he come here about, and I tell you they was six and seven and some on 'em eight year old!'

Old Henry Hackthorn leaned with his arms on the table. 'Ho! They must have had some bad characters, I back!'

'They wuz,' agreed William Busby. 'But there, we all has to learn the ways of life, don't we? Where the sea flows there's bound to be salt. We're born bottom up'ards, and we must begin at the commencement, isn't that so? When I was young I had to believe what I was told — and so did you, Henry — but when we grew up and could read good print for ourselves, that crippled 'em, didn't it? I met him some time arterwards and O my goodness! Ay! Come up! Didn't he just give me what for! I turned it off with a bit of a joke, a course, but he wouldn't have it.'

'He wouldn't?'

'He would not! No, he was a sour-minded man

and I couldn't do with him. I like a man to laugh as much as I do when there be jokes about. I reckon that's only fair. Did you know that man, Mr. Fossett?'

'No.'

'He was a very foolish man.' Mr. Busby quietly explained. 'Any old rascal got the better of him, Henry will tell you the same. Lost all his belongings and couldn't pay his way and had to begin all over again at sixty years of age. A wonderful hot-tempered man, but wonderful civil when he was inclined that way. He said to me once: "If ever you are in want of a joint of meat, William, just come to me!" And he must have had a stomach like a bear, for he'd eat anything. He would! He showed me a badger once, cut open, beautiful; its kidneys hung down like a lamb's, but I couldn't touch it. If you don't enjoy your food it won't do you no good, and it won't stop with you long. We aren't all born alike nor at the same time either.'

'William!' said a young man across the room. 'Will you make up a hand at crib?'

Busby shook his head. 'No, Charley. I love a game a dominoes. I'll play a game a dominoes with any man breathing, but as for these ere' cards I be done, ackled, green as a well.'

Just then in came George the mason. He stood swaying silently while he unbuttoned the collar of his overcoat; then he cried in a loud voice: 'I'll sing the best man in the house for a gallon a beer.'

No one answered.

'What about you, Henry?' persisted George.

'I broke my voice a-whistling, years ago,' said the old man.

'I'll sing the best man in the house for a gallon a beer,' repeated the mason.

'*You* will!' cried Tommy Shackler. And Freddy, his twin brother, echoed: '*Will* you!' They were two bachelors of forty, as like as blades of grass, who mended the roads with some decency and much conversation.

'For a gallon a beer,' stipulated George.

'We'll take you on,' said they.

'And so will I,' called out Peter Gifford, a thatcher with bloodshot protruding eyes.

'Haw! haw!' sniggered Busby, whispering to Fossett. 'Once old Peter gets started there's no stopping of him, he'll sing for two bloody year, you watch!'

'How many more on ye?' roared the challenger.

'Me!'

'You, Reuben! I didn't know your clock had got a chime in it.'

'I'll have a go at 'ee.'

'For a gallon a beer?'

'That's just about my drop.'

'Come on, the lot of ye,' said George, pulling off his overcoat with a great to-do. 'Who's going to decide the winner?'

'Leave it to the company,' said several.

'Good!' cried George. 'And the losers pay for a gallon a beer, mind ye!'

'Now give order!' commanded Busby, rapping on the table.

The singers began the contest. George blared through a ditty entitled 'The midnight mail,' with a sort of reinforced delivery that was even less soothing to the ear than the subject of the song. Old Peter Gifford quavered a couple of staves about:

> 'The ring your mother wore
> On the day she took my name.'

Reuben leaned somewhat heavily on that classic of rural taverns, 'The old rustic bridge by the mill,' while the twin brothers' duet, 'The dying buffalo,' was also rather melancholy; in fact, in the bass of Tommy it was a regular dirge, although Freddy's *falsetto* encrusted it here and there with some rather crisp *arpeggios*.

Well, then, would you believe it! The company was unable to make up its mind about these compositions, and at Mr. Fossett's suggestion they all sang again. But when each singer had delivered himself of the further burthen, the company was again shy of expressing its deciding opinion; and once more Fossett proposed a further trial.

'No, that be damned for a tale!' cried George. 'We can't fogger about all night over a gallon of beer.'

Whereupon old Henry Hackthorn spoke up: 'I tell 'ee what, George.' And he said he would join in, if so be they didn't mind, and sing a song, too.

'For this gallon a beer?'

'Yes,' old Hackthorn agreed. 'I don't mind that, as long as the one as sings sweetest and best is judged for to be the winner.'

'Of course!' The company was unanimous.

'And this time,' George menacingly declared, 'you got to make up your minds.'

'We will. We will.'

'It's agreed then,' said old Hackthorn, rising to his feet, 'that the one as sings sweetest and best wins the competition.'

'And this gallon a beer,' added George.

Old Henry elevated his chin thoughtfully, and in a thin piping voice delivered a little song with the title and refrain of 'Sweetest and best.' At its close Busby roared out:

''Pon my coincidence, chaps, if that ain't a good 'un!'

And Henry was awarded the palm of victory with jocular acclamation.

'Henry!' George sternly, but helplessly inquired, 'where'd you drop across that ballad?'

'I couldn't tell 'ee, George,' cackled the old man, 'I couldn't tell 'ee.'

'Well, I can tell *you* something!' And the mason defined clearly categorically and exuberantly what he would like to do to Mr. Hackthorn.

'That's crippled you, George!' declared William Busby. 'Shut your face and pay up.'

So it was turn-out time before Fossett could question George about that closure of the woodland path. They stood conversing outside *The Axe*, hands sunk in pockets, necks sunk in shoulders, while the other men, mumbling tunes, tottered to their homes. The moon was gone down behind the small crumpled church, the sky was steely, the air cold. George's answer startled him:

'We're building a house up there!'

'House! Up where?'

'Top a that hill.'

And then and there Fossett learned that some dastardly creature was actually erecting a house close to that lovely spot by the stile!

'But . . . but . . . who? Who is building a house just there?'

'The owner,' George said.

'But he can't *do* it!' cried Fossett.

'He's doing it.'

'He mustn't do it!'

'It's well on with.'

'It ought to be stopped!'

''Twill be finished come spring.'

'It shouldn't be allowed!'

'They'll be in afore summer.'

'Who is it?'

George pondered: 'I don't rightly know the name; it's that same party as the land belongs to.'

'But they dare not close the path — it's a public way.'

'O, we know that. They dassent do it, we know. But there it is! A course they can't stop it up really, we know that, but they want the place private-like, and so they will stop it. They *have* stopped it.'

Fossett stumbled up to his own house with an exasperating sense of frustration. The thing he liked best was gone — or going. In some absurd way he felt as though he had been forestalled and defrauded. If a house was to be built there it should have been his own, but he did not want a house of any sort to be put there at all. He would have given much to have saved the spot from such effrontery, such profanation as bricks and lavatories, ashpits and drains, plastered all over the bank where violets grew and he had seen visions. A fence and a board, too, to warn him off from looking at something that belonged to God!

VI

By the following March the house on the hill was finished. Occasionally Fossett had walked round to Clinton by the Kilpack road to observe its progress. Tiles had been laid upon the wooden ribs, the windows had doffed their white eyes, a garden was begun, and a looping road scooped out of the side of the hill. It did not look so badly now, it was indeed rather a pretty villa, but Fossett's regret was not allayed thereby; the thing was as alien as a clown at a sacrifice, it had possessed a virginity the spot had known which could never be regained. At times, as summer drew on, he was minded to ignore the warning board and climb up through the wood to renew the ancient delight, but he was a law-abiding man and did not venture. It would be better to wait, he might yet make the acquaintance of the man who had barred him out, and perhaps something could be arranged. Yet he was loath to ask favours of such a one, the creature would not understand his mystical condition, there could be nothing between them. It was all over.

A curious circumstance decided him. When at last the house was inhabited Fossett was disgusted to learn that it was not a man who had done this thing; it was, after all, a woman, a widow, Mrs. Theale who came from Gloucestershire. Her husband, the owner, had lately died. Barnes was right, Fossett was certainly illogical. He was prepared to put up with the prohibitions of a man, it was a man's world; property was his, the law was his, mastery was his, but the edicts of a woman were mere pettifogging frivolity. He grew mutinous indeed, when the August sun caressed the hills and he was imbued with longing to see the bright vale with all its lustre in the communion of those old thrice-happy days.

On a quiet evening he set off, with but one

thought in his mind — to go to the stile again. When
he came to the wood he scowled at the warning board,
broke down enough of the fence to wriggle through,
and trudged up the woodland path until he had
reached the thicket on the summit of the hill. The
sun was going down, its great arc glowed upon him
as he emerged from the thick trees, prinking each
leaf trunk blade stem and flower with unearned
riches. The wood was green, but its great bosom
flushed under that arrogant eye. One solitary wisp
of cloud was delicately pink. Chip, chip, chip, the
blackbirds briskly shrieked, the chaffinches complained. The trees listened intently, but nothing
else could they hear except the footsteps of a man
travelling a harsh road below, some quarter of a
mile away. It was so rich, verdurous and secret there
that he stood holding his breath for some moments
between the palisades of hazel crackwillow and
briar. Then he strolled on to the stile, much like an
intruder conscious of wrong-doing. There he found
the irruption was not so bad as he had feared. Not
far off, the new villa with its red tiles, green pipes,
and yellow rain-butts, set on the slope of the hill
beside a fenced garden planted with a few rose trees
in the otherwise unaltered turf. A lady was bending
over a rose tree, clipping some of its few blooms.
She looked up and when she saw Fossett sitting on
the stile she stopped clipping and stared back at
him for a long while. He was not close enough to
see her clearly, but she looked agreeable. Suddenly

she dropped both roses and clippers and ran into the house. After a moment or two Fossett became aware that she was in one of the upper rooms, watching him through a pair of field glasses. The window was wide open, and he saw her.

Fossett fancied that his sudden appearance at that spot where no stranger should have been had made the lady nervous. He disliked being stared at, and anyhow, twilight had begun and he had to return past that tree where the man had hanged himself. When he got back over the stile and was wandering homewards he realized oddly that he had not seen his 'view,' it had all been submerged in the sight of the villa and the woman staring at him.

Next evening he went again and sat on the stile as before. In a little while the lady appeared in the garden and began to clip the roses. Although she did not seem to be conscious of his presence, did not even glance in his direction, yet he felt she was aware of him; so much so that a peculiar uneasiness began to pervade him. It was as if she *knew*, as if some sly sorceress had inveigled him there, lulling him with apparent unconcern while her devilish unseen myrmidons were encircling him! With a grunt of disgust he retreated. A dozen steps along the green path would take him out of her sight, but he took only three steps — and then looked back. Ah! She was watching! Yes, she was staring after him, as he floundered slowly away.

All next day he thought of her. From the distance she had looked an agreeable attractive woman — she had even seemed to resemble someone she could not possibly be! That was because she had red hair, the only thing he had clearly realized about her. He did his daily business with a restless mind; he even made inquiries about her and found out that it was undoubtedly Mrs. Theale he had seen, and as the unclouded day wore on he realized that he was waiting for evening, and he hoped it would not rain — though rain was impossible.

At the same hour he again wandered off down through Treddle. Along the lane some children were playing and shouting in a gravel pit. Four black mares, rattling with chains and gear, the leader bearing a boy seated sideways, clumped homewards from a cornfield. As they reached the pit a fawn foal ambled up to meet them and the hugest mare, blackest and most forlorn, stopped. The foal's head at once nuzzled under her belly, snatching and sucking. The boy shouted 'Kep! Kep!', but the mare would not follow, and did not budge until a little girl clambered out of the pit and caught hold of it by the mane.

'Come along, you dirty old thing!' growled the child, 'come along!' and she hauled the dismal mare into movement, its teats spurting milk upon the road, the foal prancing prettily at her side.

As Fossett went on his way to the wood some words of his old friend Barnes plumped back into

his mind. 'A tryst, Fossett, what a place for a tryst!'
The words had sounded so unpleasant on Barnes'
lips — but they did not seem unpleasant now. Halfway up through the wood he saw lightly concealed
at the side of the patch a contrivance for snaring
foxes; small branches had been cut green-leaved
from bushes and planted in a half-circle round a
stake on which a dead brown hen was impaled. The
hen's neck had sunk pathetically, its eyes were
closed, flies were busy on its body. Somewhere
below it the sprinkled earth concealed a steel trap.
Fossett surveyed the trap contemptuously. 'Grrh!'
He kicked the stake over and the dead hen sprawled
among the twigs, but the trap was not sprung. He
had disclosed the lure, feathers, flesh, and flies — but
the trap still waited.

Up he went to the thicket, and as he emerged on
the green path the sun burst on him again. Along
by the stile it was making a nimbus round the red
hair of the lady. She was standing by the stile.
When he appeared she walked along the path towards him. She stopped when they met.

'What are you doing here?' asked Eliza.

'Why, it *is* you!' he staringly uttered.

'Are you aware that you're trespassing?'

'I don't care,' said he.

'And I don't mind!' she laughed. She was carrying a red rose, flicking it about in her hand. 'But
what *are* you doing here?'

It was the one thing he really could not answer —

what *was* he doing there? What were they *both* doing there? She was certainly the lady who had clipped the roses in the villa garden! She was there, she was here! What did it mean?

'You are looking so well,' she said.

'Um,' mumbled Fossett.

'Much better than you used to.' Eliza laughed outright.

'*You* don't,' he said.

His bluntness rather dashed her.

'But you couldn't,' he added.

The compliment restored her. 'I'll give you this for that,' she said, as she threaded the rose into his buttonhole. They walked on together nervously.

'What does it mean?' he asked. 'This house, this place, and you in it. Where have you come from? What, what, what has happened?'

The reached the stile. She looked wonderful and kind. 'Come along in,' said Eliza, and 'perhaps I'll tell you.'

'In there?'

'Yes,' she said. 'It's my house.'

'I thought it belonged to Mrs. Theale.'

'It does,' she said. 'but I'll give it to you if you like it.'

'I hate it,' he answered.

'Just as you like.'

They both leaned against the stile, looking vaguely round — at nothing. What they desired to see lay hidden in each other's hearts.

'And I suppose you hate *me* — still?' Eliza murmured.

He could not say that. 'No.' He could never say that. But hadn't she treated him abominably, treacherously? Bolted and thrown him to the devil? It nearly killed him.

'O, no, no! You *didn't* mind!' cried the astonishing woman. 'You didn't mind one tiny little bit! You never even tried to *find* me. It was just what you wanted!'

'And what in the name of God did *you* want?' he grimly asked.

'Someone to love me.' Positively, she was almost indignant. Fossett shrugged his helpless shoulders.

'And *you* did'nt, did you, Banty?'

Was she making up to him again? It was marvellous! But he was *not* going to appease her disgusting vanity, he had been fooled and despised. His glance went roving beyond her eyes to the wonder of the bright vale and the wood's loveliness.

'*Did* you, Banty?' She laid her hand upon his.

'We were married,' he said lamely.

After a while she said appealingly: 'Come into the house; I want you to see it.'

'No,' he was very abrupt. 'I won't.'

There were thousands of things to be said, but where could they begin? At last she said irrelevantly:

'I like you better now.'

Fossett grunted as if amused, and she continued:

157

'But I suppose you hate me?'

He did not answer.

'O, I can guess.' A faint smile made her look (damn it!) almost pathetic. 'And I don't wonder, I'm not grumbling, but. . . . .' She was tracing little designs with one finger on the top rail of the stile. Her white dress, her hair, face, hands and bosom, all so close to him, were full of known entice-ments. Her very audacity was elegant. 'But why did you come up here to see me, then?'

'To see *you*!' he protested. 'I didn't. I didn't dream you were here. How could I? I haven't heard from you for over three years.'

'You came up as soon as you heard though, didn't you?'

'I didn't know it was you, I tell you! I never had such a . . . a surprise in all my life. Never dreamed it.'

'You've been coming up all the week. I knew you at once, the very first moment I saw you here, and when I saw you had found me out I was glad. I did not mind, nothing seemed to matter.'

'I hadn't the faintest notion it was you until just now,' he said.

Eliza was checked by his stubbornness. 'Didn't you? I thought . . . I thought you knew me all the time.'

'I knew nothing,' her husband answered. 'But there's a heap I'd like to know.'

'If you'll come in,' she gently said, 'I'll tell you.'

'No.' He stoutly refused. 'Damn the place.'

Eliza glanced across at the villa: 'We can't stand talking here,' she said, moving away. 'There are the servants. Let us go along the path'

Fossett pulled himself together and followed her. As he reached her side he asked· 'What would Mrs. Theale say?' Eliza linked her arm in his.

'I am Mrs. Theale,' she said.

For some moments Fossett lost sight of everything, it was as though his bowels had turned completely over; but they continued their stroll along the green path. At the end they turned back and walked as far as the stile, then again retraced their steps, to and fro, to and fro, amid the twilight bloom, and all the time Eliza was explaining something or other.

It appeared that when she fled from Clapham Common she had soon got a post as secretary to a Mr. Theale, an elderly rich bachelor who lived in Gloucestershire and owned a good deal of Clinton and Kilpack. He hadn't long to live, he was an invalid, and when he died he left everything to Eliza — she was rich now. He had got to like her, and wanted to marry her.

'But he couldn't marry *you*!'

'He did.'

'But *how* could you marry him!'

'Why shouldn't I? I was nothing to you.'

'You're a liar. It's not true.'

'You were sick of me.'

'Not, not true.'

'You gave me the go-by, you absolutely drove me away!'

'Good God, Eliza, it isn't true at all!'

'You were callous and brutal and overbearing. Yes, you were!' Her accents sounded queer and strained. 'Don't you remember? It's not so long ago — three or four years.'

'Look here! I tell you it's nonsense. You are married to me, you *couldn't* marry him.'

'Well, I did,' said Eliza coolly. 'And it was the best thing, the only thing I *could* do then. He was an invalid, he hadn't got long to live, he was *very* fond of me and was always asking me to marry him. He didn't know I was married and I couldn't *tell* him. Men don't like married women for their secretaries.'

'Why not?' Fossett blurted.

'Because, well,' she stumblingly asserted, 'of *course* they do not like their secretaries to be married. I was always Miss Roberts to him. I hadn't told him anything about *us*, I couldn't tell him I had run away from you.'

'Why not?'

'It would have driven him crazy, it would have killed him; he was *very* fond of me.'

'So was I.'

'And he hadn't got long to live; he wanted to be happy — and so I let him. You see he was a Roman Catholic, he had quite a conscience about such things, and if I'd told him I was married already it would

have been no use, there was no time to get a divorce.
And besides, he was a Catholic.'

'O, the poor, poor fellow!'

'Don't be mean,' she murmured. 'I would not
marry him for some time because of course I was
nervous about that, but he was so fond of me, and at
last we had got to the stage when it was stupid not to
— it didn't seem wicked at all — and so I said "Yes",
and he settled all sorts of things on me and made me
a lady.'

'And you actually married him, really and truly!'

'Yes,' said Eliza.

'God Almighty!' muttered the tormented man.
The horizon began to rush towards him — Jesus! —
he was no more than a fly under an inverted cup.
'Bigamy!'

'I risked it,' said Eliza, 'and it made him very
happy.'

'O, sure!' Fossett grew sardonic.

'I'd nothing else to live for.'

'What about me?'

'You would never have heard of it — unless I told
you myself. I suppose it was wrong of me.'

'Pooh! Tut, tut!' Fossett was scornfully off-
handed.

They wandered up and down, not knowing what
to say. The sun was sunken and they walked in
shade.

'And he never found you out?'

'No,' said Eliza. 'He died over a year ago. He

left me almost everything. This place is all mine.
Isn't it strange — when I came and saw it I knew I
had to build a house and come and live here; some
tremendous thing was urging me that way. Wasn't
it strange?'

'Ah!' sighed Fossett significantly.

'And I had no idea that you were anywhere in the
neighbourhood. If that isn't Fate or the workings
of Providence I'd like to know what *you* think.'

'What did *you* think?' he asked, 'when you found
I was living here, close by?'

'I was glad. I wanted to see you again.'

'Weren't you frightened?'

'What of?'

'Me! I could get a divorce now.'

'Yes.' She said it timidly. 'I suppose you could
if you wanted to.'

'And you could be hauled up for bigamy.'

'Yes.'

'And you'd lose everything then?'

'Yes,' she repeated.

'Well, I can't understand you at all!'

'No, Banty, and you never did.'

'I *was* kind to you, wasn't I?'

'No.'

It was a preposterous denial, but it shook him.
'Well, I'm only sorry for one thing,' he said, 'only
one thing; I can't understand it.'

'What?'

'That you should say I did not love you.'

'But you had left off telling me.'

'But surely I *showed* you I loved you!'

'Indeed?'

'Yes, Eliza. And I never told you I didn't.'

'No?'

'And it wouldn't have been true if I had. I *did* love you, all the time, I did.'

'Ah, but the words!' said Eliza, shaking his arm playfully. 'Banty, the little words.'

Standing still, they faced each other in the gloom, and he went on morosely: 'And you never *asked* me to tell you, either!'

Eliza stared pityingly at him: 'Banty, don't you see? By asking for love one confesses to one's self that it is no longer *there*! If I had to ask for it, where had it got to? Lost, stolen, or strayed. Had you eaten it, or put it in the bank? How could a woman demean herself by asking for what you had forgotten to give her?'

'You are asking now,' he declared.

'Am I?' She shook her head. 'I almost think I could!'

When they got back to the stile Fossett did not understand what had come over him. Here he was, trysting with Eliza, an abandoned woman if ever there was one, a wife and no wife, who had deserted him, committed adultery, crashed into bigamy, and was now making him feel a monster and behave like a practised roué. He told her about himself, what little there was to tell: his love for the beauty spot,

Barnes' prophetic reference to it, and his anger at the building of the villa. The wood encircling them was a dusky sea; within, it had already assumed that mysterious polity peopled by siren fancies, mock awe, implacable umbra, and giant jaws that crumble as they wound. But there were lights beaming in the villa, it looked a refuge, secure and inviting.

'I could kill you for building that thing there,' he said.

'I'll give it to you, Banty.'

'What for?'

'To live in. Couldn't we, Banty, together? Let's begin again. We've changed and learned so much.'

'Learn!' he scoffed. 'I've learned much that I didn't want to learn. Might as well be dead, eh?'

'Don't talk of dying.' Eliza rallied him. 'That's a lesson you can learn only once — and you'll never know if it was any good to you!'

Her arms crept round him: 'Come in with me. Don't go, Banty, don't go; stay to-night, stay forever.'

'Ah,' he smiled. 'And what about your servants!'

'But we *are* married, after all, aren't we? And we'll get married again if you like.'

'What about Mrs. Theale?'

'Damn Mrs. Theale!' said Eliza.

'And I say damn that fellow Barnes. He was right about this place after all.'

'It's yours now, all yours. Come!'

'No,' he said, 'not yet, Eliza. Not to-night.'

'Why not, my dear? We *are* married.'

Some romantic melancholia still deterred and directed him. 'Let's think it over a bit first.'

'No, don't think! Forget it all! Love me again!'

'To-morrow,' said he, and to all her entreaties he would only answer 'To-morrow.'

'You promise then?'

'Yes,' said he.

So she agreed. 'I suppose you're right, Banty, but I wish you weren't!' And at last she stepped over the stile. Then he caught her hands again and stood cherishing them fondly.

'What are you going to think about?' she asked, her eyes peering close to his.

'O, lots of things,' he answered. 'Let's see — there's divorce. . . .'

'You're *not* to!' she interrupted. 'Not to at all, none of those things. I don't want you to — not for an instant.'

'Well, well,' he whimsically said.

'Think only of to-morrow.' And she darted away.

In almost utter blackness he stumbled down the path through the wood, past the fox trap, and past the hanged man's tree that greeted him with a sigh.

THE COURTYARD OF THE 'ROYAL OAK' HAS ONLY one tree, a long lean chestnut, and early one autumn evening half a dozen countrymen with names like Sam and Ben and Henry, and a naval petty-officer, were sitting on the benches under it discoursing philosophically as countrymen will, and drinking with easeful greed as only countrymen can. It was a pleasant, idle spot, feathers and dying leaves bestrewing the gravel, and the tree clamorous with the sticky mutter of starlings. A group of fat fawn hens pondered in a dark doorway, and seven white geese, corpulent and chinless, were rambling in the sunset light, their long pink noses invested with the kind of benignant fatuity that reminds you of aldermen you have never seen. The fat landlord in his shirt sleeves was cleaning a pair of boots and champing a short cigarette; at the same time, he punctuated the tattle of the men by wagging the bootbrush at them and delivering himself with imperious finality.

'Everything in this life works in circles. I mean to say, the moon's a globe, the sun's a globe, the earth's a globe. . . .'

'So's a publican's stomach!' yelled Henry.

The landlord breathed thoughtfully on the boot in his hand. A goose at his foot pecked up a plum-stone and chewed pragmatically before rejecting it. The naval petty-officer solemnly averred that science was all very well — once in a way — so long as it

wasn't overdone — but human nature had to take
its chance — same as everything else.

'You can make do without science — you had
to in the old days before the Jews — but you can't
do without human nature — and I don't hold with
so much of this 'ere vaccination. In fact — I don't
mind telling you — I don't believe in it.'

George Ponting had the shoulders of a buffalo;
his neck was short, legs and arms were short, but
the whole lot was cased in a very neat uniform. Although born and bred within a stone's throw of
The Royal Oak, he had travelled the world, and his
speech had received that infusion of cockney dialect
which comes from the superior rank of life in which
he had served. He was pleasantly pugnacious,
clean shaven and looked nice.

'And what you don't believe in — it don't matter,
whether it's science, or book learning, or a lot of
these gymnastics — it's like everything else and does
much more harm than good. In fact — I don't mind
telling you — I wouldn't give sweet damn all for the
lot of it. To give you an instance: I remember once
when our ship was on the China Station; our Medical
Officer sends for me and tells me I'd got to be inoculated. Well — everybody to his own taste — but I
don't much care about having a lot of that stuff
pumped into me. I'd been done before and it
nearly put George P. off the ratings. I found out
from the King's Regulations that I couldn't be
forced to have it done more than once a year —

that's the regulation limit. So I tells this M.O. — just a bit of a kid, you know, from one of these colleges; he'd got a mole on his ear as big as a blackberry — I tells him I didn't care about having so much of that stuff pumped into me. Of course, I was taking a rough chance with him.

'He says to me, he says "O".

'I tells him straight out I'd been done ten months before, and how the regulations provided it for once in every twelve months. Of course, I was taking a chance and naturally, being my superior officer, he didn't like it.

' "O," he says, "is that it?"

' "Yes, sir," I says.

' "You know you can't go ashore unless you are inoculated now?"

'I says: "I shall have to put up with that, sir."

' "All right," he says, "you are not to leave the boat, understand."

'And that was that!

'Well, a couple of nights after, our commander sends for me and says: "Ponting, I want you to go ashore and fetch off some broken-leave men from the club house at Cheefoo."

'I says: "I'm sorry, sir; I'm not allowed to go ashore."

' "What d'you mean?" he says, rather angry.

' "I dunno whether you're aware, sir, the Medical Officer has confined me to the ship." And I explained all that to the commander.

' "Ponting," he says, "You'll just do exactly as I've told you, and bring off those broken-leave men from the club house at-Cheefoo before twelve o'clock to-night! Those are my orders."

'Well, off I goes. I orders out the little old motor boat and it put me ashore inside of ten minutes. The C.O. had given me a bit of a sketch showing whereabouts this club house was, as I hadn't had any shore leave and didn't know the way, but, I don't mind telling you, I didn't care much about this job just then, because Cheefoo was under martial law. One of these 'ere Chinese generals had got ten thousand men surrounding it; half of 'em was bandits — they always are — and, of course, well, it wasn't the sort of job as I cared much about. Guns going off now and again, and, as it happened, I hadn't brought any arms with me — not a thing — and it was dark and lights out and all that.

'I went along the dock — nearly fell in the drink once or twice — and I blunders into some toff. I showed him my pass, and he directed me on to the club house, way up the back of the town. Someone had rounded up these two broken-leave men and put them in the club house waiting for orders. I hadn't got far when I was properly adrift, lost my way, and lights out, and I tell you I didn't feel too merry. I was dodging round trees and houses and so on, looking out for myself, till I came across a squad of Chinese soldiers at the corner of a street and they challenged me. I out with my pass, and the bit of paper with the sketch on it the C.O. gave me, and I shoved it under these blokes' noses.

'I says "Savvy?"'

'They couldn't speak English, and I couldn't speak Chinese — it's a bit difficult. "Club House, Cheefoo," I says.

' "No savvy," they says, but they passed me on to the next lot at another corner, and I shows *them* the little old sketch and says "Savvy?"

'They says: "Savvy, Cheefoo" — you know, sometimes they savvied and sometimes they didn't. The further I went, the darker it was, until you couldn't see your hand before your eye and I was properly flummoxed; you know, I didn't seem to be nowhere at all except alongside of some damn high wall. So I stops for a reconnoitre, and I hears a cock crowing and a bull bellowing, and there was only this wall and a path; that's all.

'Where this Cheefoo had got to, I didn't know; might have been in front, might have been behind me. Plenty of bright stars about, but they didn't help much; and when I stopped, everything got quiet all of a sudden and I had a nasty sort of feeling that something was just going to happen. The only sound I could make out was some little bells tinkling in a tree over the wall.

'No good cruising about like this — I thinks — I'll be into some of the bandits soon. So I turned back, and, all of a sudden I hops right into a girl strolling along in the dark.

' "Hullo, sailor," she says.

'And I answered her: "Are you English?"

'And she said she was. So I asked her if she knew whereabouts this club house was. O, yes, she knew it all right.

' "Well, if you don't mind, miss," I says, "I'd be much obliged if you'd direct me there."

' "What's your hurry?" she says.

'I told her I'd got a job on.

' "What's your hurry?" she says again. So we just stood there and wrangled for a bit, you know — talking friendly like. Course, I don't hold much with these 'ere goings on, but as far as I could tell in the dark, she was a nice girl, in fact, she told me she was an orphan and brought up in a convent somewheres in Northamptonshire.

' "What's your name?" I asked her.

' "Sal Mogundi," she says. "What's yours?"

' "That's a rum sort of name out of Northampton-shire," I says: "How did you get to China?"

'And she said — she rode over on a bicycle! Of course, that was only her joking way, though, mind you, I daresay she could have done it once she got across the English Channel to Calais or some of those ports; but the proper way is to go by boat via Suez and the Indian Ocean, same as we did. However, I rumbled to her then; I knew what she was after.

' "Gie me a fag," she says: and I gin her a fag. All the same — I thought — I ain't got many fags to spare for the likes of you! I mean, if you got a job to do, damn all that other truck; you may not care so very much about it, but it's got to be done. However, I gin her a fag; and when I struck the match, you could have knocked me down with a pin. She was a half-caste, or something in the line of a nigger, anyhow! Damn fine teeth, I don't mind telling you, and togged up to the nines; but she'd only taken just one puff at it when a hell of a volley went off, just up the road, sounded like next door, and guns began popping all over the place. It was like being in the midst of a battle. "This is no place for you, George" — I thinks — "you'd better beat it quick." And off I goes.

'I left her standing there, and I pelted off hell for leather back to the town, and after some time I fell accidentally on this club house, and eventually I got the two broken-leave men off all right. But I don't mind telling you, it was a job as I didn't care so very much about.'

George ceased.

'Ha,' said Ben.

'Humph,' said Sam.

They all drank together.

'So you didn't get annocolated, George?'

'No, Henry. I don't hold with so much of that, either.'

The landlord walked away whistling, with two boots in one hand and a brush in the other. The starlings still muttered in the trees, and another goose pecked up the plumstone.

CORNEY BARON, A HEAVY PROSPEROUS-LOOKING cattle dealer of forty, took his seat at a breakfast table in a demure little lodging-house that lay close by a hospital. The place was often used by visitors upon the same melancholy errand as himself, but the linoleumized air of the breakfast-room, with its half-hearty fire and general aloofness of the four or five tables arranged for service but still awaiting comers, had no consolation for him except the possibility of food. Despite everything, his vigil, his weariness, his sorrow, despite it all, he was hungry; and he felt ashamed, as though it was disloyal to be hungry at such a time.

'Can't get away from that, the belly rules us. In the midst of death we are in life and the belly rules. It's a bad day, too, the Lord receive it! Poor Meggie, poor old Meggie!'

Rain was streaming beyond the window into a small back-yard that a hutch of rabbits and a rockery nurturing a feeble tulip indifferently adorned.

A maid, with a childish figure and mature eyes came in and asked him what he would like for breakfast. It appeared that he would like pretty well everything there was to be had — having so satisfactorily consumed large quantities of the same provender on the two previous mornings of his stay. Those night-long ordeals at the hospital put a shameful edge on his appetite.

'Porridge, haddock, bacon, eggs,' softly whispered the maid, 'yes, sir.'

'Good morning, Mr. Baron,' cried the landlady, entering effusively, as her maid retired. Mrs. Cottring, a person of mature figure and eyes that were not very childish, was wearing red baize slippers with anklets of grey fur. She glided to the window and wrenched at a curtain.

'What rain!'

'God forgive it,' said Mr. Baron.

'*What* a rain! Any news?'

The cattle dealer shook his head. His elbows were resting on the table, his hands locked together as though they were about to wrestle.

'No,' he said, 'no.'

'Ah, the trouble,' sighed Mrs. Cottring, shuffling to the hearth rug. 'Trouble, trouble! I've known it, and so I know what it is. Heaps and heaps.'

Her small eyes drooped upon him in a way that was meant to console, but was merely confiding.

'You might not think it, to look at me, and you would hardly credit it! And only five years ago. If I never have another moment's trouble in the rest of my life, I have had my full share. Ten thousand pounds.'

Mrs. Cottring loomed in pride at remembrance of the ills she had defeated, the misfortunes she had survived. With her hands resting on her plump hips she breathed a sigh of triumph towards the silent man. 'You would hardly credit it, would you?'

Corney Baron was only a countryman, with cumbrous hands. There was something humid, pink and fulsome about his wrestling fingers, as there was about his heavy lips. But his mouth was small and constantly open and he breathed through its little fair aureole of moustache with a sort of attentive regularity, as though he permitted himself only a certain number of breaths per minute. A tinge of gloom rested in his kindly eyes.

'And nobody,' continued the landlady, 'ever understands your need when it is greatest. Friends in need! Pooh!' she sniffed, snapping a derisive finger. 'O, no. Ten thousand pounds — very nearly — and now look. You would hardly credit it. If it hadn't been for my child, I'd have gone mad or done something to myself, but, of course, I couldn't, you see. My child saved me, and now my life is hers, every penny of it, it's *for* her, if you understand me.'

'Sure ma'am,' he assentingly nodded.

'How was your wife this morning?'

'O,' said Baron, with a groan, 'she's in a bad way, altogether bad. I know it, I've known that all along, but I keep hoping. She's in good hands, you know. That's a blessing. I'd go there myself if anything happened to me — you know — anything unreasonable bad.'

'Would you! Now, I wouldn't,' Mrs. Cottring declared with a deludingly wise smile. 'Not me! I know a woman — at least, I don't know her, but I know of her — and they took her in and operated on her for a tumour, but when they cut her open, it wasn't a tumour at all; she was, well, you know, she was going to have a little one.'

'Dear God!' murmured Baron, 'didn't she know that much?'

'I think she wasn't married,' Mrs. Cottring explained, 'but, of course, I don't know. That was Dr. Headcorn.

'Headcorn,' repeated Baron slowly.

'Excuse me asking; have *you* any family?'

'No, ma'am, no. We never had any in all the seventeen years we've been married. Not one. Ha.' The cattle dealer leaned back in his chair with a smile and thrust his hands deeply into his pockets. 'The day we were married, seventeen years ago, was a very poor God-forgive-me sort of a day, dull, very dull it was, and when we had tied the knot, I had to travel off to some business at a sale, some ten or twelve miles away; so I packed my wife off home and went on to this sale. Well, I dunno, I bought a bunch of store cattle and a cow in calf, and it was pretty late in the afternoon before I started homewards, and I'd got about half way when this cow dropped in a ditch by the side of the lane and began to calve.'

Mrs. Cottring exuded a sympathetic sigh.

'It rained,' continued the cattle dealer, 'middling hard, and what with that and the cow and one thing and another, I did not get home till two o'clock in the morning. Poor Meggie! She was in a terrible stew. I was drunk, I was dead, I was gone mad, I'd run away — everything she could think of. And I'd never sweat a hair — but I was in pretty poorish fettle for a bridegroom! Ha, too bad! Poor Meggie! I think that must have been the cause of our never having any family.'

'Do you?' queried Mrs. Cottring.

'I do, ma'am,' he convincingly declared, 'I always have done, and Meggie herself is of the same opinion.'

Mrs. Cottring emerged from her bemused suspension: 'I wonder! A child is a great blessing after all the trouble, though, of course, it never understands; but still . . . as for friends . . .! Pooh!'

The door behind Mr. Baron was pushed open and a curious little girl, her hair tightly knotted with many twists of coloured ribbon, peered into the room.

'Mum! Is God alive?'

Mrs. Cottring excusably stared at her daughter and replied: 'Eugenia, look at your hair!'

'Is God really alive, mum?'

'But . . . well. . . .' said Mrs. Cottring, 'I'm not sure. It's . . . you see . . . it's hard to know that. I'll find out, presently.'

'Can't you find out now?'

'After breakfast, Eugenia. Can't you see I'm busy now?'

'And then you'll tell me?'

'O, go on, you silly thing; run away!'

At that moment the maid came and delivered Mr. Baron his breakfast, and Mrs. Cottring sailed out of the room after her dubious child and left him alone.

The cattle dealer was exceedingly weary, but sleep, that composure of mind and limb, was far from him. His gross lumbering body could batten on haddock and hog, but his mind was hovering over a bed in the great hospital, where he had waited from midnight to morn for an ultimatum — or, it might be, a reprieve. That huge bewildering sequence of wards was linked by a tangle of interminable corridors, that seemed to have no goal, but roved, diverged and endlessly retraced. Stonily, stolidly, they echoed to the tread of his robust alien figure; corridors, corridors, corridors, gloomy vistas of scrubbed iron and stone, blank varnished doors; the smell of ether, and a feeble light or two.

Between their baffling silent walls he was constantly astray. And yet, close by, behind every door was a ward that teemed with suffering, where scores of prostrate invalids were being tended in beds on dark polished floors by white-capped nurses who never seemed to rest. Twice, from midnight to dawn, he had dozed there on a bench in a draughty hall, where he had been bidden to wait for a last impossible call. Throughout the nights he was ceaselessly aware of the sound of quick approaching footsteps tracing the corridors, but whenever he raised a scared expectant eyelid there was nothing, nothing but that hole just beneath him where mice came bobbing from the plaster wall. As long as he was attending there, whether waiting alone, or sitting by Meggie's bedside, his thoughts floated capriciously away and hovered over contrary alien things; mortal cares, trivial joys; the price of fodder, cattle, prospects of market and season, or that unprofitable mare who was too damned awkward to carry her own shoes around, and quite too lazy to pull even as much as the hat off your head. But as soon as he was gone from the hospital, his mind would take a turn and he could think of nothing but his doomed wife — just as he was now, eating and mutely grieving. It was as though by the simple process of sitting beside her, or pacing the corridors, he had performed all he *could* perform, leaving the rest to those everlastingly devoted nurses and whatever fate might fancy. But away from her, it was no such matter. Grief dogged him, found him, arrested him, tore at him, and brought him back to a prison of tears, a prison that was all corridors, corridors; a labyrinth without a clue, that could end only in a catacomb. And it was a grief private and personal, a sacred burden not to be shared; how *could* a breath of it steal upon any other mind?

The first time he visited the hospital, he had stood abashed yet absorbed in the doorway of the many-windowed ward; it was so long and high, there were so many beds, and in each bed lay a woman. A number of nurses, young, robust and cheerful, were bustling in all directions. At each end of the ward, that the last extravagance of cleanliness and order served also to brighten, a large, black iron furnace burned with a lively munificence. Daffodils and tulips in jars seemed to denote that spring, like melancholy, would 'linger here awhile.' (O, *but not for long. Arise! Arise!*) A nurse, with merry sparkling eyes and a tight waist but loose bosom, came towards him. He asked to see his wife.

'What name?'

'Baron.'

'Baron?' the nurse echoed. 'Baron? Has she been here long?'

'No,' he said, 'No.'

The nurse trotted away to inquire, but suddenly he had caught sight of recumbent Meggie waving an arm to him, and without further ado he had tiptoed gently to her side.

In the beginning, she had taken a dislike to her surroundings; the bed, the other patients, the dreadful fireplace near her, the nurses — even the man who only came through with a ladder to wind up the clock; he smiled at all the women and made jokes — and the burning coal would keep falling out of the firebars all day long and all night too; it fell with such a frightening clatter upon the iron fender, it kept her from sleep. But soon she had come to like them, they were so kind and friendly; the nurses, the doctors in their white slops, the other sick ones, the man with the ladder and all; except, perhaps, that fire-place, with its dreaded recurring crashes of coal which snatched her from momentary ease and hurled her headlong down through a hundred thousand fathoms of terror. And until the dropped embers were re-stored by any nurse who chanced to observe them, the fumy smoke trailed across her pillow, and she dared not breathe. She could not sleep for the constant fear of it, and there were other noises, lacerating hubbubs, the ding and dang of knocking far away, groans near at hand, laundry baskets shrieking hor-ribly as they were dragged along, clatter of nurses' shoes as they trotted wop, wop, wop along the polished floors. Meggie wept for the peace of her own home, but she grew stoical at last, and once when a night-nurse with skirts held high had run screeching down the ward at the sight of a mouse, Meggie had suffered from a mad attack of laughter.

Sitting by her side, Corney would begin to talk of amiable casual things, anything but her illness.

'I feel terrible droopy,' Meggie would sigh.

He too would sigh and gaze fondly at her.

'Did I tell you the wind took down that old barn along yon tother night?'

'No, Corney!'

'It have.'

'So droopy — I can't get my true sleep.'

'I met old Dan Chegwidden two days ago, and he said to me: "Corney, you remember that half-grown apple standard you sold me?" — "I do," I says — "I gave you a full grown shilling for it," he says, "but that apple tree never thrived" — "Well, Dan," I says, "what do you expect for a shilling?" — "Value, Corney," he says, "value is what I expect" — "And you got it, Dan, you got it" — " I did not, Corney; it gave up the ghost, it died" — "O!" I says, "you could a made a walking stick of it, couldn't you, Dan?" — "And where'd I get the ferrule for it?" says he — "O, Lord, Dan," I says, "how much ever do you want for a little bit of a shilling?" That coopered him! "Let me see," he says and began to scratch his old head, "let me see; what was you begging my pardon for?" — "I wasn't begging your pardon, Dan"; I said, "you couldn't touch me for twopence!" — "All right, then Master Corney," says he to me, "you can go about your own burning business!" So I wished him the life of a fishmonger in winter, and that's how we parted — quite civil!'

Meggie smiled wanly and murmured again:

'I feel terrible droopy, Corney; can't get my true sleep.'

A week after her operation, something had gone wrong; there was a crisis. Corney Baron had been summoned helter-skelter and bidden remain at hand. Poor wounded Meggie declared privately to him, that the only thing to do her any good now would be some much advertised cough-lozenges; they had been her stand-by for many winters. 'Bring me some of those, Corney; it's the only thing.'

Their farm was many miles away, so he had taken

a bed at Mrs. Cottring's, but he had not slept in it. The end was near; death had not yet knocked upon the door, but it was breathing steamily as it peered through the pane. A bench in the hall of the hospital had been Corney's couch at night, and when daylight came and people began to pass to and fro again in the monotonies of a mysterious routine, he was allowed to sit by Meggie's bed until it was time for him to go to breakfast at Mrs. Cottring's.

So here he was.

And while he sat thus in Mrs. Cottring's breakfast-room, abstractedly feeding and vividly brooding, an elderly spinster came in, an attenuated knitting-needle sort of lady in a grey woollen jacket. She had weak eyes, hair uniquely twisted, and her name was Flora Field. Without a word, she took a seat at a table just in front of Corney's and sat down with her back to him. The maid served her with an orange, an egg in a pink flannel bonnet, a rack of toast, and a cup of warm milk. After perusing one or two letters she had brought with her, Miss Field sat gazing out of the window. Then, without turning, she exclaimed cordially:

'What an unpleasant day!'

'Um!' acquiesced Corney. 'God forgive it.'

And she replied: 'Why, certainly.'

'There was half a inch of rain fell in the night,' Corney continued.

'O?' said she.

'That's about fourteen tons to the acre, you know.'

'Good gracious!' exclaimed the lady, adjusting her napkin. 'There must be some good reason for all that.'

And then, somehow, somewhere between the lady's back and Mr. Baron's final rasher, it came up that Miss Field was permanently engaged in voluntary work at the hospital.

Now there were some simple things in life and business that Corney Baron could not readily grasp, and so, when he did understand that Miss Field was not being paid for her services, he felt bound to ask her why she had chosen to take on that singular form of employment. Was it a hobby?

Miss Flora conveyed quite clearly in her explanation that she came of a good family, had been expensively educated, and had travelled a great deal. Now she no longer cared for that.

'All my life I wanted to *do* something, to be of service to the poor. My time is my own, so I do this, and I like it better than anything; I am completely wrapped up in it. I don't want any remuneration — I don't need it, of course — but it is nice to know that your efforts are appreciated; after all, that is not much to expect. And the doctors do appreciate it so. They are such dears, so splendid, such untiring, devoted, wonderful men. I know them all, and they are very charming; and, as you know, they are at anyone's beck and call all day long, and all night too for that matter, from one year's end to the other. And, after all, what *is* their reward? Very often it is nothing, nothing at all. Patients are so inconsiderate, so selfish; it must be utterly heartbreaking work.'

'O, come ma'am!' Corney interposed, 'the patients can't help themselves.'

'Yes they can; they could if they would, they could quite often.'

'But surely that's why they all have to come to a hospital,' said he.

'I really do not know why some of them *do* come,' declared Flora Field, 'unless it is to criticize things they know nothing about and grumble at what they cannot possibly understand.'

'That's only to be expected,' Corney explained. 'We are ignorant at the best of times, ma'am, and when we're ill, the mind is all astray like a calf in a chapel.'

'I do think they could be a little more grateful,' retorted Miss Field. 'There are many things they do not give us credit for, and if they die, the poor doctor gets blamed.'

'You couldn't blame the patient, ma'am, not in general.'

'That's nonsense. Of course not,' she said. 'It's the disease. But these splendid men are expected to cure them at a touch, at a moment's notice. And often they don't even . . . well . . . they have no regard for anyone's comfort but their own. Not all of them, mind you, I don't mean that; but numbers do. I have often wondered why so many patients die

187

in the night. I've no doubt there is a very good scientific reason for that, but I have often wondered.'

During this little colloquy, the lady had not once turned her head to Mr. Baron. At the back of his mind Corney felt that it was undeniably splendid of Miss Field to take up this work, whatever her circumstances were, for no reward at all; in fact she was devoting her life to it, in fact it was noble of her. And yet, somewhere, still further back in his mind, a vague reflection was growing that he would dislike taking advantage of Miss Field's nobility even if he were in very great need of it — he didn't know why.

'The hospital is a wonderful institution,' she went on. 'All that science and devotion is organized and maintained for everyone's benefit. One feels' — and here Miss Field's teeth closed upon a piece of toast with the crash of a puma savouring a brittle dainty — 'that one is working . . . er . . . in the midst of great forces. Are you attending the hospital?' she asked, suddenly turning round for the first time.

'I . . . I am visiting someone.'

'A patient?'

'Yes,' Corney replied with some hesitation.

'What ward is he in?'

Corney gave her the number of the ward.

'O, that's a woman's ward.'

'Yes, a woman's ward,' he allowed, and Miss Flora thereupon resumed her gaze at the window view.

'Who is her doctor?'

'Her doctor,' said Corney, 'is a Dr. Headcorn.'

'O, charming!' screamed the lady. 'I know him very well. O, you *are* lucky. He's the cleverest and sweetest man and a most famous surgeon, too. He's a genius. You are lucky to have got him. His private fee would probably run to a hundred guineas.'

'Is that so, ma'am!' Corney was awed by the stupendous figure.

'O, dear yes; a hundred guineas at least. Now, there's a man for you! I have known him do a dozen or more operations in one morning. Devoted to his profession, a kind man, a saint, a sweet man. The nurses positively adore him.'

'Well . . . a man like that . . . I wouldn't grudge him,' said Corney, 'a horse, a house and a handsome wife.'

'Yes, they adore him,' sighed Miss Field.

'And I wouldn't grudge the nurses that, either. They are overworked.' Corney warmly maintained. 'I've seen it day and night, ma'am, day and night.'

'They *are* nice girls,' she conceded.

'I call them,' he stoutly maintained, 'I should call them — the pride of the human race.'

'Oh, I am quite friendly with a lot of them,' she said.

'But I wish,' he went on, 'I do wish they would not wear their high-heeled shoes in the ward.'

'Do they?' the lady exclaimed.

'Every man jack of 'em,' declared Corney.

'What else *could* they wear?' she inquired.

'Slippers,' said Corney, 'soft, quiet slippers.'

'O!' Flora Field protested. 'Really!'

'And there's another thing could be done, ma'am, if I might explain it to you.' And with his elbows on the table and a ponderous grave air, Corney told her of the coals dropping so often from the fire into the clattering fender.

Miss Field had no doubt there was some reason for that.

'I can't see any,' Corney said, 'and a bit or two of wire would stop it and only cost a few pence. Then there's those laundry baskets; why must they drag them scraping and screeching along?'

'Because they are too big to be carried,' said Miss Field.

'But they are not too big to have rubber casters put on 'em.'

'You may be sure,' replied she, 'there's a reason for that, too.'

'I can't think of one,' said Corney, 'and the baskets would last much longer.'

'Of course, I don't go into the wards,' Miss Field explained, 'I don't touch the medical side. Mine is all work like . . . well . . . like for a week now . . . I have been repairing the doctors' overalls, scores of them, that kind of thing. You wouldn't believe! I did a pile yesterday nearly as high as myself. Buttons, holes, rents, darns, pockets, seams and all the rest of it. It's not the doctors' faults, you know; it's the laundry women, they are so rough and reckless with the washing, they don't care, they are quite stupid.'

And then the lady loudly sneezed.

'You've got a bit of a cold, ma'am,' said Corney.

'O, it's just a little catarrh,' she assented. 'Nothing will stop it. I take quantities and quantities of medicine; it's the plague of my life. All the doctors prescribe for me, and yet there it is. I am simply incurable. '

Corney drew from his pocket a packet of the celebrated cough lozenges he had bought for Meggie.

'You try one of these,' he said. Tearing open the packet, he went across to the lady's table and laid three dark drops beside her.

'Very kind of you!' she sniffed, with a shade of amusement in her faded eyes. 'Are they any good?'

'Excellent, ma'am,' he assured her. 'Nothing to beat 'em. And cure any number of complaints beside coughs and colds.'

Flora Field popped one into her mouth.

'They are rather hot,' she exclaimed.

'That's the virtue of 'em,' he said. 'And only twopence a packet. I got 'em for Meggie,' he added, replacing the packet in his pocket and turning to the window.

'Well, I really must go,' Miss Field then said, and with a breath of weariness, she went.

An hour later, Corney returned to the hospital, resuming his vigil in the corridors, but he did not encounter Miss Field. Neither did she see him again. Indeed next morning when she began her breakfast she asked the maid:

'Who is that queer man that was in here yesterday morning?'

'Do you mean Mr. Baron?'

'I didn't get his name. He was a sort of farming man, he was sitting just there.'

'Yes, that was Mr. Baron. He's a cattle dealer. But he went away early this morning, his wife died.'

'His wife! Was it his wife?'

'Yes, she died in the night.'

'There! I knew it,' declared Flora Field. 'I was only telling him so yesterday — they *all* do. And has he gone? O, dear! He gave me quite a nice cough lozenge; I was wondering where I could get some more.'

I NEVER EVEN KNEW SHOESTONE'S CHRISTIAN NAME
until I saw it carved on his coffin plate:

Udolphus Shoestone
Aged 41 Years.

The plate, I do assure you, was of solid silver, and
the coffin was interred in a grave that later on
burgeoned into a perfect mausoleum of blue granite
and marble, all as directed by Shoestone in his will,
and all rather hideous. On the day we buried him it
rained badly, and as the white-clad priest in squeaky
boots paraded before us to the grave he held over
himself a large old carriage umbrella; we mourners
had no such covering, and indeed it would have
seemed somehow unfeeling, or lacking in due respect,
not to have braved the downpour, but I don't know
even now whether I disliked that parson or whether I
merely envied him — I know I caught a cold over it.

Shoestone had no relations at all and only one or
two friends, but for all that he was quite an amiable
clever chap and was thought to be rich, although we
had no particular reason to suppose this; in fact he
did nothing, nothing at all the whole of his life,
and he died in the midst — fell down in the track,
as it were — of his thousand good intentions without
having ever fulfilled a single one of them. Men liked
him well enough, children did not shrink from him,
and women appreciated something in him that only

women *can* appreciate — the devil knows what it is.
It wasn't fine looks — he was often a martyr to some
internal trouble — he was just an ordinary greyish
fellow who had once been auburn-haired. His
clothes never looked the worse for wear, though you
could swear they never had been new, and he had a
madness for strange hosiery — he was quite capable
of wearing neckties made of pink velvet. I suppose
these frustrated people must break out somewhere,
and Shoestone broke out in ties and tombs.

Martyr, perhaps, is not quite the right word — I
don't know — I fancy you should not call any misfortune a martyrdom if it is self-imposed. After all,
it is a poor sort of hero who has never desired to be
crucified in order to save the world. To my mind,
though, Shoestone, who was certainly not a self-
made man, was a self-made martyr. And self-willed
too, utterly capricious; but dammit, I say you
couldn't help liking him. A fool, a bigoted nincom-
poop, if you like; yet behind it all, somewhere in the
background, was a mysterious something that many
people were conscious of although they couldn't
define it. It was a sort of hidden reserve. O, it was
there right enough, but the fool never drew upon it.
Can you understand? That man Shoestone was
capable of things, immense things, of which he was
defrauded all life long by his temperament. That
is the common tragedy of ten thousand fireside
Agamemnons, and poor Shoestone was no worse
than a few, and better than most. I can tell you his

secret; he had an ideal, nothing more or less than the Ideal of Perfection. Perfection! Him! A partial invalid with the physique and activities of a hen! Udolphus Shoestone! Ah, but do not make the mistake of thinking him a preposterous egoist. God knows what it must have cost him in pride, but he realized quite early in life that personal perfection was not in him, never could be, and in fact was very far from him. You may think that a simple and common conclusion to come to, but it is not; in this world it dawns upon very few minds. It is a general conviction of mankind that its conceptions and performances are in the way of perfection. And it is a true conviction, too. If those conceptions and performances complete one's happiness, that is enough; there *is* perfection. Shoestone wanted perfection of relationship, perfection of harmony, in his life, and his ideal cost him a large amount of sense and sentiment, though not of money. For he was, in a way, parsimonious.

I wonder if I can persuade you that this parsimony was a natural part of his ideal, and that he was very far indeed from being a miser? He had, really, a heap of money, and his friends were lavishly remembered in his will. Even as a child his perverse desire to possess things, but not to use them, had dominated him, as I well remember learning on an occasion when he showed me, a few weeks before he died, a certain attic in his house; took a candle and led me up to this attic. He lived alone in a dull dump of a mansion with cold curtains and about twenty rooms in it on the outskirts of our town. There was a wall all round it, and a garden that was not cultivated to any extent but seemed to refrain from running to waste. An old woman went in daily to look after things, and sometimes her husband scraped about with a hoe; except for this Shoestone lived all alone, and although I was a frequent caller there for many years I could never persuade him to visit me. He was always promising to do so, but he did not come, and I never took my wife to see him because as a matter of fact he held rather queer views about women. I myself like women. I am fond of my wife, very fond, as of course one should be; you must be, you have to be, or why do you get married? Shoestone did not agree with me about this marriage business, although, as I told him, a few years in the army — on foreign service, like mine — would have altered his tone. We had an argument about it one winter's afternoon at tea — the very day he showed me the attic. The food at Shoestone's was always tophole, and I used to drop in on him for tea quite often. There was a lovely little Chinaman on his teapot; the teapot was very pretty, and the knob on the lid was a little fat Chinaman, very fat, who sat cross-legged and smiled at you.

'Your difficulty, Shoestone,' I said, 'is that you can't make up your mind about anything.'

'On the contrary,' he declared, 'ever since I could

think at all my mind seems always to have been made up already about everything.'

'Then,' I answered, 'it must be made up of negations.'

And he said to me: 'You are rather shrewd, sometimes!'

'Well,' I went on, 'to my certain knowledge you could have married any one of three of the most charming women in the town.' That was no more than the absolute truth, though I'll take my oath I could not understand his attraction — unless it was his money. How they guessed about that I cannot say, but women have mysterious infallible noses. And there were at least three of them after him; Chloe, Edith and Miranda their names were; they were after him, as the saying goes.

This was one of those occasions when men get into a confiding mood and tell the most astonishing things to each other. Somehow women always loom largely in such discourses. I looked at his pale face in the candlelight. Yes, he had that fondness for absurd things that made me fume. Candles! In a dark panelled house that oozed with gloom and shrieked for electric light and garlands of sunflowers or something like that in bright wall-papers! But no; there was old brass, old iron, old wood, old carpets, old window-blinds, and — goodness alive! — they weren't antiques, they were just stygian fungi! And it was not because he didn't know any better — he did, and was often proposing schemes, and just as often postponing them. He kept on postponing quite satisfactory undertakings because of the fuss and the bother entailed, or the chance that something much better still might shortly come along.

There he was, stuck among his candles, his poor face pale as a shoot under a colander, and I said:

'Why *didn't* you marry one of them?'

'It would have been so wrong, so very wrong.'

'Well, I suppose you know your own mind best, but you were pretty much in love one time and another with those very agreeable ladies, weren't you now?'

'Yes, I was,' he admitted. 'But, as you say, I knew my own mind.'

'Humph! I may have said it,' I answered after a moment, 'but I'm blessed if I can believe it!'

Shoestone fiddled about with a spoon, and blew in his cup, as though he had nothing more to say; so I went on: 'I might believe it if I could understand it.'

'It's simple,' he murmured.

'I dare say,' I said; for he was a most persuasive cuss. He could convince you very easily about his ideas, or anything else for that matter, convince you even against your will — and *that* sounds stupid — but you very soon forgot what it was he had convinced you of.

'I know my mind,' said Shoestone, 'and I know it is at war with something else inside me — nature,

I suppose. They are divided. I don't profess to understand my nature, and it is difficult for my mind to accommodate itself to my nature.'

'But that's exactly everybody's job in life,' I told him, 'and it's the way of the world.'

'The world is well enough,' said he, 'until things happen to you. Then you are no longer merely the dupe of your own nature, you become the sport of other people's, and on the whole — with a few exceptions,' he smilingly added, 'I do not like other people. I like them *en masse*; O, indeed, it is more than liking, it is a wild unreasoning emotion — sometimes I feel I could die for them — but I do not care for them individually. They make me shrink, I avoid their challenge all I can.'

I chaffed him: 'Holy St. Michael, you're not proposing to marry the women *en masse*!'

'No,' he replied solemnly, 'not any. Men can never receive from women the things they secretly dream of and long for.'

'Do you mean what the men dream of, Shoestone — or what the women dream of?'

'O, the men, of course,' he cried.

'What things?' And I began to suspect him of all sorts of viciousness. I have often noticed that is the way we generally account for anything a little out of the common.

'The things their imagination brings into the world; conceptions too beautiful to realize.'

'Devil take it, Shoestone, but what *sort* of things?'

199

'Ideals of perfection,' he answered meekly.

After a moment or two I told him frankly he had stumped me again.

'This world,' he explained, fiddling with the tablecloth and staring down at his feet, 'grew out of chaos, and that original disharmony still passes for the sublime order of nature. Huh?' he laughed ironically, 'and I want to conceive a harmony in my soul!'

'Huh!' I grunted in my turn, for the word 'soul' always disturbs me somehow.

'And,' he continued, 'that harmony can only be attained by withdrawing from the stress of life, as the world withdrew in coherence from the ancient chaos.'

Was he hinting at suicide? I wondered. Shoe-stone was such a queer card, it wouldn't have surprised me. I began gently chaffing him out of that notion, and, do you know, that made him angry. Lord bless me, I was barking up quite the wrong tree!

'No, no! I love life, I adore its beauty and its possible perfection. I want to realize only that, that alone. Death is terrible, I do not like you to speak of it.'

'My dear fellow!' I soothed him, as he turned and sat gazing into the fire with his hands trembling on his knees; and I told him that even perfection would always dissatisfy someone, that imperfection was good and in fact gratifying because we could always recognize our own likeness in it, and that there was plenty of happiness and wisdom and beauty in the chaotic old world. But he answered that he did not desire such things, he only desired perfection.

'You won't get that by sitting down and waiting for it!' I cried. 'You've got to use life, use it; grandly, recklessly, anyhow, but use it you must.'

'I do use it, in my own little way. For me,' said Shoestone, shaking his head, 'any other way is waste, destruction. I shudder at it. To waste is to die.'

'You might as well die that way!' And brutally I added: 'Better, too! Heaps better!'

'Excuse me a moment,' he said, 'I must put some more coal on the fire.' And taking a candle with him, away he went out of the room. I could hear his feet plodding along the echoing stony passages that led to the rear of the house, for he had such a preposterous unnatural dislike of coal-scuttles that he refused to have any in the house, and put himself to the continuous trouble of fetching shovelfuls of coal from the cellars — a deuce of a way off! Lord, lord, if you can't put up with a coal-scuttle! The way that man wasted his time and energies incensed me. Even such a simple matter as his teeth: he was always going to have them attended to, but having read somewhere long ago that some scientific fellow in Buda-Pest or Stockholm was discovering an entirely new treatment of renewing teeth without extracting them — Shoestone didn't know how, but he was convinced — he was waiting, yes, waiting, mind you, to hear more about it! Did he blaze off to Buda-Pest or Stockholm or wherever it was, as he quite easily could have done? Not he! I tell you, at times he annoyed me to the pitch of savagery, for it wasn't only coal-scuttles, candles and teeth, it was everything else. Nothing was ever destroyed by Shoestone, he accumulated heaps of lumber that he could not use and would not discard, and the place was like the backside of a museum. He possessed a thousand things that he could never use, while there were a thousand things that he ought to have had but never thought of acquiring.

Back he came with a shovel of fuel, which he picked out piece by piece with his fingers and so stoked up the fire. After disposing of the shovel he came back and opened a drawer beside the fireplace and carefully wiped his fingers on a duster he kept there. It was a windy dismal evening and the whole house seemed hollow. I began to smoke a pipe — a habit Shoestone had never acquired — and as I settled myself in an armchair facing him I found him staring curiously at me.

'I suppose I am a fool,' he sighed. Poor old Shoestone! I don't think it is my nature to bully people, but somehow he *invited* you to rag him; I could seldom resist doing it.

'Fool!' I assured him, sincerely and emphatically, that he was the last man in the world I should call by such a name. 'But all the same, you are timid, you know. You spend your time in proposing to do things that you never do do. You have gorgeous opportunities, but you live like a hermit crab.'

'I go to the opera, I am fond of art, I read much.'

'Yes, but you've never been to a race-meeting, or a football match, or a dance! And as for women . . .!'

'I do not care for such things.'

'Ah come! It's all very fine about racing and football and dancing, but what about Chloe and Miranda and Edith!'

He lifted his hands with a hopeless gesture: 'O, pleasant, yes; but their minds were stored with little fancy knick-knacks, nothing more.'

'Knick-knacks!'

Shoestone waved his hands again, so comically that I could not help roaring: 'What did you expect then?'

His answer was something I should never have thought of: 'Infinity,' said he.

I couldn't make head or tail of it for a long time, but it boiled down to the entire elimination of worldliness, sublimation of the spirit, and a lot of tough talk of that kind.

'I had imagined angels,' he explained.

'You certainly flattered them,' I answered.

'That is another thing,' he quickly rejoined. 'What is the use of anyone you have to flatter?'

'Women love it; they thrive on flattery, like cats on butter. The more you give 'em, the fatter the cat.' That's what I told him!

'Don't like cats,' he said grimly.

'You don't like women,' I insisted.

And then, to my astonishment, he came out with something unexpected again. 'There was one . . .' he began. 'I don't think you knew her; not Edith, or Chloe, or Miranda; after them. I must not tell you her name, but I will tell you about her. One summer she was staying on holiday, not far off, and we met — I won't tell you how — and I fell deeply in love with her. She was really beautiful, but I must not begin to describe her or I should never stop; she was *very* beautiful and cultured, and she had the rarest mind I have ever known. I told her all about myself, and she understood. We were entirely at one.'

Poor old Shoestone went rambling on about this paragon — of course he *did* describe her — and I made out she was golden-haired, dressed exquisitely, was about thirty, loved music and art and read a lot and so forth, and for the life of me I could not help grinning inwardly. There is something invariably comic, and I am apt to become satirical, about another man being bowled over. He sat forward on his chair, gazing into the fire, feet on fender, hands on knees. The wind rumbled in the chimney, and sometimes ruffled the candles.

'I loved her to distraction, and she me. I implored her to marry me, but she asked me to wait awhile. She swore she loved me, but she did not want to marry just then. I could not *see* any reason for delaying, but although I could not understand or guess it I felt there might be something it would be indelicate to probe her about. I adored her too much to do that. And then — I can hardly bring myself to confess it — it seems so crude — but — we became lovers — suddenly. We had not intended — we had not foreseen — I mean we were taken by surprise — a disaster — but — there was no turning back. And there was bliss as well as torment in my soul, for I had never known a being like her; it was as though imagination itself, born in Paradise, was being blown on a cloud across the ruins of the world. We used to spend the long summer evenings on the sand dunes out by the harbour, watching the gulls and the waves and the little yachts coming in, until the emerald lamp was hoisted on the pier head, and high aloft the ruby beam of the lighthouse began to blink, off — on, off — on, red — black, love — shame, off — on, and the air would cool in the gloom and a little bell would tinkle, sweetly yet sadly. And there, to my horror, she told me she was already married. *That* was the little secret I had not guessed, which I had been too timid to probe into! For a time I was near madness and death. My bird of Paradise was strung to a hoodie crow. But she, she was all tears and adjurations and surprise, and even anger — surely I *must* have known it, or guessed it, all along? And why, why should such a stupid matter so upset me now in the face of the one great thing — it made no difference at all! She had never really loved anyone but me; we were united in spirit and in flesh; it could make no possible difference at all! Alas, it did. It sounded the most dreadful blasphemy to me, and as soon as I had found out more about him I went off to London to interview her husband.

'I went to her husband and confessed my fault. I did not feel myself to be so utterly damnable and blameworthy, but the guilty seldom believes in his own utter guilt; he has always a defence, excuse or justification, something that makes black look very nearly white. Her husband was a large vital man, excusably bitter. I told him, and said I was prepared to pay the penalty.

'"Hell!" he said, "That's the sort of debt you can never pay. What do you expect me to do?"

'I asked him to divorce her.

'He said: "The more often she's divorced, the more she'll want to be!" And he laughed outright at his own quip.

'But I did not laugh. I tried to explain to him what she and I meant to each other, but he seemed to have no kind feelings at all for her. He grew impatient, kept snarling "God! God! God!" until at last he seemed to tower up in the room, and he burst out: "Listen to me, you thistle for a sow! You've seduced my wife: well, you're not the only one — by a dozen! She tells you she has never really loved any man but you; you're not the only one — by a dozen! And she's the kind of woman, I'll take my oath on it, who will wait until I'm going to the scaffold for murdering you, or some of her other paramours, and then, just simply then, she'll say to ME that I . . I . . . I . . . am the only one she has ever truly loved all her life long! And I shall say: 'Dammit, you might have told me that before!' And she'll answer: 'I would have — only the telephone was out of order!' Bah, you buffoon, you toad, off with you out of my sight!"'

Shoestone, poor devil, was quivering with breathless emotion.

'What could I do?' he went on. 'What more could I have done? He was right. Life *is* just buffoonery, it is impossible; it is constantly organizing itself for a regular tragedy, difficulties, danger, despair — and then, Pop! The whole thing rattles down like a clock, or cries "Cuckoo", or something grimaces at you, and you cackle because you are saved and grief is defrauded. I tell you,' he cried, beating his knees with his hands, 'I do not like to be defrauded; it is stupid!'

I waited for some time, but he did not go on, and I was impatient to hear the end, so I asked: 'What happened then?'

Shoestone shrugged his shoulders: 'He was a fearful man. I left him and hurried back, but she was gone. I have never seen or heard of her again.'

'Humph!' I sat silent, not daring to look at the poor devil. There is nothing one can do or say in such a case, and I felt very uncomfortable. Because — hang it all — you couldn't blame the husband of such a hussy. Whether Shoestone believed what he heard then I never knew, for all of a sudden he got up as if to change the subject and said:

'I've never shown you my attic; come and see.'

He took a candle and we stalked up the wide stone stairs until we came to the top of the house, and there he unlocked a little room, and in the room was just a collection of toys. Nothing else, all old-fashioned toys: rocking horse, sailor doll, trumpet, yacht in full rig, toy sword, buckets and spades, engines and soldiers, all the usual things and all as pristine as on the day they were bought.

'What the devil are these?' I asked.

'They are mine,' he said, 'given me when I was a child.'

'But they have never been used.'

'I never played with them,' he said, 'I did not care for them.'

'And you've hung on to them? All these years!'

'Yes,' said the chuckle-head.

'Never even played with them!'

'I wish I had,' said he. 'I dust them and clean them now and again, just look over them and keep them tidy. And sometimes, do you know, I have a mad desire to rush up and play with them now, and begin all over again!'

'Well, begin, for God's sake!' I roared. 'Get on the horse.'

It was a hefty dapple grey and Shoestone wasn't a big fellow at all.

'No,' he said in a whisper, 'It's too late!'

Something in his voice, so utterly forlorn and dejected, struck me then. I put my arm around his shoulders coaxingly.

'Come, come, old friend. If you don't want them, smash 'em up, burn 'em! Don't go on like this, don't recall the past; you can't live on memories.'

'I have nothing else to live for,' he said.

'There's the present,' said I.

'I wish it were past.'

'And there's the future.'

'I wish it would never come,' he sighed.

I could make nothing of him at all. The candle wax was dripping on to the floor. He was wasted, starved, worn out seeking perfection, and he had run back to his toy cupboard.

All life long he had sought for something that was not to be found, that never came, that could never be realized; that no one, not even himself, ever knew anything about. But Shoestone *had* realized perfection in one way, and in one way only; he was — God forgive me for saying it — a perfect fool.

VINCENT'S PRIDE

THERE WERE FOUR OF THESE GAFFEKINS; THE professor, his wife, their son Vincent and their daughter Hilda. The professor's wife was a handsome sprightly woman who bred Siamese cats and sang in the Choral Society, while the professor himself was absent-mindedly polite and peered at you with myopic eyes as if speculating: 'Is this some person I do not want to know?' They had two children and apparently plenty of money — when the professor quietly and incalculably died. There can, really, have been no need to remove a professor of Oriental literature to a sphere where his studies can have no peculiar value, but die he did, and Mrs. Gaffekin was left with the problem of a son aged ten and a daughter aged seventeen.

With the remnants of a larger home they went to live in a tiny Chiswick house that was stuffy with nooks and shadows and bannisters and bird's eye maple, where chairs, brackets, mantels and couches were arrayed in chintz, and lace was disposed under things like unusable teapots and empty caddies, and candlesticks glistened freshly from that backward mirage of time known as 'yore'. Here Mrs. Gaffekin, bereft of cats and husband, and despondent of voice, had leisure to regard her son Vincent who had once been destined for Oxford, if possible — Cambridge if otherwise. She knew that men of genius sometimes began as infant prodigies, though quite often they were either stupid or misunderstood, and so she watched him and waited expectantly, for one of her convictions was that provided you could wait long enough you never waited in vain. Unhappily she was deprived of any such consolation; when he was twelve years old the poor lad was stricken with paraplegia, a wasting disease of the legs, which left him a partial cripple with a hopeless future.

For a while he shuffled about on crutches or perambulated himself in a wheeled chair; then, as he grew up, he could make a fair shift for himself with a couple of sticks and certain metal supports strapped to his disabled legs; but meanwhile Mrs. Gaffekin had died, after solemnly confiding him on her death-bed to the care of his sister Hilda. With the proceeds of the insurance and the remains of the paternal fortune these two, brother and sister, found themselves still not intolerably circumstanced, and they continued to dwell in the little house in Chiswick.

Hilda Gaffekin was a beautiful creature, with the disposition of a martyr more or less unconscious of martyrdom, a disposition that would have provoked resentment or contempt even in a less subtle mind than Vincent's, for at twenty-two he was a difficult burden for anyone to bear, and there was no one else to bear it. His career was destroyed; there was no Oxford, no realization of genius, no branching into flower from the bud of such promise; there was, indeed, no life, nothing but failure, and he was pitied by all, though there was nothing he so much resented as pity. Perhaps this was due to vanity, for he was a handsome fellow from the waist upwards — a circumstance which in itself made his predicament all the more fearful — and he took some revenge by visiting his venom upon the patient head of his sister, who had a very human desire to lend a hand to Providence, whether he wanted it or no — and who could tell? Vincent annoyed her, it seemed as if he practised to annoy her, by saying things she did not like about the things she admired. In her mind was a vague esteem for ancient Greek art, and her own appearance recalled to her admirers — and there were many — the carvings of that agreeable age.

'Your Greek women were much like the run of women nowadays, vain . . .'

'They had something to be vain of.'

'Harridans, fat bulging things, long bodies, waddling as if they hadn't any ankles.'

'Not the goddesses!'

'There never were any goddesses.'

'I can believe there were.'

'I can't.' He affected to despise interests he could not hope to experience, and derided those ideals he found it impossible to pursue.

'They were beautiful divine devoted things,' Hilda averred.

'Devoted! They were hopelessly immoral. But I grant you they *could* run twenty miles. *They* didn't ride about in penny omnibuses or chew meringues.'

Hilda not only *did* do those things, she was the kind of girl who constantly *would*.

'No,' she retorted, 'for they were always hunting, or doing those discoboluses and things!'

'Sacred Myron! And what did they do when it rained?'

'I never think of it raining there,'

'It never seems to do anything else here.'

'O, but Van, it is very nice in the garden when the rain is dropping on the lavender — you can smell it then! And what do you think? I noticed a crocus and a wallflower already out in the Bastable's garden to-day.'

'Well, I wish the damn weather would get drier and warmer; that's its proper job. It's February already and I can't move an inch, I shall never get my book done.'

He was writing a book, and it was his fancy that he could not write it indoors, but only in the garden outside. There was very little other escape for him; his malady had anchored him, he was almost immovable unless a friend would give him a drive out in a car, or Hilda wheel him into the park. He could shuffle here and there, handing himself on from table to door, but his infirmity nursed a shame that he seldom outfaced in public, certainly never alone. Like a desperately wounded animal he sought for solitude with the wounds of his grief; only in utter loneliness could he avoid the pitying eye and realize the depths of whatever was in him, passion, exaltation, oneness with life. All in vain, the way was barred with humiliations; he was like a tack on a wall, that hadn't even a picture hung upon it. All the brightness of life passed him by, he could not go with it, he could no more than mentally peer at it without hope of participation or possibility of purchase. 'To be, *or* not to be' was not his question; it was rather 'To be, *and* not to be.' The things that happened everywhere were inexorably odd; they happened to everybody but they did not, and could not, happen to him. Life had no purpose, anyhow; it had only possibilities, and even those infinitesimals must beg for opportunity. Gaffekin would have attended an execution very amiably, even with joy, provided of course that it was not his own. So he sat on a chair and wrote letters to newspapers, brooded over chess problems, or read accounts of famous trials; often he would imagine himself conducting the cross-examination in place of that fatuous prosecuting barrister:

'Prisoner at the bar, be good enough to tell the gentlemen of the jury . . . why . . . if so and so . . . and so and so . . . you . . . etc. and so on.'

And the abject criminal would quail at Vincent's tone and be carried moaning from the dock!

There was nothing else to dream about except his motile boyhood, poor matter for a man grown savage with frustration. Ageing generations dreamed of good old days and sighed for the past happiness which until now they had scarcely recognized; the younger were ecstatic about the future, a millenium of movement, freedom and joy; but he was of no generation, he was fixed, time passed him by. It was his fate to be ever filling the bucket, yet never to find it full, and seldom as much as a dram to moisten his parched desires. Little wonder then that he could rage violently about a lost button or a delayed newspaper.

'O Van, why do you let these small mean silly little things impress you so?'

'How can I avoid them?'

'How?'

'Yes, you tell me, tell me how! Life is made up of all such miserable things.'

'Our life do you mean!'

'Well, isn't it?'

'No, not at all, surely not!' Hilda was positive and comforting.

'It's what's the matter with mine,' he gloomily contended.

'What is?'

'All this significant insignificance.'

Of lovable things in his life there had been only his mother — it is astonishing how boys go on loving their mothers long after their fathers have ceased to do so! Vincent had loved her in childhood, adored her in youth; he had loved her till she died, and now her memory was his only treasure. He could not extend that fervour to his sister, so patient and

so kind and as amiable as she was beautiful, for
Hilda abounded in intractable enthusiasms. Her
thoughts effervesced, they were as bubbles. The
things the world misunderstood! The forgiveness
she prescribed for offences uncommited! The
virtues she found in villains and vixens — and the
vices she sometimes imagined in the blameless! She
was also lovely and virile and had access to all those
opportunities denied *him*, and for that reason alone
Vincent hated her with a bitterness that would
have shocked her had she been capable of divining
it. His thoughts about anyone at all soon grew
malicious; it was a sort of evil anodyne, it enabled
him to reflect a little comfortingly on the divine
infallibility of injustice!

Her friends the Bastable's, too! He hated them.
Tom Bastable, a somewhat noisy stockbroker of
thirty, was in love with Hilda; he and she went about
a lot together, and Tom often came in to sit with
them of an evening. A tall powerful fellow in pointed
shoes, with hot pressed hair, tight black jacket and
striped trousers, he would discourse of shares, of
foreign places he had visited, of some new under-
wear he had found, and he would tell funny stories
— stories like that one about the wife who had
grown so tired of her husband that the poor man kept
on buying newer and gaudier pyjama suits for
himself to wear in the hope of striking her fancy
once again. They must have been funny, for he
always laughed very heartily at them himself, and

217

only stopped laughing to ask: 'You see the point, don't you?' And then he would go on laughing again.

Vincent privately thought him a jackass. Bastable enraged him with his silly thin plastered head and his long vital legs sprawling under all the tables and chairs that always impeded legs like his, but the man loved Hilda, and Hilda probably loved him — for she always laughed at the things he said, even the tritest, with genuine mirth — though Gaffekin knew his sister would never marry, or not until he himself was dead. It was Bastable who took them for drives in his car, it was Bastable who did this, that and the other for Vincent, and it was Bastable who proposed and arranged that lamentable visit to a night club which left such a permanent gash in Vincent's pride.

One frosty March morning Vincent was scanning *The Times* by the fireside. He usually began with the death notices, and when he came to the end of them he often, for some reason, appeared to be disappointed. What was Hilda doing? Hilda was standing by the garden window holding a red shoe in her hand. She had on a green wool dress, a ridiculous tiny white pinafore, and from a saucer of paint on the window sill she was repainting the heels of her crimson shoes.

'Why are you doing that?'

'Tom wants us to go with him to The Rotunda to-night.'

'Us?'

'You and me.'

'What for?'

'For a little diversion, Van. There's to be dancing and so on.'

'What good am I for dancing and so on?'

'No . . . but it will be a nice change for you. It will be very gay.'

'I shan't go. Are you going?'

'But Vincent, you *can* go! It will be perfectly simple to take you, and it's very comfortable there for anyone who doesn't want to dance.'

'Is Bastable going?'

'Of course!'

'In the car?'

'Yes.'

'O well, go then!'

'Not without you. No, Van, I shouldn't dream! You *must* come. It will be quite easy.'

'O, easy as skating! Are you going to dress yourself up?'

'My new crimson silk! You haven't seen me in it yet.'

'I don't want to.'

'Wait till you see! I'll get your dress clothes ready this afternoon and . . .'

'This afternoon!'

'Don't be silly. Tom will come for us about ten.'

'Why the devil *do* people always want to dance at night?'

'They've no other time.'

'There's day, isn't there?'

'Everybody's busy then.'

'Busy! Everybody! What at?'

'You silly! Doing the world's work, of course.'

'World's work! Bosh! They're all like curates and railway porters, wondering what the devil to do with themselves.'

'You'll like it very much.'

'What am I going to like?'

'The Rotunda, it's . . .'

'I'm not going to any Rotunda, I shouldn't dream of it this stinking horrible freezing weather. Whatever made you think I'd go to a show like that?'

'But you don't know what it's like.'

'Of course I know!'

'You've never been.'

'Of course I haven't!'

'Its simply ripping.'

'O, stop using those foul words! What is The Rotunda, anyway?'

'It's a night club.'

'That's it, a night club! It'll be raided by a lot of fat-headed policemen and we'll all be carried off to gaol.'

'When you don't know,' said Hilda, brushing the paint meticulously on her shoe, 'be an optimist, Van!'

Now the truth of the matter — as her brother had already guessed — was that Bastable had privately asked Hilda to go alone with him to the club, and she had regretfully declined — she could not leave her brother for so long. Whereupon Bastable had urged her to bring him, too, and Hilda had determined to persuade him. If it came to the worst she would go herself and leave Vincent to the care of their maid, although he hated to be hovered over by that creature.

By the superior divination of the infirm Vincent had guessed all this, but as the day wore on his petulance subsided and he grew amiable. At ten o'clock, when Bastable arrived, he was ready.

'Full dress, eh!' chaffed Bastable gaily.

'Dress! My God, I'm positively wearing a crinoline!' declared Vincent.

Tom proposed to carry him out to the car, but the cripple insisted on walking unaided; with a stick in either hand he shuffled along the garden path, and swivelled himself into a back seat of the car. It was frightfully cold and the moon was straining under heavy clouds. The radiant Hilda prepared to merge herself beside her brother, but he abruptly ordered her to sit in front with Bastable. She obeyed, but then leaned over the back of her seat and asked:

'Are you sure I'd not better sit with you, Van?'

He did not answer, and the car moved off. In time they came to a small dim square surrounding a railed garden, and drove up to a brightly lit porch.

'Let me give you a lift up these steps,' urged Bastable.

'Ah, to Hell with that!' Gaffekin answered, and with difficulty he shambled up and along into a lobby, where they discarded their outdoor wrappings.

The chief room at The Rotunda was a high circular one, relict of some Masonic fancy, with a glass dome supported by four vast marble columns rising from the polished floor. When erected in The Rotunda the pillars had no capitals, and it was thought they looked somehow unfinished until some capitals made of plaster were stuck round the necks of the pillars. Even then it was generally admitted that the capitals themselves looked impoverished, and it was decreed that they should be gilded; so gilded they were. All round the circled wall were richly cushioned lounges, dark blue and gold, with oblong tables in front of them, leaving the central space between the pillars for dancing. The great chandelier in the dome shed a million beams upon the floor half full of languid couples when our visitors sat down amid a sequence of *vivace* strains that bobbed, swerved, tottered, and recoiled. According to Vincent the orchestra was disseminating dactyls, while the dancers ambulated in elegiacs.

'S'truth, what a saturnalia!'

Bastable ordered drinks, but he soon took Hilda away into the dance. Vincent had laid his two sticks at the back of his seat and sat twirling the stem of a wine glass. 'A waiter ought not to wear button

boots, like that, and he ought not to squint either —
it's unlucky.' There were as many people sitting
down as there were dancing, and every table was
equipped with a telephone — of all things, a telephone! There was one standing on Vincent's table;
it was numbered in prominent figures 21. There
was one on the left hand table, a few feet away,
numbered 20, and one on the right numbered 22.
At number 20 a man with an abdomen, a nose,
and a troublesome cigar, was speaking into his
telephone.

'Yes, yes. My dear Jessie, I most certainly will.
But listen; I'm becoming quite moral.' A flick of
the cigar. 'I've lately taken to liking the husbands of
my girl friends almost as much as I like the girls
themselves. Ha, ha! What do you say to that?'
A puff at the cigar. 'I do hope it doesn't become a
habit. Ah well, life, my dear. *You* know . . .'

Gaffekin perceived that this number 20 man was
a fat degrading clod — and yet, and yet, he could not
help but envy him! Those women! That easy
assured access! Vincent was a romantic soul,
defrauded of the possibilities of romance. He was
inexorably cut off from agreeable women, or he
thought he was; and what Vincent Gaffekin thought
upon any subject was apt to assume such an air of
cosmic affirmation that none had the hardihood to
dispute it. To be as handsome as his sister, and yet
lie entombed in an infirmity, with the door left
half open upon an Eden whose farers passed him by,

was to consume each hour in Tartarus. The dead was dying in its grave.

As each dance ended Hilda and Bastable returned to the moody cripple, plying him with drinks and conversation; or Bastable brought along people he knew, several indifferent ladies and a half-tipsy turf agent who swayed on his heels as he grasped Vincent's hand with petulant affability: 'Mr. Gaffekin ah! It's the first time I've had the pleasure of meeting you before. By my blessed holy soul, it is and all!' And he lounged at Vincent's side for some time after they were alone, showing him a packet of bawdy photographs, and nudging him with his elbow: 'Eh, what!'

But on the opposite side of the room sat a lady richly and bluely dressed, a double string of pearls around her neck, smoking a cigarette in a long black holder. Small, and beautiful, and alone; but quite self-possessed; sweet white arms, feminine fragrance, auburn hair. Whenever the crowd of dancers parted Vincent's eyes sought her, and at times her own questing glance met his. Was it fancy, or was it madness, that led him to think she . . . O, lunacy of course. All lunacy consisted of . . . well, what *did* lunacy consist of? She never danced, she was alone, she was staring at him, and as she stared she stretched out her hand to the telephone on her table. But she did not use it, she did not call to anyone. When the crowd hid her from him the fat clod at number 20 was speaking into his telephone again.

'But Jessie, you must! I'm rather under martial law to-night, just a wee bit, rather. I'll tell you later. It will be quite all right. O, pooh! That's imposs! You tell him to go and talk to his grandson. No. Yes. No. Yes. It will be quite all right, I tell you.'

What the devil is that all about? Vincent wondered. And what a fatuous thing to do — laying telephones into the holy sanctity of your club, right on to your private table! Bad as having an octopus in your bath. Surely you could leave your blessed business outside for an hour or two?

'O, boy,' cried Bastable when Vincent asked him about it. 'That's the cream of the show — what *are* you thinking of! Those lines are only laid from table to table, they are not connected outside. You just ring up anyone you see sitting around, anything that takes your fancy, and speak to it. It's just a bit of fun.'

'Fun!'

'It's so free and easy. You see a pretty girl over there, don't know her from Adam, can't get an introduction, here you are, ring her up! Catch as catch can!'

'And is this fellow then, at number 20, just ringing up somebody in this very room?'

'That's all.'

'But he knows her, why doesn't he go and speak to her.'

'Search me!' grinned Bastable. 'Here you are,

ring him up yourself and ask him: *Number* 20, *what's your dirty game?*' And pushing the telephone stand towards his friend Bastable whirled away with Hilda again.

Presently, when the floor was clear of dancers, and Hilda and Tom were away sitting with some strangers, Vincent again courted the attention of the lady in blue. She did not appear to be attached to any set; there were people sitting drinking, eating, and smoking near her, but she neither spoke to them nor heeded anybody, none but Vincent Gaffekin, and him she was frankly observing with a sort of favouring curiosity. She was alone at her table and on it was a tall glass in front of her, half full of yellow wine. What took his gaze as potently, however, was the figure 4 displayed on her telephone. Gaffekin's senses were uncoiling; she was noting him, approving him, and the flattery of her regard was exquisite. Yet it aroused some sadness, too, for he was a broken thing; she did not know that yet, and it would be dreadful to have to reveal it. But her whole being was a summons, a summons to him alone in all that room, which he could not put aside; her eyes were flashing gentle greetings to him. The delight! A marvel! Surely a miracle could happen! When the music resumed its demented flatulence and the dancers hid those smiling eyes from him, it was as though a heavy cloud had blotted out the sun, and the chilled man, sighing with hope and fear, was almost sickened by the emotions swirling in his breast. He might go across to her and sit beside her — why not? He could manage that much — though it would only expose his wreckage. Yet why not! Why, why, in the name of God, why not? The audacity of the idea brought sweat to his brow, and as he sat wiping his face with his handkerchief the telephone bell on his table tinkled. He stared and stared at it. Startled by its sound he stared at the trembling bell as though it were a thing to be wary of. It trilled again. With nervous hand he snatched the receiver and put it to his ear.

'Hallo?' he said.

'Excuse.' It was a woman's voice, with a slight foreign intonation. 'Is it number 21?'

'It is, yes.'

'I am sitting at number 4.'

'Ah, yes . . .! I know, I know. How splendid of you!'

'You recognize? I am dressed in a blue gown. How do you do!'

'And you have beautiful hair.'

'Do you like my hair — no?

'Enchanting, so is all of you.'

'Are you interested! I have been peeping at you!'

'And I at you.'

'Not very much. No!'

'Very very much! I cannot bring myself to look at anything but you. My eyes refuse to.'

'That is a flattery.'

'It is God's truth.'

'Ah, monsieur — you must have your eyes looked into.'

'By you! May I?'

'You are much alone.'

'Alas, I am.'

'And I, too — pity me! I have no friends.'

'Nor have I — pity me!'

'O, fie! Monsieur, do you dance?'

'No,' he said glumly.

'Never?'

'Never. But won't you tell me your name?'

'My name?'

'Yes, and I want to know *all* about you.'

'Come and dance with me. I will tell you then. It is a l-o-n-g name, very long. I will have to murmur it, in your ear.'

'But I cannot dance!' Vincent spluttered his distress. 'I am so sorry. Really, I cannot dance at all.'

'Come. I will teach you how. I am very clever.'

'Ah, you must excuse me. Nothing in the world could give me such joy. It would be heaven. Forgive me, I'm a cripple, quite unable to dance. But I would give my soul to please you.'

'Ah, my dear! What a shame! What can we do? I will come and sit with you. You are so interesting. We will talk of everything — yes?'

'No, no,' he said. 'Wait! It is not so bad as all that. I will come across to you. Would that bore you?'

'No, no, no! I shall adore. And you will promise. . . .'

'Promise? What must I promise?'

'Promise to be tired of me at the right time!'

'Not while I live, mademoiselle!'

'Mademoiselle! My name is. . . .'

'Stop! You shall tell me your name when I come; you must murmur it, in my ear.'

'Ah, monsieur, you quiz me!'

'No. I'm coming.'

Gaffekin looked vaguely round for his sister and her partner. The orchestra had flogged itself once more into a mild hysteria that was muscular rather than musical, the dancers grew gloomily intent on deportment, but the great chandelier and the colossal pillars were rich with singular dignity. He got his two sticks, heaved himself up to his feet — and then was hideously betrayed. The metal contraptions supporting his feeble legs gave under him, something snapped, and he pitched headlong to the floor at the foot of one of the pillars. Few people saw his mishap, he was mercifully hidden, the orchestra blared on. The near-by dancers, thinking him drunk, just swerved aside from him and amusedly scanned his prostrate body as it struggled in vain to rise. Suddenly Hilda saw it all, and with a faint shriek she darted there followed by Bastable.

'O, Van! Van!' she cried, kneeling beside him.

'It's that blasted clip has broken,' he groaned. 'God, what luck! Help me up, I can't move myself.'

229

People began to crowd round them now.

'What about a doctor?' asked Tom.

'No, no. Never mind that. Get me up! Get me out of this! Can't you get the car! At once! At once!'

'O, Van!' Hilda was almost sobbing.

'Shut up, you fool!' he gasped between his grinding teeth. 'Can't you get me into the lobby? Get me out of this horror — O, quick — for Christ's sake!'

Bastable at once picked him up and, bearing him across his shoulders like a dead sheep, stalked quickly from the hall, followed by frightened Hilda carrying the two sticks. The orchestra leader turned a nonchalant eye upon them as they passed out, and continued to wag his baton. As though he had been blinded Vincent held his hands across his face until they had got him into the silence of the lobby; then he opened his eyes and whispered humbly:

'Thanks, Bastable; many, many thanks.'

'You get his coat,' said Tom to Hilda, 'while I carry him out to the car.'

A porter pulled open the door.

It was snowing; it had been snowing a long time. The world was very white, very quiet, very cold.

ONE FINE DAY I TOLD THIS TALE TO A STRANGER, and he turned up his nose, as to say it was not true! Well, well; be as be may, there is much in a fish's eye the poor moon does not see. All sorts of truths live and die in the world, but there is one truth we seldom lay our hands to and that is: the truth that has no neighbour in ourselves. We cannot make a stomach for that. Yet there is the truth of likeness as well as the truth of fact: has not many a man been called a murderer though he only destroyed a villain?

It was going on my way to the fair at Asnamorig, and halfway between the goosebridge and the haggard I met this wholesome carpenter and his dog.

Says he: 'Good day.'

I said it was fine.

So down we sit and I tell him the tale.

Had I — then said he — a chew of tobacco?

I had not. I offered him the little pear the girl O'Stancy had given me the night before, a sweet round pear.

'Take it,' I said.

And it was then he declared the tale not only was untrue, but it never could be, never would be, true in life or time, and he should not believe it. Well, I didn't want anyone to believe it then; but now, if you read on, you may get used to it and I'll not care whether you believe it or no.

Dunky Fitlow's the name. It is the name of a man not too young, and not too old, and rather huge; nobody else's coat would ever fit him and he, for sure, could never slip his foot into the throat of another man's shoe; but his life was full of poetry and sleep — rather more of sleep than the other. Sometimes he would only wake up for an hour or two in the week, and then he might say a few marvellous golden words of the poetry, and off to sleep again. Or maybe he would eat like a wolf, and then off to snoring sleep — without any of the poetry. And once in a while you might see him drifting through the fields of summer, watching the corn grow and talking with the old men.

'The song of the oats,' he would say, 'is better than the song of the wheat, but the song of barley is a tangle of vipers hissing.'

'It is so,' the old men answered, 'but all's one to the thresher.'

'The thresher's arm,' he would say, 'flogs draf and grain alike, though a sheaf of corn is twin to a lovely woman.'

'It may be so,' the old men answered, 'but all's one in wedlock.'

It was time, everybody said it was time, for him to be thinking of making a marriage. But what woman in her senses would ever seek a match with the like of Dunky Fitlow? He had coaxed them all, the fine, the lovely ones — they said he had no beauty. He courted all the rest, the widows, the crooked, the sour spinsters — they said he was no ways industrious. So there was only the camel-faced woman left then, but her he would not pursue.

'What is the matter with that man?' the camel-faced woman asked when she heard of him.

'There is something astray in his heart,' was the answer of one and all.

'Well,' said she,' if the heart is dull in his breast, said she, 'let love unlock it,' she said. 'I'll marry him.'

She laid her traps for him, but there was no nice appearance on the woman.

'Bondage is the doom of all, be it life, or love, or labour; wealth, woe, or wickedness. Sleep is deliverance — I'll be free.' So Dunky lay in his snoring sleeps for longer than before, and when waking he was always harder to come at.

But it is a poor fowler that never rejoices in the coy bird. One day, as he was going down from his sleep, Dunky met the camel-faced woman coming up the stairs. He made to go past her, right by, without any small word of greeting.

'Hi! What's this?' cried she.

'What's what?' And Dunky yawned a very great yawn.

'O, you know! Well enough you know!' the camel-faced woman replied.

'I don't know a thing at all about it,' said Dunky.

'Ho!' says she. 'You don't, do you!'

'Go on. Keep your distance,' Dunky said.

'Where are you going, my little poeteen?' she asked him very tenderly, her eyes looming at him.

'Ah, let go of me!' cried Dunky, quivering like an aspen on a grave.

But she would not let go of him, she never did, and in no time at all it seems they were to be married, and great preparations were made, for she had much wealth and was lavish in her ways.

On the day they were to be wed Fitlow rose up early and went forth to take the bright air. The lake was a bowl of silver in the golden hills, swans were rafting along, and a heron brooded in the reeds like a sentinel at prayer. As he was walking by the lake Dunky spied in the road ahead of him a marvellous bloom of white, all flashing and moving. When he came up to it, there lay a large dewy turf upturned, and on it were scores of butterflies, all white. Dunky's shadow disturbed them for a moment and they fluttered up idly into the air, but soon they settled on the turf again into one huge lily-bloom, throbbing and alive. He stood admiring it before he went on. He had not gone a score of steps further when he heard a cart behind him, and he looked back.

There was a man in the cart and a woman with him, and they pulled up beside the bloom of the butterflies.

'What are they doing and all?' the woman asked. Her voice was harsh in the pure morning air.

'Breeding,' the man replied.

'I don't care to be looking at that,' said the woman.

The man sat in his cart, flicking his whip at the butterflies, and every time he struck some of them down the woman laughed. The man said nothing — just flick, flick, flick, in his stern duty, until they were all killed.

Dunky walked on to the church. It was early yet, and the camel-faced woman had not arrived, so he sat down on a bench to rest his bones. When his bride came Dunky was in a snoring sleep, and none could wake him, not bride or priest or people, and they had to leave him there in the church, and he was sleeping for three days. Each day the bride and priest and people came and nudged him, or pulled his nose, or thumped his loins — all lost labour, for nothing could ever rouse Dunky from his slumbers. But on the fourth day he rolled over awake, rubbed his eyes, and married the camel-faced woman.

She took him home. 'Early to bed,' said the bride, for she was stone weary waiting for him. When Dunky followed her to the bridal chamber the poor woman was already asleep.

'Ah me, ah well'; sighed Dunky, 'I was never a one to disturb a woman sleeping.'

Off he dropped again, while the bride slept on, unkissed and curst. Thus it continued between them for many days and nights, each asleep when the other was awake. She was what she was, and he hadn't the heart to flatter her. And then one time

Dunky awoke, and there was no one there at all, he was lying cold. Up he got, did on his clothes and went to the room downstairs, but there was no one in. The house was empty, she was gone. There was a bowl of roses on the table, but the dropped rose leaves were lying in a heap all round the bowl — she had been gone a long time, gone for good and all! Then Dunky felt the pinch of loneliness, and he sighed for her. She was gone entirely, and there was no more left for him to do but what he had always done before he married her: to sleep, to wake, to go into the fields, to talk to the oldish men with their beards and long coats and walking sticks.

'O, this is no life at all,' sighed Fitlow, as he passed the time o' day with them. Winter and summer they wore the same long rusty overcoats, their beards were white, and they would doddle hither and yon. Now their eyes drooped as if from too much gazing in the sunlight.

'We have just come out,' they said, 'to pass the time away.' And they would count the lambs, or watch the fish cruising about the idle streams. Happen a hare would rove through the paddock of the old windmill. Whenever they saw a man crossing the fields any way off they would peer after him and begin to ruminate: 'Now who be that man? He's going towards the north. We ought to know that man. If we did, we'd know where he be going.'

Or it might be the springtime, when sleep had

forsaken him altogether. Daffodils had begun to peer in the gardens, and bare trees seemed to stretch out their arms to catch something Dunky could not perceive, which only they were aware of. As he walked along he could see, a way off, a tree nobly proportioned and perfect; yet when he got to it he found it was two trees, one behind the other, and neither of them much to look at by themselves.

'O, it is no life at all!' he sighed. 'Time's will is on the wing, and I go lingering on, lingering on.'

The camel-faced woman was done with him; he was not too young, not too old, but there was no enjoyment of him; she was what she was, and he hadn't the strength to flatter her; she was done with him.

Then one day, in the height of summer it was, she was struck down in the glaring sun and perished of a stroke. With half a heart Fitlow went to bury his wife, and when he had buried her and come out of the church he burst into tears and sobbed like a child. Close by the porch stood a man, a middling sort of man, and when he saw the grief and the true tears of Dunky Fitlow, this man asked:

'What is the poor fellow crying like that for?'

'Hush!' murmured the neighbours, 'He has just come from burying his wife.'

'O, the foolish creature!' said the man. 'Tell him, tell him I'll chop my old wife for his dead one, and pay all expenses I will!'

'Hush, hush! For shame!' cried the neighbours

all. And of course the neighbours were angry, but the other did not care.

'Foolish man!' He kept on grinning and roaring. 'I'll chop him, I'll chop him!'

And Dunky was all in black, save one of his shoes was laced up with a bit of green cord. The camel-faced woman was dead and gone, unkissed and curst — he too, he knew it. 'Darling', he whispered; and he was weeping like a child.

THE FOGGY FOGGY DUE

BONNER FOGG WOKE UP TO DESPAIR. HE NEVER had had any money, and at the age of forty was still living on his wife's private income, still trying to borrow money from her, always unsuccessfully, for wildcat projects. The night had been glorified by a dream that someone had left him a million pounds; he woke up — it was not so. The only brightness was in those scarlet military braces (his aunt had given him them at Christmas) dangling from the buttons of his black trousers which had about half-a-crown in the pockets. Ghastly! For he wanted to buy, he had simply *got* to buy, a present for Grace Capstick's birthday. Grace was his wife's bosom friend (Eva adored her) and Grace was married, too; but she was very discreet, and so, well, after all, what was a man to do? A man had to live, somehow, and Harold Capstick was a pimply oaf who ought to have married some market-gardener's daughter.

Moodily he arose, but he breakfasted fairly amiably, Eva being one of those early risers; she was already abroad with Grace, having a riding lesson on the marshes from Tillion the jobmaster. Bonner Fogg took his walking-stick and went out. Just as he emerged from the stores after buying a shoe-horn he almost ran into the side of Grace's husband, Harold Capstick. For a flashing moment

239

Bonner fancied that Harold was attempting to ignore him, but Capstick looked so queer and distraught that Fogg hurried after.

'Anything the matter, Harold? You look ill,' he said, pressing his friend's elbow and peering down at him.

'I'm not ill,' replied the other testily, jerking the friendly hand away. 'I'm going for a stroll over the links.'

'I'm going that way,' said Bonner, who was possessed of any amount of Christian spirit. They walked on together in silence: Capstick, a short neat plump dark oily-faced man with glasses that seemed clamped to the hollows of his forever startled eyes, and white ostentatious cuffs in his short sleeves, striding jerkily; while Fogg, who dressed anyhow — you never noticed how — fair, slender, and slightly bent like the stalk of a hyacinth, lumbered along beside him, trailing his stick.

'*Is* anything the matter?' Fogg inquired again.

'Not much; no, nothing to speak of.'

If ever a man conveyed the implication of mute suffering stoically borne, that man was Harold Capstick. And it was a fine day, too!

'But I admit I do not like it,' he added, after a moment.

The links were green and inviting; little shorn hills and plats of tees and boxes of sand and red flags. The white windmill, twirling its arms in mild breezes from off the sea, cluttered amiably as they walked by. Suddenly Capstick stopped to confront Bonner Fogg, and he hissed out:

'How would you like it if you found out your wife was untrue to you?'

The astonished Fogg could only ejaculate· 'But . . . but . . . she's not!'

'I tell you she is!' rapped Capstick, glaring at up him.

'Are you out of your senses, man! Excuse me, Capstick, you'll admit that I know a bit more about it than you do?'

'But . . . good God! . . . what do you mean?'

Very sternly Fogg answered the bristling little man: 'I mean what I say. Every time. If it's a joke it's in very bad taste let me tell you. I don't like it, naturally.'

'But what have *you* got to do with it?' shrieked Harold.

'O, nothing, nothing! I've got nothing to do with it.' Fogg condescendingly sneered. 'She's only my wife, I suppose — or isn't she?'

'I'm not talking about *your* wife! What the devil are you thinking of? I'm talking about *my* wife!'

'O! *Your* wife!' breathed the enlightened Fogg. 'O!'

'Of course I am.' Harold snorted.

'I beg your pardon, Capstick. I quite thought — from what you said — I quite thought you were referring to Mrs. Fogg. And, naturally . . .!'

'Mrs. Fogg! Eva! Good God! You don't

imagine, surely, that I would joke about a thing like this, at my time of life, do you? I'm not joking. Let me tell you it's no joke, I was never more serious in my life. My wife is untrue, she is untrue to me. Ha, ha, ha, ha, ha! Grace! I can assure you she is damn faithless, Bonner. You never expected to hear that, did you?'

Off he went, stumbling jerkily over the grass, followed by his companion. As they went, he threw over his shoulder: 'And *I* never expected to hear it either, Bonner!'

Fogg was silent, in fact he was shattered; he wanted to run away, but the little man seemed to be dragging him in his wake. And, of course, it was monstrous! What could he, or anyone else, do with a screw of a man who accosted you thus in public, who blurted out things like that? And it was not the first time Capstick had done such a thing, not by any means. (He had told people, really anybody, that he had a fistula when he was eleven and stole a fountain pen from a curate. Why did he do that — people would ask. Because of the fistula — Capstick would answer. The fountain pen had been full of green ink, and they had traced the delinquent through his use of it. And to this day Capstick could not understand why a clergyman had used such green ink.)

'You never thought to hear that, did you?' Capstick repeated and waited for his friend. 'And I never thought of such a nasty thing, either. But it's true.'

Some sort of relief began to flicker in Bonner Fogg's guilty bosom; he mumbled that he was deuced sorry.

'Imagine *me*, then, Fogg; imagine me! Such an idea never dawned upon my poor shrimp of a brain. Now I am nothing; I am completely nothing.'

Perhaps — Fogg hinted — perhaps he was mistaken, after all.

'Why *should* I be! Why do you say that, Fogg? have you heard anything about it?'

'No, no. I haven't, not a thing. But I know Grace, and I think you must be making a mistake somewhere.'

'O, pish!' cried Capstick, much as though it would annoy him to be so mistaken.

'But listen, Harold! It's a mistake any man might make, and I dare say many men *have* made it.'

'Have you ever made it?' interrupted Harold.

Fogg leaned over the irate husband: 'Me! How should I know, how does any man ever know?'

'There you are then! Very well!' Harold retorted.

Fogg continued, temporizingly: 'What I want to say is this — is that — well anyway — after all — it is the kind of thing that might happen, in these modern times, to any one of us. In fact, if you look at it in that light, it is bound to happen. As long as there's a forbidden tree, I suppose women will flock to it.'

'Bound to, you say! O, dammit, but why *me*, Fogg? Why me? Why not you?'

'Why not me?' Fogg solemnly responded. 'It *has* happened to me!'

'O, O! I didn't know.' Capstick was momentarily abashed.

'Well, of course, I don't actually *know*,' Fogg went on. 'But I think it *may* have; in fact, there's really no room for doubting it.'

On they went walking, they went walking on. Capstick did not seem to be as impressed by Fogg's revelation as Fogg expected, but a man engrossed with his own private grievance of that nature is cursed with many degrees of self-indulgence; the salt sea might drown the Royal Family, or the Apostles might burn to an ash before his very eyes — he would scarcely be aware of it, or only mildly interested.

'I didn't know that, of course, Fogg. But still . . . you must pardon me, I'm not myself, it's really most upsetting, let us turn back.'

They turned back. 'Who,' began Bonner Fogg, 'is the — er — fellow?'

'Ah, that's the point, that's the mystery, Fogg!'

'It always is,' Fogg sighed.

'Who is he? I have yet to find out,' Capstick confessed. 'But I shall, I am going to, you may rely on that. I have yet to discover who the viper is, but the important point is that I know about it; I have got some inkling, in fact she doesn't deny it, but as for his name — she defies me! And that makes me think of things that cause me to shudder, because I have not, up to now, been a very violent man. But still, we shall see! I have my idea. I tell you, Fogg, I have my suspicions. I have. O, yes.'

'Who do you suspect?' Fogg feebly inquired.

'O, I can't go screaming it out here, man! How can I? Would you? Don't be obtuse!'

Fogg mumbled apologetically. Capstick tripped on, muttering to himself, until he once more turned and stopped.

'Do you really wish to know?' he demanded with a minatory glower.

'Well . . .' the other lamely answered. 'Of course, I . . .'

'Then I'll tell you, Bonner Fogg, I'll tell you!' shouted Harold. 'I suspect you!'

'Me!' exclaimed the horrified culprit. 'Don't be such an ass, Harold! What scandalous nonsense!'

Capstick glared at his companion as though seeking to probe him to the soul. Then the glare slackened disconsolately.

'Isn't it you, Bonner, really? On your honour?'

'On anything you like, Harold.'

'Well, it might be you — why shouldn't it be! I suspect every man that I know she knows, every man jack. That's the state I'm in now. God help me, what shall I do! I wonder what I can do?'

After a few moments he turned away and went stumbling back towards the links. Bonner Fogg did not follow, but watched him in silence, a comic figure, though it seemed to be retreating insurgently.

Then Fogg trudged back through the little town until he came to the Gun Garden on the cliff. The Gun Garden was just an acre of sweet turf with a path, some seats, a flagstaff, and six big guns. Fogg sat down upon a seat to survey the sea and wonder what he should do about it all. It was damned serious — that fatheaded Harold going prancing and bawling all over the town. What in the name of hell had Grace been telling him?

Six ugly rusty old cannons captured in the Crimea or somewhere, and dumped here to show off. National pride! Piffling popguns! And people as proud of them as they were of their main drainage and the railway station! Not an atom of use, neither for ornament nor destruction or anything else. But perhaps there was something in this national pride after all? National — rational! Good solid basis for society. Up with your flag, pinch the other fellow's guns, teach him a lesson!

It was all very fine though. Why must she go kicking over the traces just now? She had always been so discreet, so clever, in fact she was damn good, well-bred, and you could rely on her. Absolutely. Always. But still, you couldn't be too careful.

Fogg's gaze ranged over the sea. It was pleasant to sit up in the Gun Garden and watch the waves purling over, little wool-white waves. Although it was early in the season half a dozen people were already bathing, and a red-faced elderly man on the shore in a pink dressing-gown was stalking deliberately as though every step was intended to be a footprint in the sands of time; he was also carrying a black furled umbrella.

She mustn't do it. She mustn't let on. But there, of course — she can't? Absolutely staunch. Queer cattle, women! They don't mind telling you how sweet they are on somebody else, but they will suffer to be hung rather than say who! It was blessed serious, though.

Fogg took her photograph out of his pocket-book. Head and shoulders, a dark debonair little creature of about thirty, looking as tricksey as an antelope. Sweet round face. Her hair lay in plaited bands around her head from ear to ear. The eyes were bright with a sharpness that might have made you wary of her anger, but behind their hard brilliance was a well of comfort and sweetness.

Thirty yards off a gentleman marched up to a vacant bench, sat abruptly down, and unfolded a newspaper.

'Major Macalister!' muttered Fogg. He had not seen him for a long time. Macalister was a retired military personage, reputed to be rich, who hunted a good deal. It was ironically hinted of the major that he hunted more than foxes, his idea of human relationships expressing itself towards men in terms, first of social policy, and then in terms of sporting opportunity. Towards women, however, it expressed itself in terms of opportunity, sporting if possible, otherwise if necessary. It was not so long ago since he and the Foggs had been rather friendly; Eva, despite the rumours, had thought him most agreeable; but of late they had been quite out of touch. Fogg moved along and greeted this gentleman with factitious geniality.

Major Macalister, a very hairy, much shaven, trenchantly jowled man, glanced at Fogg and answered frigidly: 'How d'ye do.' Nevertheless, Fogg sat down by him and they got into conversation.

'Any news in the paper this morning, major?'

'Heaps! Haven't you got one? Here you are.' The major held out his copy with a dire gesture.

'No, no; not at all,' said Fogg. 'I never read newspapers.'

'Then you ought to,' retorted the other severely, 'instead of picking up information at second hand.'

'I was only wondering what Mawbash Opal Mines are quoted at to-day,' Fogg coolly said.

'What do you know about opal mines?' was the quick inquiry.

'Only a little,' answered Fogg, 'but I am rather interested in some.'

'So am I. I can tell you all about opal mines, particularly Mawbash. Now is the time to buy their shares if you haven't got any; if you have any stock, double it, treble it, and hold on for three months. Now's your time.'

'I know, I know,' said Fogg with a pensive air. 'But I can't get hold of the cash.'

'Well, borrow it,' snapped the major.

A mood of simple madness began to swarm over
Bonner Fogg He cleared his throat:

'I suppose, major, you couldn't lend me forty or
fifty pounds?'

'I could not,' the major said, instantly resuming
his perusal of the news.

'For about two months — three at the outside?'

The major said: 'Humph! I see Barraud's Preferred dropped one and ninepence yesterday.'

'I wouldn't bother you,' Fogg persisted, 'it's not
my form at all, but I would like to get in on this
Mawbash business.'

'Ask your bankers.'

'Can't. I'm overdrawn as it is.'

'I'm not a moneylender,' Macalister informed him.

'Of course, I've plenty of money coming along,
but — always the way, isn't it! — it's held up just
when I most want it. I've plenty of security for a
small loan, though.'

Macalister looked up at him and said stiffly:
'There are only two reasons for lending money; one
is for profit, the other is for friendship.'

'Quite so, I understand that,' answered Fogg.
'And what sort of interest would you require? I'm
not very flush, but anything that's reasonable — you
know.'

'I've told you once that I'm not a moneylender!'

'Will you lend it for friendship, then?'

'Wouldn't dream of it!' said the major.

Bonner Fogg felt deeply wounded: 'Oh, major!

I've known you a good long time. You know me, and we've always got on well together — we've always been friends.'

'What nonsense! I *have* known you for quite a while, yes; but I haven't any friendly feeling towards you, not a scrap!'

'Well, well! I didn't know that,' Fogg sighed. 'Good Lord, I thought I hadn't a single enemy in the world.'

'I'm not your enemy,' retorted the major. 'Don't deceive yourself. But I can't lend you money for friendship.'

'Lend it for charity, then,' the reckless suppliant suggested.

'Charity,' was the reply, 'doesn't deal in loans — she makes gifts.'

'I'm not asking for a gift, Major Macalister.'

'I'm not offering one, either!'

'I'm not asking for a gift,' repeated Bonner Fogg. 'I just thought you might be willing to do me a business favour.'

Having returned once more to a fixed scrutiny of his newspaper the major made no comment, and for some moments there ensued an uncomfortable silence.

'So that's how it is!' at length said Fogg, with truculent disgust.

The major nodded: 'Yes, Mr. Fogg, that's how it is.'

Fogg leaned back with his legs thrust out, pushed

his hands into his trousers pockets, and pursed his lips in scornful meditation. He was not surprised, but he had been so often rebuffed, so many uncharitable gibes had been meted out to him, that he lived in a sort of furtive hope that people would not see through him or his designs. It was obviously time to get up, to depart, to leave this cursed army jack to stink in his opal mines, but Fogg seemed to be fastened to that seat and he sat on in the fond belief that he was putting a bold face on a hideous situation.

Who should come sauntering along then but Harvey Ritson, another rich man. The major affably made room for Ritson to sit between him and Bonner Fogg, whom they both specifically ignored. Ritson was a deep-voiced bellowing giant, noticeably heavy with his aitches, their recurrent aspirations cleaving his speech like a blast from a tunnel.

'Jinks, my dear major! At the club just now! Jinks of the extremest altitude, I do assure you. You know the small Capstick — that profound little fellow?'

'Yes, yes.'

'He is having some trouble with his Dulcinea. Illicit gallantry, I believe.'

'Yes, well?' grunted Macalister.

'I understand she has been distributing her favours rather recklessly. Very low and lamentable! And the joke is, the point is, with whom!'

'Well, who?'

'He does not know!'

'Bah!' the major gurgled. 'Then what's all the fuss about?'

'Fuss! Dear major, have you no feeling heart?'

'I'm not married,' rasped the major.

'So I am bound to believe,' the other bellowed with a significant howl. 'But Capstick is, he is tremendously married. And first, he pours his lamentations into your ears, and then he implores you to confess.'

'Confess?'

'That you are the naughty man.'

'Who?'

'Whoever he happens to be talking to! Dozens of fellows!'

'O!'

'It's all over the club, it is all over the town!'

'What is?'

'His pathetic state, my dear boy. Desperate! There's a tinge of homicide in the ball of his eye.'

'I don't believe a word of it,' said Macalister. 'A lot of sniggering, bar-parlour scandal-mongering!'

'Major,' declared Ritson, 'you must agree that she is a very attractive little lady — isn't that so? But women are what they are, although we do not realize for some time. And then, then things like this happen — although it is hard to believe it at first. Inevitability! Inevitability!'

Macalister folded up his newspaper and pushed it under his haunches.

'They do say,' continued Ritson, 'that she has been about a good deal with that fellow Tillion.'

'Tillion?'

'That riding-master.'

'O, him! Humph!'

'I don't know anything about it positively, not myself, but what one sometimes hears one sometimes remembers.'

'It wouldn't surprise me,' said the major. 'It's as likely to be him as anyone else, I suppose.'

'She's a cut above him, certainly,' Ritson went on, 'but women are what they are, although we may not realize it for some time.'

'What are you chewing?' the major abruptly asked.

'I have a slight catarrh,' explained Ritson. 'I am sucking horehound candy.'

'What?'

'Horehound. It is a very good household remedy. Can you smell it?'

'You positively stink!' Major Macalister replied.

'Then let us go and liquidate the offence, shall we, dear major?'

The major sprang up and he and Ritson went off together, in step and pulling down their jackets, without even a nod to the other man.

Bonner Fogg sat on, gloomily reflecting. Tillion! Toby Tillion! The idea was farcical. The riding-master was a brisk clean-shaven ostler with cropped hair and spurs, whose life had been, and still was, devoted to the instruction of elegant ladies and some children in the accomplishment of ambling and gambolling on horseback. His wife, who had never been on a horse at all and wore worsted stockings, had laboured so long in a stationer's post office that her very soul had become cream laid, and her blood was ink.

'Well, what's to be done?' mused Bonner Fogg. In accordance with the habit of a lifetime he soon concluded there was nothing to be done. And, of course, he would contrive not to see Grace for a little while, until the rumpus had burnt itself out.

In the end he did not see Grace again, neither in a little while nor for ever, because in a few days time the little town was electrified by the news that she had flown, bolted, gone to America.

'And with Major Macalister, of all people!' snapped Eva Fogg. 'That gross toad!'

Bonner Fogg was utterly wrecked; he was harrowed, galled, shorn, reduced and ruined — in short, he was quite miserable. He could not bring himself to believe in this lacerating denouement, he simply could not believe it — not of Grace. He could, indeed, believe anything of that infamous army potwallopper, but of dear enchanting Grace — no, no! There must be some other solution of her incredible defection; she was not *that* sort of woman. Given a little time, everything would be explained, and she would come back to laugh in triumph over their credulous folly.

Meanwhile Eva gabbled so viciously of the perfidy of her dearest friend that one might have been excused for thinking Grace had stolen off with Eva's husband! Never had she trusted her, never, not for a moment; she had suspected her all along of some abominable treachery.

The tale, alas, was proven truth; the elopement was a fact. Harold himself came to visit them and confirmed it. He was unexpectedly cheery.

'I wanted just a word with you, Bonner; just a brief chat, you know. I made a fool of myself on the links the other day. I'm sorry for what I said to you then, I apologize, I'm sorry. You *will* forgive me?'

'Not another word about it, please!' murmured Fogg. 'I'm naturally shocked at this dreadful affair, I had no idea! What are you going to do, I mean what steps are you going to take?'

'Do! What? They're gone, aren't they! I can't rush off to America and kill him, can I? Pooh! Not me. Not now. There are just as good fish in the sea. What more could I do?'

'It's too wicked; she ought to be punished,' Eva sharply declared. 'That's what I think. He's a horrid deceiving brute, and she ought to be punished, somehow. She ought not to be let off like that. But you wait — you will see that her conscience will pay her out in the end!'

'You know,' Harold argued mildly, 'I don't think she carries very much in the way of a conscience, I don't honestly think so.'

'Oh, she has!' Eva asserted. 'Or she will have. That's the doing of the Almighty; it's put there by the Almighty to punish us that way if He can't manage it any other. She *ought* to be punished, somehow or other, for it's a scandal. She ought to *be* punished.'

And Bonner Fogg, pondering upon all those friends who warn you against your friends, and upon those lying fraudulent greedy swashbucklers who clump through life like juggernauts, snipping off whatever takes their fancy and giving nothing in return; Fogg, pondering thus, murmured with affectionate sympathy:

'We must hope it's for the best, Harold.'

IN TIMES LONG AGO, BEFORE AN ENGLISHMAN'S home had become his castle, there lived a sturdy old fellow by the name of Groggo. He was a cheerful man, and I declare there is nothing more pleasant than the sight of a jolly old chap wearing a big flower in his buttonhole — which was what old Groggo always seemed to be doing.

'Neighbours,' he said, when they chaffed him about the blooms, 'I'll have me a flower now, for there's a deal of grass to grow when my bones are mouldering in the valley.'

Which was good truth, in a way — as the neighbours all agreed — but not very much of a reason.

'Reason enough for me,' said Groggo, 'as long as it be true.'

It was his fortune to live alone in a garden amongst a fair spread of proper neighbours, and in the garden was a mere scrimp of a cottage that did contrive to ward off wind and water but had small share in any comforts of the world. No wife, neither cook nor maid, had ever made its bare estate look seemly, no hearth had ever warmed its barren walls, and for the use of a fire Old Groggo always squatted round a pile of burning logs outside his cottage door.

'How can you bear to live in such a daft way?' the neighbours asked him abusingly. 'A wise man sits within his house to have the cheer of home. There's your house, with its bed and a bracket for the flower pots; it has the means within, but you only sleep in it, and here you mope without, exposed to weather, all weathers, and things creeping and crawling and making a set at you!'

'What things?' Old Groggo inquired.

The neighbours took a considering look around his garden full of marigolds, for in truth they had not thought very deeply of what they were complaining beyond their need to complain of something or other: 'Well, what about these slugs?'

'Slugs!' cried Groggo. 'They dare not come anigh me, for if they do I poke them in the fire.'

'You ought,' they said then, 'to build yourself a fireplace in your house and have a proper chimney.'

'For why?' Groggo shouted.

'And sit inside your house.'

'For why?'

'And dwell respected and respecting.'

'For why?'

'Everybody does so, and everybody should; it is the law of the land, the rule of life, and the custom of the world. You ought to have a chimney, and sit beside your hearth!'

'Ought! Ought! Ought!' Groggo grunted. 'If any man came to me and said: "Dost want a chimney, Groggo?" I would give him my thanks and say, "Nay". I tell you, you cannot wind your clock with any other man's key. The question is not what I ought to have, but whether I want it so.'

'That is *not* the question, Groggo,' they explained

to him. 'It is the question of right or wrong, good
or bad, and as God is our witness it must be good, for
without it what should we be but miserable cast-
aways? And it must be right, for we all follow it.
That is sound sense and good knowledge, so why
do you set yourself against the rest of us in this
matter? You have the time and the skill, and there
are stones in the quarry.'

'Ha! It's no load on ye to say that!' replied
Groggo. 'But I have done without a chimney all my
days and years, I do not care for a chimney; I want
the free air and my clean smoke rising, and no call
to be badgered with shovels and soot to keep a
chimney clear.'

'But a house,' they said, '*must* have a chimney, and
chimneys must be cleaned.'

'Turn away, you,' said Groggo sourly, 'and walk
on!'

And he sat on in his garden throughout the season
and into the rasping winds of winter, watching his
woodsmoke flounder and stream.

The priest came and passed him the time o' day.

'Brother Groggo, you have a house, it is true, but
it is a cold empty miserable thing. Four walls and a
roof of thatch you have, but for the most part they
languish and you mope without, your eyes are
weakened by these stinking fumes, you are blind to
the treasure you might kindle from a spark within.'
And he tried to persuade him that a chimney was his
need.

'Sir,' said Groggo, 'I've no call to that career. What should I do with a chimney?'

'You could have a pure fire within.'

'I have my pure fire without,' said he.

'And when you peep up it,' continued the priest, 'you shall see the stars by day.'

'I can see them all at night,' answered Groggo, 'without a chimney, and I want no stars by day when there's the holy sun.'

Thus they argued for an hour.

'And as to the sweep!' inquired the priest. 'Were all men of your mind, how should a sweep continue to live?'

'I live without a sweep,' Groggo said: 'let him live without me.'

'Selfish man!' was the priest's cry. 'Were all men of your mind, I doubt even a priest could live.'

'Ah, your worship!' And Groggo gave him a grin. 'Don't shove the bear to the bee's nest! Were all of my mind, I doubt they would want a priest at all.'

'You are full of dirt and doubt,' the priest told him. 'There is no goodness in your way of life.'

'I doubt the good may still be very nasty,' said Groggo.

'Nasty! Why, silly man, if it be good that is impossible.'

'O,' said Groggo. 'There's physic, and abstinence, is there not, as well as smoky chimneys?'

'I see now,' the priest sadly said, 'that you are dogmatical, full of false dogmas; in other words, your are an ass!'

'Brother,' replied old Groggo (for he was a rare hand at banter), 'I am only dogmatic about my doubts.'

'Get you a chimney,' retorted the priest, 'and I will take care that you keep your chimney clean.'

'Turn,' said Groggo. 'Turn away, you, and walk on!'

And he lived as before until the summer bloomed again, and then he would go walking along the high cliffs by the sea. The hills rolled back smooth and steep from the cliff edge and up towards endless sky, and there Groggo would lie down to watch the gulls gliding, or listen to the audible vain passion of the waves and the wind moving with soft footstep in the hoarse gleaming grass, over the banks of trefoil, the warrens of bugloss, and the stonecrop and the seapink.

The parish constable met him there and passed the time o' day.

'You must build you a chimney, Groggo, against the winter comes.'

'Winter is far off.'

'Ah, but you must build betimes. None of your this year, next year, now or never.'

'I'd give a bushel of cherries to hear no more of that chimney,' Groggo said.

'Ho, ho! There is such abundance of cherries this

year, Groggo, as I never saw before! They hang so full on my tree, it would break a soul's back to pick 'em and bear 'em away.'

'Pooh, you no call to worry about that! I never saw starlings hatch out so fast as they hatched out this year, and starlings are the neatest cherry-pickers that mortal heart could wish for.'

'Ah, but I mean a man, Groggo, a man with a ladder and a basket.'

'A starling carries no basket, and I never saw one with a ladder, or breaking a bough — leave alone its back. They will strip your tree for you, and I do declare there will be no twinges, master constable!'

'Touching that matter of your chimney. . . .' began the other. . . .

'I must walk away,' broke in Groggo, rising up, 'and walk on.'

Not long afterwards Groggo received a letter from the by-laws, and the by-laws said it was not lawful for a house to lack a chimney; they summoned him to build a chimney with all convenient speed and thereafter dwell in accordance with the law of the land, the rule of life, and the custom of the world. Lacking a chimney he would be haled before the by-laws to show cause or submit to judgment.

Now Groggo had no regard for other peoples' fancies or opinions, but he had a vast respect for the law; he felt he could no longer contend with the majesty of such solicitude.

'Alas and alas, how shall I strive for a mark that

lies beyond me? A heavy quoit wrings the wrist.
Let it be; I'll have me a chimney. Very well.'

That was his answer to the by-laws, and so while
days were long he set to work; by the time the days
had shortened a fine chimney was sprouting like a
March bulb from his rooftree. On the day of its
completion Old Groggo invited his neighbours,
and they came in the evening to make merry. The
neighbours said: 'We have come to light your fire,
Groggo.' They set logs on the new hearth and lit
them, while Old Groggo went outside to watch the
smoke twirl up from his chimney, making long tails
in the moonlight. Then he drank two noggins of
gin and danced a dance.

'Bravo, Groggo, good for you!' And they all
declared he was a worthy fellow of the flock.

For a while it went well. No one in the village
had ever been so fastidious as Groggo in the charge
of a chimney; he exceeded all bounds in his devotion, it was cleansed in the oddest times and seasons,
whether or no. The earliest man afield would spy
the brush poking once more from Groggo's chimney, and the night-owl grew weary of his zeal. The
soul of man is seasoned with strange savours. Why
was it so? Was it the convert's fearful joy? Was it
pride in a flue, or care for the by-laws! It was not!
It was not! The embers on the new hearth were
always warm and handy, he tended them as one
would tend a votive sign, and the chimney itself was
a proud piece of adornment, but the presence of fire

within the house summoned an unknown dread to
Groggo; the firebrand's menace, flame in the thatch,
the rafters falling and himself caught by the neck,
or the smoke strangling him! Care, not reason, lay
on Groggo, and in the deep of night he would
flounder sweatily awake and blunder pell-mell into
the street, scaring the neighbours with his 'Hip!
I smell smoke!' They would call out to him:
'Peace, peace! there is no smoke, Groggo!' But
although that was true Groggo was hard to pacify,
and he came this caper so often that the vexed neighbours began to curse the day when Groggo built
himself a chimney. Prudence was a virtue, true
enough; but prudence bought so dearly was apt to
mortify the flesh and derange the spirit.

Of Groggo and his deep fear — what shall be
said? Had he obeyed the secret wish of his heart he
would have thrown the chimney down, and with
his own hands swept the hearth away, but Groggo
was a man, a truepenny. The weathercock, veering
to every slant of the wind, knows nothing of man's
pride or the dignity of his gods. The force of nature
is strong, but the spirit of man is a vulture looming
above a grave, and Groggo was too proud to return
to the habits he had loved, too fond to abjure the
approval of his kind. But he was not too proud to
build him ladders of wood to the loft window, to
contrive sundry escapes, cages to catch sparks, or to
plant waterpots in every angle of the rooms — enough
withal to cradle a shoal of fish! And he hung a barrel

full of water in the rafters over his bed, thinking to pull it with a cord when any fire broke on him in his sleep.

And that, alas, was his undoing, for one night in a scare of alarm he pulled madly at the barrel. He snatched at the cord, the barrel smashed upon him — it broke his skull. Down dropped Groggo, and he never rose again.

As to the fire there is no more to be said than that his fear had deceived him.

'What a mad wretch!' cried the neighbours when they found his corpse. 'A fool like that,' they said, 'should never have known a comforting fire at all!'

A LITTLE HARBOUR AT THE MOUTH OF AN ANGLIAN river. On the far side, a mile away, a tiny town gleaming quietly in the sunset, with two church towers an ecclesiastical college and a home for ancient mariners. On the near side, wharves, huts, sanddunes and a solitary inn called *The Ferry* which had some daffodils in its half-a-perch of front-garden; beyond that, pastoral heaths, windmills, and hamlets.

Evening was placidly enfolding the harbour. A few rugged smacks nudged amiably at the wharves, fumes of tar and fish drifted from the blocks, cordage and tackle, and sea odours rose from the fallen tide in the river. A man by the name of Billings who was squatting on a bollard got up and slouched away into the bar of *The Ferry Inn*. There is no keeping some people out of some public houses, and Billings had the mystical compulsion. He also had a sea-faring hat with a red paper flower fastened at the corner of the peak, and gold rings in his florid ears; a fair man, a tall man, a man in a blue jersey, with brine in his voice and long wading boots up to his thighs — in short, a fisherman. Into *The Ferry* goes Billings, and 'Good evening' to him says the land-lord, Alan Starr, a fraternally dapper person with avid eyes and a waxed moustache; his white shirt sleeves were rolled up above his elbows.

'A pint,' replied Billings.

'Nice evening, Edward,' repeated the landlord, and Billings grunted, 'Ah.' When he had taken a good quaff of ale he said: 'You ain't seen my brother-in-law yet?' And he lounged easily against the counter — he was the sort of man that always leans.

'No, bor; I ain't seen Abel for three or four days.'

'I'm expecting him by and by.'

It was a dim faded taproom and seemed too shy ever to have been painted — it had been cleaned so well. A couple of tables scrubbed to the bone, some hard chairs, and framed photographs on the walls of wedding groups twenty years ago, beanfeasts, and cricketers wherein Alan Starr might be guessed at as the knowing young man with cap cocked awry and a ball in his fist. But the worn linoleum on the floor, streaked grey and white, had a suggestion about it of the entrails of some glutinous leviathan. There was not a great deal of profit to be made out of the custom of *The Ferry Inn*, and Mr. Starr augmented his income by crafty deals in antique clocks and life-saving dogs.

Two flat-faced tidy strangers sat at one table, stoutish, with pipes protruding from their faces. The landlord, addressing them, resumed an interrupted yarn:

'Well, it was in the time of the Fenians. . . .'

'Just fill that mug again,' one of the stout strangers commanded.

'Yes, sir!' cried Alan with ferocious alacrity. As

he gave the handle of the beer engine a coaxing pull he repeated: 'In the Fenian days it was. . . .' He set the pot in front of the customer, who then asked to be obliged with a postage stamp. Alan disappeared into his private parlour in search of a postage stamp.

'It's a good tale, this Fenian tale,' the one man remarked to his companion.

'It *was*.' The other puffed at his pipe stolidly.

'But it wants telling, you must realize that. It wants *telling*, in a certain *way*, delicate.'

'Yes, yes; and I heard it twenty years ago,' said the other with an air of contempt.

'So've I. Five thousand times. But a good tale is worth hearing over and over again, Harry, so long as it's well told. It's the art of it.'

'That's right enough, Sam, and I had a queer experience once, I did. . . .'

'It *is* funny how experience keeps on cropping up!'

'A very funny experience. . . .'

'Wherever you go, experience is a great thing, Harry. It carries you through all the troubles and trials of life. And you never forget it.'

'I was there for three weeks once. . . .'

'Where?'

'Edinburgh.'

'Don't I know it! I been there. A noble city, wide streets — aint they? — and very well educated I should say, such a lot of bookshops.'

'The streets are all blooming granite and the books

are all religious, but I was only there for three weeks and three days, I was. . . .'

'Just long enough, Harry. Just long enough to love what you like. That's the main factor, aint it?'

'I was ordered to go on guard. . . .'

'D'ye know, that's a duty I always liked when I was a soldier. Most chaps didn't, but I did. I liked being on guard.' Sam swilled down a hearty draught. 'Go on, you tell your tale, Harry, you tell it.'

'Well, it's a good 'un. Just give me half a chance, Sam; if you'll only listen, and my God it's good.'

Then Harry began to mumble so secretively to Sam that Billings could not overhear any more. Back came the landlord:

'There you are, sir!' he cried, and laid a postage stamp before the inquiring man, who thereupon tendered him sixpence. The two friends waited mutely until the change was brought. The landlord then, after a furtive glance round, rested his hands oratorically upon their table and began: 'As I was just about to tell you. . . .'

A woman with a jug came in at the door and stepped up to the bar counter.

'It was in the time of the Fenians,' shouted the landlord, retreating to his lair. 'I'll tell you in a minute. Yes, ma'am?' He picked up the woman's jug and hovered over his handles. 'In the time of the Fenians. . . . Beer, did you say, ma'am?'

'Stout,' answered the woman wearily, counting some coppers from her purse.

'Pint, ma'am? No — half a pint, of course.' He pulled and paused. 'Stout, I think you said, ma'am! Lumme, this cask is nearly empty; I must go and see to it.' And after serving the woman he trotted down into his cellar.

Harry resumed his colloquy with Sam, while Billings still leaned, watching for his brother-in-law, Abel Staple. Tap, tap, tap; the landlord was adjusting his barrels. His wife, an unpleasant woman with red hands and an agate brooch came into the taproom and lit a hanging lamp. The two men ceased their whispering until she had finished. Then a labourer entered.

'A pint, missus,' he muttered.

As she was supplying the drink the labourer said quietly to her: 'I just been along to see Albert, and, O, he's dying fast; he can't last another hour.'

'O, O,' the landlady intoned distressfully, and quickly put the pot on the counter. The man drew it towards him and laid down his pence. She pushed the money away. 'No, no, I could not take it. I'm much obliged to you for coming and telling me. I must run along at once and see the poor thing.'

She flung on a cloak and bonnet and called down to her husband in the cellar that Cousin Albert was just dying. As she and the labourer left the taproom together Alan Starr came up to the bar again.

'Poor old Albert!' he said to Billings. 'How that man have suffered! Operation after operation, in and out of hospital like a bee in a hive. It's a funny thing, though, but if your bladder's got a slit in it it grows with a sort of selvedge edges and won't come together again. Stands to reason, flesh won't grow together unless it's raw. There's no arguing about that; you can put your two fingers side by side, like that, but they won't join up — not unless you skin 'em, mind you, and scrape the flesh raw and bind 'em tight together, *then* they might, but not without. Poor Albert, it's a funny business! Dear me! Poor old Albert!'

Turning briskly towards Harry and Sam he cried: 'Well, gents, about these here Fenians. . . .'

Both men instantly arose.

'Must bid you good evening,' said Sam.

'What! Are you off, gentlemen?'

'Yes, we are off.'

'We got to go,' added Harry.

'Aye, aye. Good evening,' Alan said, 'and thank you.'

In silence after their departure the landlord meditatively filled his pipe; having lit it he marshalled his hopes once more with a sigh and leaned upon the counter:

'Did I ever tell you that tale about the Fenians, Ted? I don't think I did, did I?'

Billings slowly shook his head: 'I can't call to mind I ever heard it.' The landlord glanced at the clock.

'Well, it was in the time of the Fenians. . . .'

'Just a bit,' the tall fisherman interposed. 'Give us another pint, will you?'

'Pint, Ted? Certainly.'

Billings drew some coins from his pocket and selected a shilling. The landlord pushed the filled pot towards him. 'Yes, it was in the Fenian days. . .' But the coin slipped from Alan's wet fingers and went rolling and wriggling across the taproom floor as though escaping from some dire tyranny.

'Hoi! Hoi!' The landlord trotted round after it. 'Now where are you gone to?' He stooped, peering under the hard chairs and the tables after the lost coin. 'Did you see where he went, Ted?'

No, Ted had not observed that. Alan sunk upon one knee and struck a match, searching here and there.

'Come out, you shameful thing!'

But the shilling lay low, and the landlord was soon exhausted by the pressure of his belt and the constriction of his breeches.

'Well, may I be boiled alive!' he cried. 'S'gone hopping off like a frog in a tunnel. Must be here somewhere.'

'I din see it go,' Billings said. 'You had it.'

'Yes, I had it, but I din see it go neither. I'll find it,' he said, rising, 'to-morrow morning. It must be there, I know it's there.'

Returning to the bar he composed himself once more. 'Well, I was going to tell you. . . .'

Again Billings interposed: 'What about my change?'

'Your change! Ah! What was it you give me, Ted?'

'I give you that shilling.'

'O, ah!' sighed Alan, 'that darned thing!' He glared into the dark corner of the room where the coin was last seen. 'I know it's just there, I see it go. Let me get a candle; I'll soon have him out of that.'

So with a lit candle he searched, and after much gaping and groping and groaning he found the shilling just as the door was thrust open and Abel Staple came in.

Staple was a clean-shaven ruddy countryman, clad in fawn corduroy that reeked of sheep, and his shrill voice was so powerful that it produced tangible vibrations in the air. He lived in a village a few miles off, where his wife Fanny, a sister of Ted Billings, had died the year before.

'How goes it, Abel?' was the landlord's greeting as he returned to his counter.

'O . . . there's beef and butter, and the bread's none so bad!' grinned Abel.

'Ain't seen much of you lately.'

'Well, what with the time o' year and the time o' life, and the time o' day I can't stand the pressure of these late nights. Five o'clock in the morning you'll see me in my bloom! A pint, please.'

'Pint? Five o'clock, eh? The Almighty never put it in my power to behave like that, Abel. I could not do it, not for the Emperor of China and fifteen pound a week.'

'You can always get up if you got anything to get up arter.'

'Pooh!' replied Alan, 'it's only a habit!'

Abel paid him from a leather purse, and then turned to his brother-in-law:

'I got a rabbit for you, Ted.'

'I got a dozen herring for you,' answered Ted.

'This rabbit ought a bin a hare.'

'They're longshore-uns, but half of 'em has tidy roes.'

The two men moved over to a table in the corner furthest from the bar counter and sat down side by side.

'What about my change, Alan?' Billings sternly called.

'Din I give it you?'

'If you did, I ain't seen it.'

'If you ain't seen it, Ted my boy, then I reckon I can't have given it to you.'

He brought the change and handed it to Billings: 'Nothing like honesty and a free mind.' Then he went humming away to sit in his private parlour.

Night had grown dark outside; there were no sounds from the harbour or the sea, for the wind was still. The old clock in the bar was ticking loudly.

'Have you thought of any little thing to put in the paper?' Abel asked in a lowered voice. 'Any little bit of a jink that's nice and proper?' And Billings, extracting two or three scraps of paper from somewhere under his jersey, replied: 'I got one or two snatches here.'

They were proposing to insert a joint notice in the 'In Memoriam' column of the local newspaper; Billings read out from one of his paper scraps:

> *In fond memory of Fanny Staple who fell*
> *asleep May 12th. Gone but not forgotten.*
> *From her sorrowing husband Abel and her*
> *brother, E. Billings.*

The sorrowing husband emitted a doubtful 'Humph!'

'I think that's a good one,' Billings declared. 'Don't you? It 'ull cost two shillings. Or you could have a verse of a hymn or a text from the Bible and that 'ull be half-a-crown.'

'I don't much like that fell asleep talk,' the widower commented.

'It's only a manner of speaking, Abel.'

'Yah. But sleeping is sleeping, and when you're in your grave it's something else or different. I go to sleep, but I get up again. Five o'clock of a morning, my angel, year in year out.'

'It's only a manner of speaking.'

'I know that; but, dammit, she died, didn't she!'

'Well, all right; what about a hymn?' her brother suggested. 'Fanny was always partial to hymns — it runs in our family. I like a song, myself.'

'God bless us and well I knows of it! She'd howl her eyes out over a hymn.'

'You mustn't forget she had a tender heart,' Billings maintained. 'Right from girlhood she had.'

'No call to! Not as I could ever see.'

'I dunno . . . I dunno. . . . Some has a smile for one thing and a sob for another and you can't understand the reason for either.' Billings seemed to be mournfully affected by some recollection. 'If we could understand that, Abel, we should know a lot more than we do.'

'You's looking for the place where the cat put her paws, Teddy. You know she's bin and collared the cream, so what does it signify? Fanny was as good a wife as ever trod on this earth; cooking, washing, mangling, mending — every mortal thing the heart could wish for — except a child — and that she never had. That was her downfall. She come to me in her prime, pretty as a lamb, a laughing girl, but she soured early and took to other ways. I tell you honest, Ted, she gave me a fair sickener of hymns and tears. You can cry tears till your breast is wet and you dream of nothing else; you can drop your tears all over the furniture — I've seen the spatters, ah — and then you can go and drop them all over the garden, but tears don't make the beans to grow. So much psalming is all very well, and we has to put up with it, but out of season is out of reason, I say. I've been religious and soulful, too, in my day — we all of us have, ain't we? In my young time forty year ago, when I was a boy, Parson Froggett took me through my confirmation and he was a good old Christian vicar as ever tipped a shoe. I can remember him marching us all off from the schoolhouse one fine morning to go for the blessing of the lord bishop. (Just such another day, it was, as that fine Whitsun when Fanny and I got wed; lilacs, laburnums, and the grass sweet as an apple.) I can remember him now! Off we goes across the fields to the church, boys in front and the gals behind all dressed in their white muslins. And we boys got the devil in us somehow that morning, it was such a pink of a day, and the bell ringing, and we rooshed along over stiles and through hedges till the gals puffed and blowed and tore their frocks to tatters, and old Froggett — he was very fat, fine old face, stuttered a bit — he calls out: "S . . s . . s . . steady boys, steady; n . . n . . n . . not so fast in front there!" But we boys got the devil in us that morning and we made their backs sweat for 'em. He were a good old Christian man, Froggett; kept up a good house though he was never married hisself; cook, coachman, two maids, and Eva Martin's daughter cleaned his boots for years and got tuppence a week for it; but I'm blamed if he didn't go and poison hisself arter all. I liked old Froggett.'

The fisherman ruminated, with puff puff puff at his pipe.

'Twarn't so much the eyes,' he said, 'it was the mind weeping.'

'I shouldn't ha' said she was weak-minded, Ted.'

'Nah, well,' Billings sighed. 'What are you going to put in this notice? We got to put in something or other — or ain't you going to, arter all?'

'Sure?' cried Abel, 'I be game enough.'

'Cause if you ain't,' Billings declared, 'I'll put it in myself.'

'You've no call to say that,' Abel soothingly answered. 'You've got a brother's full heart, I know, I know you have, but she was my wife whether or no, and I'm not renagging.'

'There's this one, then.' Billings fingered another paper scrap: *Till we meet again.*'

'Well, ye know, that's pretty much of a hymn, too!'

'She was fond of hymns, very fond,' Billings steadfastly declared.

'She was, O, she was, Ted; but my heart was never a crock for that sort of pickle. Let's have something cheerful and a bit different now it's all over. *Peace, perfect Peace,* I reckon is the best. We don't want a lot of palaver about a silent tear and that sort of chatter. It's all over. Let's have *Peace, perfect Peace.*'

The brother was silent. After waiting some moments Abel inquired:

'What do *you* say, Ted?'

And Ted said: 'O, have it your own way. I'm agreeable.'

'All right now,' Abel answered. 'That's settled then: *Peace, perfect Peace.* Of course next year, if God spares us, you can put in whatever you've a mind to; that's only fair. Now you look arter it, Ted, will you, and see it goes in the paper the proper time. When *is* the date of it?'

279

'Week after next.'

'Course it is! Whatever was I thinking about! Time flies so. *Peace, perfect Peace*, then. Landlord!'

Abel rapped loudly upon the table with his empty pot. Alan came forward: 'Give us a couple a pints.'

The beer was drawn. Alan Starr pocketed the money and lingered with a smile on his face as the men gulped deeply; then, suddenly leaning upon the table, he began once more: 'It was in the time of the Fenians.' It would be unmeet, however, to pursue that story to its close, though the prospects of impropriety, however reprehensible, are very alluring. At its conclusion the two men prepared to go home.

'Here's your herring,' said Ted to Abel.

'Aye, aye; here's your rabbit,' Abel replied.

'And what about paying for the memorial notice? Half and half you said, Abel.'

'That's right, I was near forgetting. Tell ye what, Ted; I don't mind tossing ye to see who pays the lot.'

'Call to me,' said Ted grimly.

Abel called and lost.

'My, if that ain't a blow from a pig's tail!' he cheerfully cried, as he handed Billings a two-shilling piece.

DOE

THE REVEREND PHALAROPE DOE, FONDLY REFERRED to by his choir as Sammy, was vicar of a village in the South Country. His church and his vicarage, hung over by pastoral elms, were hunched beside a lucid stream near a bridge of stone; the water smiled under its arches, the fish hung dreaming in its tide. Just beyond the bridge the road forked at a triangle of grass where two vast lime trees towered above a tiny tiled hut with a padlocked door; the hut, never opened, and plastered with bills of circuses long remote in time and place, harboured a sort of fire-engine that had never been used, that only a few old men had ever seen. Then you came to the village on the flank of a small hill. It was an undistinguished heap of houses with a burden, no doubt easily assimilated, of the frequent traffic of trains; two long chimney shafts projected from a lime kiln that had died in its own pit and an iron-works that was decaying into rust. The place itself looked rusty, harassed alike by the roar of passing trains and the poverty of its trade.

Here, where incentives to virtue were not impressive, though vice seldom ogled with its alluring eye — at least, not observably — for forty years the Reverend Phalarope Doe, portly and ruddy, had ministered, and seldom had a vicar conferred so fair a lustre on so mean a village.

281

'His sermon never said or showed
That Earth is foul, that Heaven is gracious.'

For he was kind and wise, and, he was *so* forgiving —
he could forgive anything. A pat on the shoulder,
and something, somehow — *you* know.

'Now tell me,' he would ask some erring maiden,
'why were you so careless?'

'Oh, sir, he decaptivated me!'

'There, there; you shouldn't have done it. I
shouldn't do it again, you know, not that kind of
thing, if I were you. It's wrong; at least it's not
quite right, you know. I shouldn't do it again, not
if I were you.'

Sammy's pleasant home was a little too big and his
income a little too small. Too big for what? Too
small for what? Well, he was a bachelor for one
thing, and the vicarage — to say nothing of the
garden — was larger than the church, and as he
could afford neither curate nor gardener he revelled
personally in both activities at the expense of muscle
and high-mindedness. Kindness was his hobby, his
pastime; he played for the pleasure of giving — and,
in his turn, taking — as one played bridge or golf.
And what a player he was! When his wristbands
became frayed he cut off the ends of his shirt sleeves.
Concealed in his study, behind an almanac of 'The
Light of the World,' there hung a certain map of
his own neighbourhood which he had marked with
different coloured spots, each spot denoting the

homes of agreeable souls on whom he could rely when rambling afoot. A green spot signified a place where he could be sure of a bed, a red spot meant lunch, blue merely tea, and so forth.

'Ah, splendid souls!' And, as it were, his very heart would give them a smile as he took his stick again to trudge the homeward path. At the first tree he came to he might pause awhile. These beautiful leaves! They grew and they died. The trees became bald, like himself, like the aged; their beauty was but skin deep; yet the *idea* of tree, the spirit manifested in its passion for continuity, its beaming leaves, was eternally beautiful. How unlike man, whose idea here and now, was not in life alone, but whose destiny was assured!

One day he received a letter from a man with a vaguely familiar name, who lodged in apartments at Twickenham. Rowfant? Ellis Rowfant? It turned out to be an old college chum he had known forty years ago at Oxford. They had had rooms in the same college, the same scout had served them on the same stair, they had swotted for a degree together, taken it, and had gone down together. And then no more. That was all. Doe had been ordained and disposed of; Rowfant had vanished quite away and he had not heard from him, or of him, until now. The two men began a cordial correspondence, and the long lost friend soon came to pay Doe a visit of several days.

On the appointed afternoon Doe walked along to

the small parched railway station, whose station-master had a permanently dazed appearance caused probably by the ignoring rush past of so many trains that never stopped. Its grey granitic design seemed to invite the meeting of extremes, for when the weather was at all cold it was colder there than it could decently have been elsewhere, although if warmth were the order of the day it was here that the temperature multiplied.

'What a fine day!' exclaimed Mr. Doe.

'Ah,' retorted the stationmaster, 'we want plenty of this, and more of it.'

'It is sumptuous indeed,' said Mr. Doe.

The parson idled up the platform and down the platform, reading every placard quite seriously, even the notice which declared the railway company's resolve to transmit explosives only under the most stringent conditions, and that coal, coke, shoddy manure and statuary would be carried only on similar terms.

'Well, well! But really, you know . . .' the parson was reflecting as the train came in.

There could be no doubt that that queer figure was Rowfant. He was the only passenger to emerge, and he came peeringly up to Mr. Doe.

'My dear friend, do I see you! Good heavens, yes; do you know me?'

'I see you,' Doe assured him. 'We have trebled the years but there is little change.'

'I fear we shall treble the change in vastly fewer years!' Rowfant rejoined.

'None of your pessimist whim-whams now, Ellis. I remember you, O, I remember you very well. You were always a regular Hamlet.'

'Deplorable!' grinned Hamlet. 'I hope you don't mind me appearing like this? I've come straight off the river—must change directly we get to your place.'

'Come on,' said the parson. 'Come on.' And he picked up the traveller's bag.

Ellis Rowfant was an amiably vigorous gentleman in the sixties, with a slight round-shouldered stoop and a large clean-shaven magisterial face. But when you caught his gaze through the round spectacles you saw that he had quite childish blue eyes. A small pink cap with a monogram was clapped upon his head in a way that seemed to fasten it there; his jacket of navy blue was flashing with buttons, and a pink tie adorned his throat. His trousers of blankety flannel were of such voluminous vastness that they fluttered audibly as he walked along.

'I've no car,' explained Doe, 'but it is only about ten minutes walk to the vicarage. I hope you had a pleasant journey down?'

'Most exciting! We had a fellow in our compartment reeking with asthma, and he kept on snorting and spitting out of the window until a lady sitting opposite to him couldn't bear it any longer and complained.'

'Dear me. How? What?'

'She asked him to control himself. Ha! Ha!'

'Well, but really . . .'? the parson said.

'Oh, he was a regular hard-boiled case. He just argued with her.'

'Argued! He should have left the carriage.'

'That's just what he would *not* do. She hinted at it, then she suggested it, then she bluntly requested him to, but he replied — and very politely, I *must* say — that that alternative was hers.'

'By Jove!' the parson said.

'So then she told him that he was the rudest man she had ever met, *and* the most disgusting! But he sat tight, he would not budge, and I am bound to say it got more provoking than ever. At last she burst out again: "This is insupportable! *Cannot* you control yourself?" "Madam," he says, "I can no more control myself than you can control your appearance. There are many things in life we have to put up with, afflictions and inflictions all very disagreeable. We are both suffering from the defects of nature. For instance, I do not care for your appearance" — he said — "I do not like it at all, it is repellent to me. But do I complain about it? Do I beg you to do something for it, or ask you to leave this compartment? I do *not*" — he said — "Heaven forbid! I just mutely suffer." "Well, I wish you would suffer a little *more* mutely," says she. "Madam" — he says — "it is impossible to suffer mutely from asthma." And they were still wrangling when I got out here. Ha! ha! By George, he *was* a rascal, he gave her such a dressing-down. I — do you know — I positively rejoiced at it!'

286

'Oh, but really, Ellis!'

'Can't help it. I'm sure you would have been the same — though I'm not much of a Christian these days. Anyhow, I'd almost bet they are very good friends before they get to their destination.'

'Of course, my dear Ellis. I'm sure they will be.'

'I wouldn't be too sure — it didn't strike me as a very promising beginning for romance.'

'Romance!' echoed the puzzled parson.

'Oh, she wasn't bad looking,' Rowfant explained.

They turned the corner by the lime trees and in a few moments there was the church with its untiring spire, the vicarage trees, the lawn garlanded with peonies and hedged with may, and in the water under the bridge the fish were gliding. A little bow-legged maid with a squint in her eyes took the visitor's bag. Ten minutes later they were drinking tea on the lawn, and Rowfant, admiring the old red wall with its topknots of saxifrage, the squat house and its bow windows, the simple peace of the garden, murmured in envious tones his appreciation.

'You are most welcome here,' his host assured him with a beaming look.

'I'm not much of a religious these days, I'm afraid,' Rowfant went on.

'Well . . . of course . . .!' Doe smilingly sipped his tea.

'It was never quite in my line, you know,' explained Rowfant.

'And I,' Doe responded, 'I'm a professional.

Forty years, my boy. And I rejoice in it. I would not change, I could not.'

'Nor could I,' said Rowfant, 'but I love your home. You never married?'

And Doe answered: 'No. That was not in *my* line.'

'Nor mine,' said Rowfant abruptly.

For many days Rowfant abode there, lingering on and on under pressure from his friend. He soon learned that the parson's familiar name was Sammy, and he too used it fondly. Their old affection had bloomed once more and they were happy. Time and again they rambled in company to spots that were marked red or blue on the vicar's map, and when the parson was otherwise engaged Ellis would lounge for hours in the garden. On Sunday morning he sat there in a dream by the old red wall; the bells had chimed cheerfully, the voices and footsteps of assembling worshippers could be heard passing by. Then there was silence, a silence that itself seemed holy despite the chirping of birds, until the chanting of the choir stole across the road, threaded through the odour of the may, and filled him with melancholy joy. Mysterious melancholy, inexplicable joy! He had not once been into the church during his stay — such a sweet old church! He ought to have gone, at the very least he ought to have gone once. They sang well in there. He would go to-night, it would please Sammy.

When Doe returned Rowfant warmly praised the singing of the choir.

'Pretty good,' the vicar agreed. 'Two fine tenors, you know. Jerry has a glorious voice, perfectly topping. Arnold's tone is not so pure perhaps, but it's a shade more ineffable. I like that.'

Listening with affectionate amusement to his old friend, Rowfant would forget that there was no disparity of years between them; even when a parishioner came with some trouble, preposterous or profound, Rowfant, noting old Sammy's anxious care, would laugh to see him as a boy might laugh at his funny uncle. When he went visiting in his parish Sammy's pockets bulged with little gifts, the deuce knows what; peppermints for a child, it might be, some crochet cotton for a dame, or a packet of quassia chips for cleaning Sergeant Tullifant's roses. Was Doe working in the garden? Then he would be in his shirt sleeves and heavy boots, humming as he hoed and sweating as he dug.

'Ellis!' he would bawl across the lawn, 'Do you think that poet was sincere when he said: "The cut worm forgives the plough"?'

'I think he was ignorant.'

'Not ignorant, Ellis!'

'Well, he can't have known anything about the psychology of worms.'

'O. Should you think that worms *have* a psychology, Ellis?'

'They ought to have, Sammy, to carry their forgiveness to such extremes.'

'I don't know. It strikes me as a very profound

utterance. I do hope it applies to spades, in gardens.'

Surely he was a happy man? He had his little life, so neat, so simple; his little desires, so pure, so few; and his little dreams of a very large heaven — while he, Rowfant, what had he got? Even his tragic memories had grown dull, posthumous heaven was a forlorn mirage, he lived in some rooms in Twickenham.

With all his asceticism old Sammy was man enough to enjoy his food to the uttermost — at night — in that low-pitched dining-room with the four Arundel prints on the walls — desperately devout *they* were — and photographs of college teams — *not* so immaculately pious — including one of Rowfant and Doe in a Corpus Christi torpid of eighteen hundred and . . . . Good God, how incredible! No rugs encumbered the polished floor, no cloth the table, and not even a clock on a shelf anywhere, for why have a clock when you've always a watch in your pocket? But there was a huge block of wood in one corner of the room that served as a stand for a tray.

'What *is* that lump of timber?'

'That, Ellis? Oh, that is quite unique. I got hold of it years ago. Do you like it? It's an ancient butcher's block.'

'Sweet!' grinned Rowfant.

'Don't you like it?'

'I might — in years to come. I must present you with a pole-axe to go with it.'

'Oh, forbear, Ellis! My dear chap, forbear!'

Dinner at night was a ritualistic indulgence by a soul that deserved every hope of the punctual benediction. Each forkful the reverend gentleman shovelled into his mouth caused him to close his eyes and smile. Paradise! He took a gulp of wine, and whispered to himself. Having consumed his heap of spaghetti, his piece of mutton, his apple and his orange, he settled down with a pair of crackers to the nuts and his second glass of wine — white this time in place of red. Selecting the nuts with care he would rattle them with a frown against his ear, and discard some; later, his toothpick came into play, raking his hollow teeth with the felicity of a rapier.

'And now, my dear Ellis, what about a game of draughts? Or dominoes? Any little excitement of that kind?'

And they would play on until the nightingales began.

These homely days exercised so beguiling a pressure that Rowfant almost forgot his own creeping age. Though youth was dead and gone, though the future had got all his destiny slyly tucked in its fob, wise old Sammy was friendship's mellowing sign, simple, steady and devoted, and the prospect of leaving him again for Twickenham's barren complexities filled Rowfant with many qualms. The years ahead of him might be few, or they might be many — one could not live for ever — and this lodging alone was a trashy affair; but one could live well with Sammy. Why *not?* Rowfant had a small income that freed him from the embarrassments and futilities of work. The parson's home was large, but his income was small, smaller even than Rowfant's own, and with their resources pooled the two of them might dwell in ease for Sammy and some grace and harmony for himself. One night after dinner he spoke of this:

'Sammy, would you care to put up with me?'

'Put up with you?'

'For good. Could you do with a lodger here?'

'A lodger!'

'Yes, me! Tell me truly if the idea fills you with hatred, but I am making you a proposal, Mr. Doe. I want to live with you, to live here, always, and all my worldly goods on thee endow.'

The Reverend Phalarope listened intently while his friend dilated, outlining his resources and propounding his hopes.

'What do you think? Would it be possible?'

'It would be terrific!' cried Sammy. 'Nothing could be more terrific. It is . . . good gracious, my *dear* Ellis . . .' — he jumped up to grasp his friend's hand — 'a superb idea.'

'But could you really bear it?'

'My *dear* boy! Say no more, it shall be exactly as you wish.'

'No, Sammy, it is to be exactly as *you* wish; just as we are now, and you must throw me into the river as soon as you grow sick of it — poison me, poleaxe me, and dump me in a sack!'

'A sack!' shouted Sammy. 'I couldn't put you in a sack!'

'Then don't bother about the sack.'

'And you really mean it?'

'From the bottom of my heart.'

'It is settled then.'

'Settled it is, old friend.'

Again they clasped hands upon it. The parson stood for a few moments with closed eyes and Rowfant knew that some blessing had been invoked on their renewed alliance.

'I must go back to Twickenham, Sammy, for a couple of days, to clear up everything, and then. . . .'

'Then you'll come?'

'I'll come. You don't mind harbouring such a barbarian?'

Doe gazed wildly at his friend. 'What do you mean by that, I wonder?'

'My not being a church-goer.'

'Pooh! You don't object to *my* going!'

'You see — I never could stand that holy capital letter of Holiness.'

'Ellis, that is merely a printer's fad.'

'Really, my dear Sammy! You'll shock me, you know!'

'If I could, my boy, you would be more than half-way to grace!'

'To grace!' Rowfant shook his head sadly. 'No,

Sammy, I don't think so—ever. But there *is* something I must tell you if I am coming to live with you down here. It is only right that you should know all about it beforehand. I've been going to tell you . . . but . . . don't you see . . .?'

'What *is* it?'

'Well, it will take some little time — shall we sit down?'

'Ellis!' cried the parson protestingly. 'Are you going to relate the story of your life?'

'More or less.'

'Have you a hideous past?'

'Yes.'

'O Lord! O dear!' Sammy wrung his hands and emitted a whimsical sigh.

'I *must* tell you,' Rowfant insisted. 'And you've *got* to hear it. So just squat down, there's a good chap.'

Down they sat, and Rowfant began his story.

I I

'When I went down from Oxford forty years ago I lived with an aunt in Gloucestershire. I was an orphan, you know, and my Aunt Susie was a widow; she had looked after me since I was five years old, in fact she was a mother to me, and she adored me. I suppose I was fond of *her* — I hope I was, for she was the soul of goodness — but I am sure that my feeling for her *now* is stronger than it was *then*, all that long time ago. And it isn't exactly love, either; it is more like admiration. Or perhaps it is only gratitude? She gave so much and got so little; somehow there is nothing *inevitable* about such a situation, it is not *always* conducive to love and possibly not very often — what do *you* think?'

'I find it rather hard to think that, Ellis.'

'But it *is* so, I am sure. She was not what you call rich — just comfortably off — and we had a small house and garden, and one servant maid named Elizabeth — Lizzy Lee. I was supposed to be going into the Government service but there were all sorts of difficulties and I made a mess of one or two exams. I was a pretty ineffectual sort of creature in those days; my aunt thought I had weak lungs or a heart or something like that, but the truth is it was laziness, I was *born* like it, really lazy. Do you know, she never employed a gardener and the two women — she and Lizzy Lee — managed the garden by themselves, digging and hoeing, and so on all at the proper times, and I never stirred a leg or lifted an arm to help them. I love a garden, but I dislike gardening, and they seemed to revel in it. Of course there was nothing physically the matter with me at all, never has been — I've rowed all my life, and still do — but at that time I was reading a lot of poetry and things and I fancied I could make some sort of a shot at composing a poetic drama. There was quite a vogue at that time for poetic dramas, and I went floundering about with my head in a fuzz of fatuous dreaminess which my Aunt Susie thought was a sign of genius! So did I, but it wasn't — it was mere cheek. Well, after about a year of this my aunt died, and *that* wiped my eye pretty thoroughly because most of her income came from a marriage settlement which ceased on her death. She left me the house though, and a block of shares in some African gold mines which had brought her in about two hundred a year, and she bequeathed thirty pounds to Elizabeth. Of course I ought to have buckled to, then, and begun some sort of a career for myself, but I didn't. I decided to carry on the house and write my poetic plays. O, dear! I soon got a shock — two shocks, in fact. One came when I found out what wages my aunt had been paying Lizzy Lee — Elizabeth. It was fifteen pounds a year. At that time I was imbued with a lot of radical notions and it seemed to me dreadful to pay anyone such a miserable pittance, especially as Elizabeth was a model domestic. She was young, about my age, and rather pretty, but I assure you it wasn't *that* that did it — it was my socialism. I was really *shocked*, and I doubled her wages at once.'

'Humph! That was rather a jump,' exclaimed the vicar.

'O, she took it quite as a matter of course; it didn't make any difference, she was as near perfection as a servant could be; but I soon got my second shock! The dividends that year, my dividends on aunt's gold mine shares, were cut down by a half, and in the end I was only getting a bare hundred pounds. Still, I didn't regret having doubled Lizzy Lee's wages — I was very bigoted in my views in those days — but quite soon, as you may imagine, I was in desperate straits for money, got into debt all round for household necessaries and so on, and at last it came to the point where I decided to *sell* the house, *move* into a cottage somewhere cheap, and get rid of Lizzy Lee. Had I had any sense I would have hold her the truth, but I was too stuck-up to do *that*, I couldn't bring myself to do it, I could *not*, so she knew nothing at all about my financial bust-up, and managed the house in the same style she had always done. And I was absolutely on the rocks! So at last I had to tell her that I had arranged to move to a cottage in the Cotswolds and that I shouldn't require her services there. I told her the cottage was very small, that I intended to do all the work myself, in fact I talked a lot of Tolstoyan nonsense — even to her! And I gave her a month's notice. She said "Very good, sir." I can remember it even now. But before the month was up she offered to stay on, at her old wages, and seemed quite anxious to come to the cottage with me. That was out of the question, of course, and besides I simply could not afford to keep her on — though I didn't tell her *that*! She asked me if she had "done anything wrong", but you can understand that as I had donned the high hat by doubling her wages I was too cocky to own up that I couldn't afford her at any price *now*.

Worst of all, it never occurred to me — I was *such* a numskull in those days; I am still, I suppose — it didn't occur to me to ask her what she was going to do, not until the very last day when she was packed up and about to leave.

' "Where shall I send your letters?" I asked her.

'She said there wouldn't be any. I said I'd better have her address in case anything turned up. She said she was going to London, she didn't quite know whereabouts until she got there.

' "Where's your regular home?" I asked her.

'And she answered: "I haven't got one!"

'That was the whole truth of it: her parents were both dead, she had nowhere to go. I hadn't known that, you see, and here was I, throwing her out on to the world! Not intentionally, of course, but still, I was a thoughtless ass, oozing with fatuous blank verse and having no notion of responsibility. She was about my own age, twenty-four or five, and — did I tell you? — she was really quite beautiful. There were tears in her eyes, but she kept a stiff upper lip and didn't suffer them to fall — not while I was looking. I could see though, and I simply *had* to ask her to stay on. I told her I had had no idea of her circumstances, that of course I could not let her go off like that, and she had better stop with me until she found another situation. O, a lot of palaver! But she was rather a proud young woman and her pride wouldn't let her accept my belated offer, and though I wasted a lot of words and remorse on her

I could not induce her to change her mind. Away she went, after promising most solemnly to write and let me know how she got on in London. Of course she never kept that promise.'

'Didn't she?' asked the parson with a dubious frown.

'No. Well, within a week I moved to my new cottage; I took what I wanted of my aunt's furniture and sold the remainder with the house. And it turned out to be quite a good stroke of business. In a month or two I paid off all my debts and was left with a couple of hundred pounds in the bargain. I saw I had been altogether too hasty. I wished I had had more foresight and kept Lizzy Lee to look after me. I could have managed it easily after all, but as I say, I did not hear from her, she did not keep her promise to write. By that time she was very much on my mind or my conscience — I don't know which; I expect they are the same thing? It's no use having a conscience unless your mind directs it aright, it's a boat without a compass. I remembered that she was a woman, young, good-looking, though possibly my romantic fancy endowed her with ethereal glamours at times, for poetry does really play the deuce with you in your salad days. Quite often I had a cranky notion of trying to find her — goodness knows how! for she did not keep her promise to write me — but if I could have got into touch with her again I *would* have had her back, for it is not all honey looking after yourself when you're lazy like I was. Besides, I'd got enough money after selling the house to go on paying her her proper wages. What made it more annoying still, in a way, was the fact that in a couple of years those confounded gold mine shares went soaring up again, so that I could even have kept on my aunt's old house, had I but foreseen it!'

Rowfant paused, and fixed a musing gaze on the print of some martyred saint who was being cauterized by demons with a few red-hot harpoons. 'It was very tantalizing, you know.'

'Well, but Ellis,' said the smiling parson, 'you have nothing to *reproach* yourself for.'

'O, haven't I!' exclaimed Rowfant. 'I haven't told you yet.'

'O! Indeed, O!' Mr. Doe said.

Rowfant went on to describe his efforts to compose poetic dramas, efforts which were frustrated time and again by such trivial impediments! His cottage was on the side of a Cotswold hill, it overlooked a woody valley and a stream. There were horizons too, threaded as it were by long belts of beech trees, a lofty uplifting view which so stimulated him that he found it pleasanter to work sitting in his tiny garden rather than at the desk in his room. In that serene and open purview thoughts seemed to flow in him, ideas bubbled, and his imagination became as frisky and glittering as a fountain. But the fountain will not play for ever; bubbles are merely bubbles. The thoughts, although they flowed and flowed, did not flow *out* of him; they swirled, and then they subsided to depths he could never fathom. Ideas came, but they came and went untamed. He imputed this defeat to the languorous airs of summer, the distractions of birds, of bees, of clouds — to anything but his own want of genius. To-morrow would do, it would go better to-morrow. Every passing cloud or sign of shower was an interruption of his mind's airy play; their exquisite designs were invitations to dally, to postpone. To-morrow would be time, it would be better to-morrow. When autumn came along he felt a revival of vigour, a glow of renewal, but on the other hand the sharp air made it no longer agreeable to meditate out of doors, and the chill of life got into his mind when the rigour of the season got into his bones and drove him back into his cottage. There with his books he would sit by a drowsing fire, lying in wait for inspiration as a fox waits for a hare, until the idleness bemused him and the tick of the clock became a noisy nuisance past all bearing; he would stop the clock, forget time, and snooze.

'Ho, ho, my dear fellow!' cried Doe. 'You will be able to write *here*. My, yes! Play after play. I believe *I* could write a play. We must do one together, for the village school.'

Rowfant smiled wryly. 'You know, Sammy, I might have done a real good play if it hadn't been for those infernal shares. You see — they had caused me to do a mean thing, sacking Lizzy Lee, and then they turned on me and gave me all I wanted. It was very significant.'

'I don't quite see the . . . er . . . significance?' remarked the other.

'Don't you! Well, I was selfish — selfish enough, God knows! — but I never really wanted anything at that time except to write my plays. When the shares slumped and I sacked Lizzy Lee I did her a great wrong, it was a vile thing to do. If I had not done that all would have come right in a few months; but I hadn't the sense, I did the dire thing, and then those shares waxed fat again as though they approved of what I had done. They were certainly cursed; they made me do things I should *not* have done, and they prevented me doing the things I *ought* to have done. It was over twenty years before I got rid of the brutes — and it was too late then. I sold them in a boom year I may tell you!'

'Well, ah,' Mr. Doe blandly commented, 'I'm all for castigating Mammon, but it sounds rather as if you were biting the hand that fed you, Ellis!'

'Wait, Sammy, wait. Let me finish my story!'

'Haven't you finished yet?'

'Good Lord, no. Listen. I went on dithering in the Cotswolds for six or seven years. By then I had got a regular lump of money in the bank; the shares paid hand over fist, and I spent little. I got into the way of dodging up to London fairly often to see plays, and on one such occasion I put up at a private boarding house in one of those squares just off Hol-

born. I had been to the theatre and I had gone home
to bed. It was one of those places you just blunder
upon, goodness knows how. Fate, I suppose. I've
never been there since. And I was fast asleep when
something woke me up with a great start. It was a
cry, a loud cry, it was like the cry of some . . . well,
of some lost soul! I sat up in bed and listened. The
room was in darkness, pitch-black. I heard the
shriek again. I lit the candle. It was two o'clock.
My watch I remember was ticking very loudly and I
watched it, almost breathless, for five solid minutes
actually, but there wasn't another sound. So I blew
out the candle and snuggled down in bed again. At
that very moment I heard something more, and I half
rose up and listened; you know — I listened *furiously*.
I heard a voice wailing aloud: "O, won't somebody
give me a match? I'm all in the dark and I'm terri-
fied. Can't you hear me? For Christ's sake someone *give* me a match! I want to get up to my own
bed. I'm all in the *dark*! For God's sake give me a
match, can't you! I'm all alone in the dark and I'm
frightened. Can't you hear, someone? For Christ's
sake give me a match!" Just like that, on and on,
and very loud. I could not make out where the voice
was coming from, upstairs or downstairs, man or
woman, but it was certainly somebody in the house.
I waited and trembled and waited, to hear what
would come of it, for something to be done, but
nobody took any notice. Nobody else seemed to hear
it, and that awful wailing went on until I could not

bear it a second longer. I *had* to get up, and light the candle again, and pull on my dressing-gown. When I opened my door I could hear that the noise was downstairs, so I got hold of my candle and crept down the first flight. No one there, so I crept down the second flight to the hall. The crying had stopped directly my light appeared and halfway down I couldn't see anybody, in fact at first I only saw a grey skin mat at the foot of the stairs and a pot of very white geraniums shoved under the hatstand, but when I held the candle up high I could see a lady sitting all lopsided on the doormat with her hat cocked askew. And she was tipsy! *That* was it. A handsome woman and elegantly dressed, but tipsy! She said "Hullo, I've been here *such* a long time. What the devil's the matter with you all? Nobody ever takes *any* notice in this rotten house. You don't, do you? Who are you?" She seemed to think I was one of the servants. I put the candle on the hatstand and helped her to her feet. Her breath stank of rum and she tottered a little, but she just picked up the candle and made for the stairs. Of course I followed close behind her. She pulled herself together and held the candle up to look at me. "Rather nice," she said. "Haven't seen you before!" She had on a sort of cape, and she walked quite jauntily, carrying the candle in one hand and lifting her skirt with the other. I followed her as she stumbled up two flights of stairs. She opened a door quite close to my own. "Come in," she said; but I stopped in the doorway.

She flung off her hat and cape, kicked off her shoes, and then she began to undress. I called out: "If you've got a candle of your own here I'll light it for you." "Don't you trouble, my dear," she said! In a minute or so she had got her own candle alight and brought mine to the door. I said: "Thank you, good night," and was walking off with my candle when she hissed out: "Are you all alone?" I thought it best not to answer, but she bawled: "*Are* you?" So I replied: "Yes, I am, thank you." "*Too* bad!" she said. "*So* sorry. Au revoir!" or something like that.

'I didn't get off to sleep again for a very long time. The sight of anybody intoxicated always distresses me, but a young woman beautiful and boozed is simply shocking. I couldn't help wondering who she was, and what she had been doing to get like it, and why no one had answered her cries, for I thought the whole house *must* have heard her. As a matter of fact I found out later that nobody *had* heard her! She had been staying there for quite a long time and had a latch key. This night she had been out to a party, got fuzzy with rum, and had fallen down in the pitch-dark hall.

'I met her the next morning. I was all alone in the breakfast room when she came in, looking *radiant!* I didn't quite know whether I ought to greet her in such circumstances, but directly she saw me she came bang up to my table and said "Thank you for last night." "A pleasure!" I said. "May I sit here?"

she asked. "Do" I said; "what will you have for breakfast?" She sat down, she stared at me, and she suddenly exclaimed: "Mr. Rowfant!" And then I saw it was our Lizzy Lee, dressed in the pink of fashion and looking like a lady. Of course you could have split me with a paper knife. Such a surprise! "Why, whatever are you doing here, Elizabeth?" I said. For a long time I couldn't get much information out of her except that she was now a Mrs. Robinson, but we talked and talked and she became quite fascinating you know. It is extraordinary what nurture and dress does for some women. At last I asked what she had to do that morning. She said she had no engagements. "Shall we go out?" I asked, and she said, "Yes." "Where shall we go?" "I don't mind." So off we went and took a hansom as far as the Royal Academy. "Shall we go in?" "Yes," said she. I can remember the details of that visit perfectly, though I have forgotten all about the pictures we looked at. When we got into the court-yard of the Academy there was a baker's cart stand-ing outside the door of the Astronomical Society. The horse had gots its nosebag on and some sparrows were waiting and chippering at the horse's feet and Eliza-beth had to stop and watch them. It made her laugh because the birds would chirrup and the horse would sneeze, and every time he sneezed he blew a handful of oats out of his nosebag, and the sparrows would snap up the grains and go on chippering encouragingly for more.

'Well, we saw some of the pictures and then we sat down in one of the galleries. I asked her about her marriage and so on, and then it all came out with a vengeance: she *wasn't* married, she had never been married at all, but, you understand, she *ought* to have been. The Mrs. Robinson name was just assumed for propriety's sake and convenience, but she wasn't married. Gradually I got the whole story. It appeared that when she left me and went off to London she was unlucky and could not find another situation. She tried for months and months, until her savings came to an end, and she was absolutely on her uppers. Then, of course, the inevitable happened — she was a handsome creature — she went as housekeeper to a certain man who was quite unscrupulous, although he was kind to her in a way. I think he died, and then there were one or two other episodes of that kind. Once — she said — she was an actress, but I discovered that she had only posed in some suggestive tableaux for a threepenny gaff travelling round the fairs. At last she had become the mistress of a rich man who was already married. All this filled me with dreadful remorse, but at the same time I was very angry with her. "Why in the name of all that's sacred didn't you write to me?" "Write to *you*?" said she. "Yes," I said, "as you promised?" "What do you take me for?" she answered (and with a good deal of spirit, by Jove!) "You had thrown me out, homeless." "No, no! I didn't," I said, "and you promised faithfully to write." "Well, it was all your fault," was her reply, "but it doesn't matter now."

'I couldn't believe it of our innocent Lizzy Lee, not for some time. I was appalled to think I had been the unwitting instrument to send her into such a way of life. She was quite insistent that it *was* my fault, and of *course* it was, I *saw* that it was — it was only too awfully true.

'She sat on one of those lounges, looking really beautiful, better than any of the paintings I saw, and no one looking at her there would have dreamed she had been drunk on the doormat at two o'clock that very morning. She asked me why I had been so anxious to get rid of her, and I told her, then, the reason, the proper reason. That seemed to puzzle her. "You were hard up! I had no idea," she said. "Why didn't you tell me? I did not think it was anything like that at all." "What *did* you think it was?" I asked her. "O," she said, "I've forgotten now, but I'd have stayed on, of course I would, for nothing if I had known. Instead of that — you just threw me out!" She repeated that it was all *my* fault, as of course it *was*, this mess she was in. My fault, my helpless fault! And as I deeply realized it then, my guilt, my imagined guilt if you like, affronted me and I felt that it was my solemn duty to get her out of it; I could not rest with a thing like that on my conscience. I told her that I had wanted to get her back again as soon as my affairs had recovered, but that I hadn't known where to find her. "Do you want me back now?" she ventured. "Would you come?" I asked. She laughed; "What wages would you pay me?" Saucy, wasn't it! We didn't say any more about it just then, we just dropped the subject, because in spite of everything she had become a very charming companion. For the next week we were inseparable, went about day after day together, and she behaved well, very well indeed. To cut a long story short I stayed on in that boarding house. I got very fond of her and didn't want to leave her, but it wasn't *only* that. I felt overwhelmingly that some reparation had to be made to her, from me, absolute reparation for the hideous harm I had done. Not intentional, of course; I had been careless, and it had brought this disaster on her. I felt I *had* to make amends — if only to redeem myself — and the best way as it seemed to me then would be to marry her. I began by asking her to give up this man who was keeping her. That made her look sad, so sad, I can't describe *how* mournful, yet when I asked her to marry me she just laughed aloud! But she soon realized I was not joking. I was serious, very serious, and I kept on at her until at last she agreed to marry me. And she did marry me, yes, absolutely! I gave up my Cotswold cottage and we took a little house at Brighton. I made Lizzy destroy every stitch she possessed in the way of clothing and personal belongings. She had heaps, but I was very squeamish about her retaining any of those things, and to do her justice she agreed with me. I spent a heap of money on refitting her, and the only thing she retained was a Bible her mother had given her; it had her name inscribed in it: "To Elizabeth, from her distracted mother on the day of the operation by Dr. Fuller to her nose." '

'Her nose!' echoed the parson. 'What was the matter with her nose?'

'Oh, it wasn't *her* nose,' Rowfant explained. 'Hers was fine, sort of Grecian, and she had an abundance of bright hair and the bluest eyes. No, it was her mother's nose — a polypus, I think. Lizzy was splendid and for over a year we seemed to be living in Eden itself, but after that things began to go wrong. It may have been my own stupidity, it may have been the cussedness of nature, or it may have been a conflict in myself that betrayed us, for I do know that the more deeply I loved her the more I came to loathe the thought of that awful life she had once led. I thought I had accepted all that, I had taken my share of the blame and supposed I could dismiss it from my mind, but that was very far from being so — it became a dreadful canker. And Lizzy, too, she had grown used to some of the extremer luxuries, was extravagant, ran into debt, began to drink again. Once more I found it difficult to make ends meet; my savings were all gone, my income was inadequate, and in short I did not know which way to turn. I could not give Lizzy the sack this time, even if I had wished to and I didn't wish that, though I was horribly hurt by some of the things she was doing, but a climax came when I found out that she was once more corresponding with her old paramour, had actually seen him again, and I guessed she had resumed relations with him. When I taxed her with this she admitted it, and left me, and went back to him. Yes, that's what Lizzy did. Ah, well, I can't describe the horrible bitterness of it, indeed I couldn't if I wanted to, for thirty years is too long a time to remember a grief. I know that I wanted a divorce. Now divorces are most expensive affairs, though it *is* so cheap to get married, but I still wanted to get Lizzy on to the right path again. I wanted that very much. This man was a widower now, and I imagined he would be very glad to marry her if she were free as well. Perhaps he would have done so, but as it turned out he did not. For three years I stinted and starved myself to get money enough to launch proceedings, for I was determined to pay the costs myself, no matter what was the award; it seemed a ghastly immorality to win her redemption — and mine too — with *his* money. Idiot! Fool! Blind besotted owl that I was! Well at last I got my decree, but it was a sorry business for her man entered a defence and the case lasted several days and those confounded news-butchers made a great to-do in their newspapers. I got my decree, but it didn't avail poor Lizzy very much: within a week of its being absolute she died.'

Rowfant stopped at last. Apparently he was finished with his story.

'Dear me,' said the parson, 'how very sad that is.'

Rowfant blew his nose, using his handkerchief meticulously. The parson coughed. There was a silence lasting several moments. The parson coughed again. At length he said:

'You have had a very sad time, Ellis, a very sad time. But you behaved splendidly. There is something wrong about it all, somewhere I feel. I don't know. But you behaved splendidly, Ellis, you did, indeed.'

'No,' said Rowfant. 'No. All that starving and stinting to pay the costs was monstrously quixotic, and it was thrown away, wasted in the end. I didn't mind for myself, but for poor Lizzy I *did* mind. Don't you see? If I had been less of a fool, if I had thought more of her and less of my own precious scruples the poor girl would have been divorced and free a couple of years earlier at least. And she could have been married to that man and it would have put things right for her in a sort of way. But my stupidity prevented even that. And she died, and — well — what about *her*?'

Soon the parson came and bent over his friend:

'All is well, my dear boy, all is well. Believe that. Now — ah — just forget all about it. I wonder,' said he, glancing around the room, 'I wonder, Ellis — would you care to play a little game of dominoes?'

'Why, yes,' Ellis responded brightly, 'yes, I should love to.'

'Very well then.'

They played.

III

A few days later Rowfant was installed at
the vicarage with his pink cap, his waterproof
tobacco pouch, and a lot of books that Sammy declared he would certainly have to look at — some
time, later on. From the day he turned his back
upon the blandishments of Twickenham and was
inducted as it were into the pale of the church Rowfant's heart was aware of revivals and renewals he
had not thought to experience again. And there
was no betrayal this time. The two old men in
friendly bondage shared a home, a life; and they
shared their thoughts, snoozing and brooding in
the garden under the leaning trees while the sun-
inspired brook inched warily by. In some half-
maudlin mood Rowfant perhaps would ask: 'What
is Life?' And Sammy would tell him.

Or Sammy would bridle with domestic ambition:
'We might put up a little greenhouse here, Ellis. I
am very partial to cucumbers — do they disturb
you?'

Or there would be intimate wanderings over the
sleepy fields, for the parson was no longer a lover of
the open road.

'I really regret the dust, Ellis, the dust of the old
highway. It often gave me real pleasure, thirty
years ago, before the roads were so hardened and
polished and thousands of wheels going where there

were only ten before. Traffic was so small then, and it was genial, too; just a wagon, a butcher's cart, the squire's barouche, or a fleet of bicycles. And you could pad along so softly in the roads with a luxurious inch of fine dust under your footsoles; rich historical dust, too, gloating over ancient Britain and Julius Cæsar, and the sun flaring at you while the sweat oozed and ran. And then, to come to some bosky chestnut tree at the corner of some turn with a pond and a goose deliberating on it! O dear, O dear : the tree and the pond may be there still, but the goose is gone!'

And Rowfant found that he too lamented the dust that had gone to dust indeed. He found that his own divergent thoughts were often of the same cast as his friend's, though he seemed to use them as stepping stones to directions Rowfant had always shunned. Despite his secular bigotries he found that he liked hearing his comrade pronounce the benediction at their meals together. One day Sammy said: 'Will *you* say grace, Ellis?' and stood with his venerable head piously bowed, never doubting his friend's response. Rather than grieve him Rowfant submissively invoked a blessing in which he had no belief. He found that it pleased him immensely to please Sammy; he had no belief in God, but he believed in his friend.

Once he had asked Rowfant to be a good chap and go with him to the church and ring the bell for the evening service.

'Why, what is the matter with the sexton?' Rowfant enquired.

'Drunk,' replied Sammy. 'He is imperiously drunk.'

It seemed such an agreeable quandary for a parson to be in that Rowfant was delighted to oblige — just for once. But somehow things were never done 'just for once' with the inexorable Sammy. You were taken for granted, you were inveigled, you were roped in.

'We ought to do a Nativity Play at Christmas,' declared Sammy. 'Yes, to be performed in the church. And that's just your line, Ellis, isn't it? You could write something extraordinarily good, it's a beautiful theme, one of the finest the world has ever known — O, immeasurably! You just knock off the words, not too much spouting you know, but action and simple piety, and I will find the performers — as many as you like, the more the merrier.'

It was a waste of time for Rowfant to plead his entire unfitness; he had to renew his acquaintance with the Gospel according to St. Luke and to plan his Christmas pageant. Naturally this required — and it was somehow quite *quite* natural — his occasional attendance in the church, where a robin had once had the cheek to build its nest in a hole in Sammy's lectern and put five eggs in it. It ended in Rowfant's becoming a sort of lay clerk to the implacable Mr. Doe, in his sitting below his pulpit and responding to his Amens in no browbeaten manner.

'Wouldn't you like to read the lessons, Ellis?'

'No. You must excuse me, Phalarope.'

'I should like you to do that, Ellis.'

'I could not do that. I would not *mind*, but I do not feel myself *fitted*, you understand — *fitted*. I am interested in it all, you know that, but the fact remains that I am entirely insusceptible to any sort of religious emotion, utterly and entirely. The ceremonies are quite agreeable, they are pleasant, but beyond that they *mean* nothing to me.'

'Why should they? Ellis, what are you afraid of?'

'Afraid! I'm not afraid of anything. But I do miss something, I want some clue. I can't break through the crust of all these ceremonies and contradictions and find the thing I'm after, the thing which sometimes I find in myself, which satisfies *me*. I suppose I can't *find* what you call God. I can't believe in Him.'

'It is all very simple, Ellis. The Kingdom of God is within you.'

'No, Sammy. The soul is not really man's identification with God, it is merely the *possibility* of such identification. Now suppose — just listen to me for a moment, Sammy — suppose there *is* a great Jehovah sitting in the skies or wherever you like to have Him. That *may* be true, I won't argue about it, just suppose it. But even then it is quite easy and natural to suppose that this life of ours is the beginning and the end of things for mankind, isn't it? And what then?'

'Suppose! Suppose!' The Reverend Phalarope Doe wagged his head and smiled indulgently. 'I am not able to suppose any such thing, Ellis. And you have forgotten Jesus, haven't you?'

'I have not. Even He envisages this world as the centre of the universe.'

'Why not?'

'Why not! Don't you realize that our world is but a gnat in the galaxy of a million worlds?'

'I do.'

'He had no conception of any other world save Heaven.'

'Nor have I, Ellis, nor have you. To apprehend omniscience one must have an omniscient mind. All else is impertinence. You could put out your tongue at the Lama of Tibet, but even he would disdain to take notice of the gesture.'

'The Lama of Tibet?'

'Yes, you believe in him, although you have never seen him and never will.'

'But I *know* of his existence. I have read of him.'

'I have read of Jack the Giant Killer.'

'And do you believe in him!'

'No. But I have read of God, and his blessings confront me day by day. God's miracles are numberless, but in face of them all, Ellis, I am sometimes tempted to think that mankind's one stupendous miracle is greater than any of His. I mean the Miracle of Unbelief.'

'That's no miracle, Sammy!'

'To me it is. And I would like you to read the lesson sometimes. You could do it beautifully. You read the Bible to yourself and it gives you pleasure, isn't that so? To put it at its lowest it gives you great pleasure. Now?'

Rowfant sighed. 'It's a duodecimo emotion, Sammy; not like yours, a folio in full calf.'

'Never mind the binding. Penny plain is no less than twopence coloured, which costs twice as much and means no more. Don't be selfish, Ellis, I'm not asking you to take a Sunday School class!'

So Rowfant read out the Word of God and feared no evil. He wrote his play, he rang the bell, he did whatever Sammy required him to do. There was no end to their exchanges of belief and unbelief, but there was no division between them; their differences were no more than a crude brush across a surface of velvet, as marked as the advance of a harrow across a pasture — and as fugitive. Sometimes while listening to Sammy's exhortations Rowfant would fall asleep, and when he awoke Sammy would be gone away somewhere, to the garden, to his study, or into the church. 'Ah,' Rowfant would despondently sigh, 'he disapproves of me!' But it was not so, never so. The two old friends were in bondage to an affection that time and thought had no wish to subvert.

'Why did you never get married, Sammy? Don't you care for women?'

'I love mankind.'

'But women, Sammy.'

'And their children too.'

'Humph! I don't think I love man, really.'

'I do.'

'Not in the proper human way, not in any *wide* sense. I don't accept him as an equal, I'm afraid, but still I am content with him.'

'I am not content with him, Ellis, but I love him.'

What would have been impossible to Rowfant, or absurd in him, was so firm and beautiful and appropriate in old Doe, who was so fond and ever faithful, that Rowfant could not find it in his heart to oppose him. Against Sammy he could somehow advance his reasoning only with small shuffling steps, like a man on a tight rope balancing a rod that was no security against a fall. The multitudinous permutations of man's mind, its diversity of measure, its warp that would plait only with the woof of its self-sown views, left Rowfant without hope of ever sharing his dear friend's belief and bliss, but he lived gratefully in its reflected beam. The beam might be a mirage and lead no further than the grave — but what then? What pangs and what misery had such innocence avoided!

The autumn faded upon them and winter eves approached with the wild cries of those wounded winds that harried every obstruction, thorn, gulley, barn, garner, fold and fence. The sere skeletons of dead herbage were snapped on their fields and scattered. The clouds that hung above the firmament's meek frill of light were coloured like the inside of a shell. The surfaces of flat objects, such as the top of a well or the bar of a gate, had a grey doubtful lustre, but a rare planet sparkled aloft with a benignity bland as a prophet's faith. But the heart of a prophet — thought Rowfant — hears only the echo of its own sighing.